WALTZING LUCIFER

*

A Isobel Sutcliffe

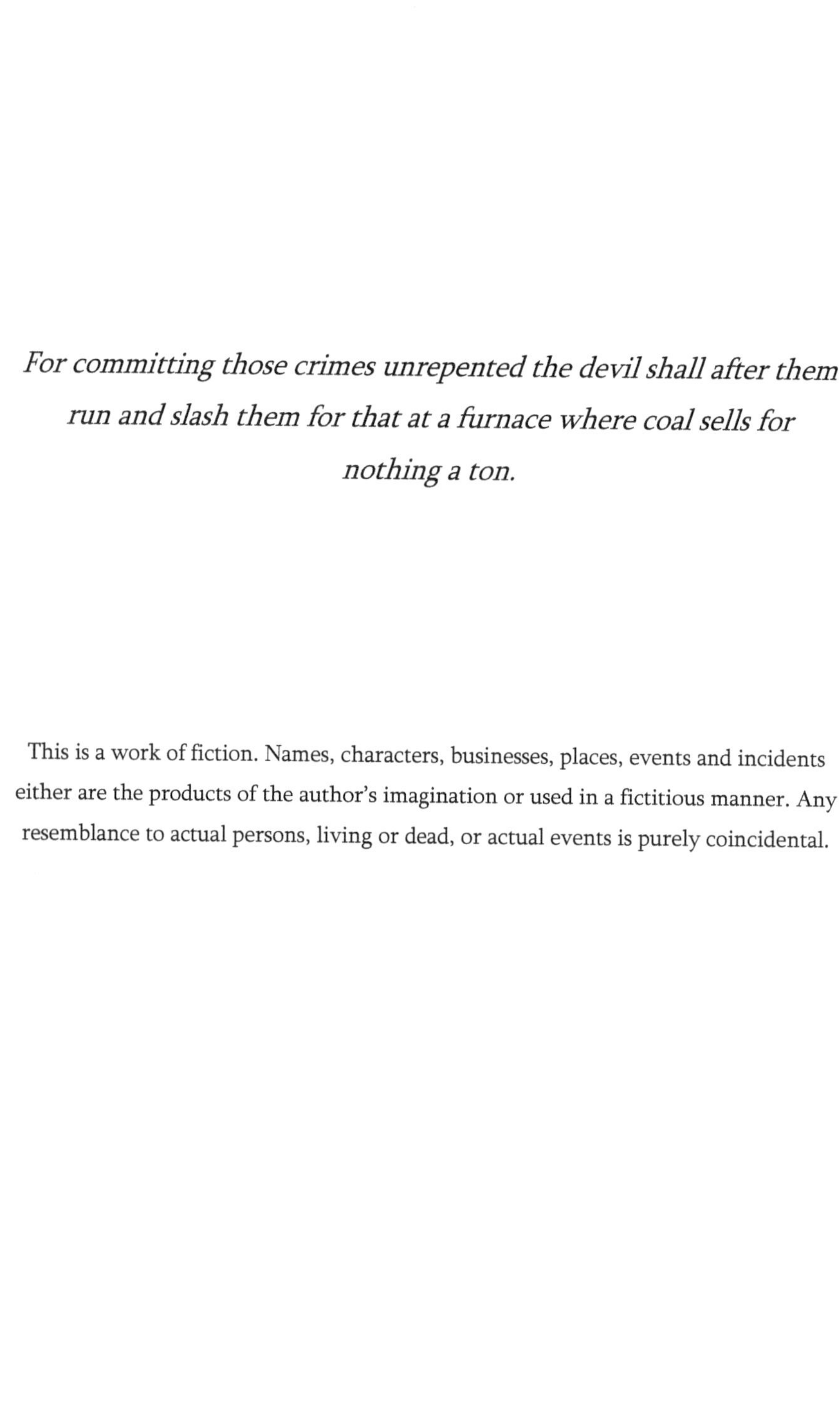

*For committing those crimes unrepented the devil shall after them
run and slash them for that at a furnace where coal sells for
nothing a ton.*

JaCol Publishing Inc.

Copyright 2017 by JaCol Publishing Inc.

FIRST PRINTING

November 2018

JaCol Publishing Inc.

195 Murica Aisle

Irvine, CA 92614

818-510-2898

ISBN: **978-1-946675-31-6**

JaCol Publishing

AUTHOR'S NOTE

I am a child of the sixties. I grew up in the Sunshine State of Queensland, Australia. Like most of my generation, I frittered away my young years, living, learning, and preparing for the years ahead, oblivious to the dark underbelly that existed in our state. Unaware of the depravity operating between the cracks. There were no mobile phones, no internet, no social media, and political correctness lay dormant for another several decades. Security cameras were rare. Homosexuality was illegal. Rape within marriage did not become a crime until 1989. While the government that held power through the years covered in this story presided over what many called a broken system, it is said that their predecessors were every bit as corrupt. For this book, I have chosen a non-partisan approach. This is a story of what might have happened.

****

Table of Contents

ACKNOWLEDGEMENT

Dedicated to my husband, my son and my daughter. My brothers and sisters whose humour always inspires me. To Randall Andrews, my editor and writing coach, thank you for your patience and inspiration. To Karen Brosinsky for her wonderful artwork. To the beautiful people of Writers World, you inspire, educate, and amuse me.

1.

The Kinanes 1967

Mikey cringed as his father's eyes tracked left to right across the lines of his dishonour. This encounter might end with a hard boot in the arse. Barefoot and in his pyjamas, he fidgeted as his father's shoulders sagged.

Tom Kinane flapped the letter. "So, now what are you going to do, Mikey? How do you propose to get that senior school certificate you so badly want when you've been chucked out of school in grade eight?"

"Sorry, Dad, but those bastards deserved it."

"What exactly did they do to deserve a beating?"

"I didn't beat them—not really."

"Well what did you do?"

Mikey braced himself and confessed. "I flushed their heads in the toilet and kicked their arses. One tried to kick me in the nuts so I pushed him into the piss trough, too."

"You fought them all at once?"

"No, one at a time."

Tom Kinane's mouth twitched. "That's quite an achievement—there were—" he paused to look at the letter, "three of them."

"I locked them in the sports tackle room and did them one at a time."

His father made a noise in his throat. "Your organisational skills have always been admirable, Mikey, but why? Why did you do it when you knew you were on your last warning?"

Mikey's older brother stepped in the room. "He did it because they were calling me a fairy, Dad." Craig lifted his chin. "Again."

Mikey Kinane was the youngest of seven. Five boys and two girls. They lived in a big old house in the inner South Brisbane suburb of Highgate Hill. As usual, on a Wednesday night, his father arrived home at ten thirty after a long day running the Valley Star Hotel across the river in Fortitude Valley.

"It really shits me when they say that, Dad. Craig's not a fairy." Mikey's scowl moved from his father to his brother. "He's not! He's really good at playing footy and cricket."

Craig grinned. "Thank you, Mikey. But listen, kid—you don't have to defend me—I don't care two hoots what those snotty nosed little twerps call me."

"Well you should."

"I am what I am, Mikey, and the sooner the rest of the world gets with it the better off we'll all be."

Tears brimmed Mikey's eyes. "You're not a fairy! You can't be—I—you don't have to be. Just get a girlfriend or something!"

His father patted his shoulder. "Go and get into bed, Mikey. I'll come and talk to you shortly."

His father gave Craig a one-armed hug as Mikey left the room. Craig was seventeen and in his last year of high school. Mikey didn't want him to be different. It was weird—why did he like boys and not girls? Tall, handsome, and athletic—how could he be queer? The bedsprings squeaked as Mikey rolled in and pulled the sheet up.

Liam and Aiden sat up, twin grins shone in the darkened room.

"Well tell us," Liam inquired.

Aiden pressed. "What did he do?" The fifteen-year-old twins lauded their little brother's expulsion as the pinnacle of his academic achievement. They'd been trying for years. His failure to alert them before he flushed three heads and pushed one into the urinal their only complaint.

"Nothing yet—"

The twins ducked under the covers at the sound of their father's footsteps.

"Okay, Mikey." Tom Kinane sat on the bed. "Here's what I'm going to do. I've already discussed this with your mother and she agrees."

"I'm sorry, Dad—Mum was really upset with me."

"There is a little over a week left in the school term, you can come and work at the pub—no, wipe the grin off your face. I've got a long list of jobs for you to do. Dirty jobs."

Contrition chased the smile from Mikey's face. "Then what, Dad?"

"We'll talk about it in the morning. You get some sleep, you should have been in bed over an hour ago."

"Those guys were asking for it, Dad."

"Mikey, you are not your brothers' protector. They are all quite capable of looking after themselves. Craig has been taking care of himself for years—he doesn't need you to fight his battles. Promise me, no more heroics."

"Okay."

"Good, now—"

"Dad, what's wrong with Craig?"

"Nothing is wrong with him, son."

"But—"

His father ruffled his hair. "Go to sleep, Mikey."

"Good night, Dad."

Mikey rolled onto his back and sighed. If the other Kinane brothers were clover, Craig was a rouge poppy, distinguished by his flamboyance. Mikey loved Craig as much as he loved all his family but wished he wasn't different. Craig hadn't had an easy childhood but he survived to develop strength and resilience. His ability to deliver a sharp rebuttal was his weapon of choice. His reputation as a pugilist his coat of mail. His movie-star looks broke hearts; his Irish charm earned him a host of friends and admirers. Mikey watched and learned; of all his big brothers, Craig was the one he wanted to emulate. Even their stature was similar.

But why does he have to be queer?

2.

Kitty

Katrina Olsen climbed onto the veranda rail and craned her neck; she wanted a closer look at the new neighbours. She jumped back to the floor and skipped into the laundry.

"Mum, can I go and say hello. Please?"

"Kitty, you might get in the way."

"But you and Dad went over, why can't I? Please, Mum?"

Her mother sighed. "Okay, but you can only stay for a minute and then you must come home."

"Thanks, Mum!" Kitty picked a bunch of roses, jumped on her bike, and rode down the hill. The farm next door had sat deserted for weeks with a 'sold' sign on the gate. Eight-year-old Kitty hoped to find kids her age and she'd have new friends to play with on the weekend.

The Kinanes were friendly and invited her in for a drink. It disappointed her that the youngest Kinane, Mikey, was a tall thirteen-year-old. Undeterred, she shadowed him and longed for his attention. She bombarded him with questions and giggled at his droll answers. He teased her about her big blue eyes and rosebud mouth.

He tweaked her nose. "I got your conk, Kitty-cat."

"Why are you so funny?"

"It's the Leprechaun on my shoulder. Can't you see him?"

"What's a Leprechaun?"

"A little Irish rum-soak."

"What's a rum-soak?"

"One day you'll find out."

"Tell me now."

"Don't you have a doll to play with or something?"

"My doll got burnt."

"Burnt? How?"

"I set fire to it with a magnifying glass."

He had an easy laugh. "Why did you do that?"

Kitty shrugged and pulled a face. "I wanted to see if it would burn."

And so the years marched on; Kitty started high school—she in grade eight and Mikey in grade twelve, his final year.

****

Mikey begun to pay Kitty a different kind of attention. Her big blue eyes and rosebud mouth had always set a fire in his loins but her child's body had extinguished the flames. Now, the girl from the farm next door was the prettiest girl he knew, he'd watched her develop from child to adolescent, her breasts budded and grew. Her body changed from girl to woman in a matter of months, she went from the carefree tomboy to a self-conscious teenager with little concept of her beauty. Mikey ran off several rivals who announced they would like to seduce her. He bided his time; in his heart he knew Kitty would be his.

As he grew older, Mikey had come to understand Craig but he wished his brother would fit into the norms of society. Craig told him he shouldn't let it bother him but to Mikey, it mattered a lot. He wanted him to be like the rest of his brothers. The world had never been kind to people like Craig, but as the sixties gave way to the seventies, an attitude of tolerance began to dawn though acceptance remained years away. Like many of that era, Mikey wondered why anyone would choose a pariah's lifestyle.

The move to the farm at Nambour, two hours north of Brisbane, changed life for the Kinanes. Tom stayed in Brisbane with Craig who followed his father into the hotel trade. Their mother, Mary, shared her time between the farm and the pub. The eldest, Jimmy, took on management of the farm; something he had always longed to try. The girls, Nola and Fiona, moved to Nambour and opened a fashion boutique. The twins left school and joined the army and in his last year of school, Mikey surprised everyone when he won the position of school captain.

3

1971

The bus roared away in a cloud of diesel smoke and dust. Kitty clutched her school bag to her chest; Mikey slanted his body her way and his arm brushed her shoulder. Their feet crunched on the gravel road to where it forked to their respective farm gates.

He stopped and a cheeky grin broke the smooth lines of his face. "Kitty, why do you hold your bag like that?"

"Like what?"

He pulled it from her grasp. "You're covering your titties, aren't you?"

Heat rose in Kitty's face. Mikey had a wont for exposing the torturous secrets of puberty. She craved his attention but when she got it, she had to resist fleeing. "No I'm not—"

He moved closer, his voice soft in her ear. "You've grown a nice pair, Kitty, don't cover them." He handed back her schoolbag and vaulted the gate. "Shooting lesson tomorrow afternoon?"

Kitty nodded.

He winked over his shoulder. "See ya then, Kitty-Kat."

A trembling mess of adrenaline-laced jelly, she gazed after him as he strode along the narrow road. Mikey was seventeen, tall and handsome; a grown man to her eyes. His cheeky compliment had set her heart racing. An endorphin rush propelled her home and she bounced in the back door.

Her mother paused from dicing vegetables. "Katrina! What have you been doing? Your face is red as a beetroot."

"Nothing Mum, I just ran home—I—need to pee."

****

Mikey's family were keen sporting shooters and competed for the title of best marksmen. He'd gained permission from Kitty's parents to teach her how to use a gun and he spent hours patiently training her—any excuse to spend time in her company.

On a warm Saturday afternoon, he lounged against a wall of the shed and watched Kitty bite her lip as she concentrated on holding the rifle steady; she squeezed the trigger and...

"Now you're getting the hang of it, Kitty-Kat!" He smiled as she danced at the third hit in a row of the target. "Next week I might let you fire one of the big rifles."

"Let me try now."

"You'll need a bit more practice with this one first, you'll have to hit the target every time, you've gouged a fair swag of dirt out of the backstop." Mikey took the rifle from her, clicked the safety catch, pulled out the magazine and stuffed it in his back pocket.

Now is your chance, Mikey.

One hand held the rifle, the other pulled her against him; the top of her head just reached his shoulder. Her eyes widened as he stooped; his lips brushed her cheek then covered her pretty mouth, easing her lips apart. She trembled like a captive bird in his arms.

Mikey threw caution against the corrugated iron wall and revealed his heart to her. "I love you, Kitty-Kat," he whispered, her face warm against his cheek.

Kitty nodded, her flushed face intensified the blue of her eyes.

"I'm a little old for you—your dad would kick my arse if he saw me kissing you."

Kitty bit her lip; her eyes reflected his silhouette against the clouds. Her lips framed words her throat failed to produce. The chatterbox kid was speechless; Mikey continued his one-sided conversation.

"Let's keep it to ourselves until you're older, okay?"

She nodded.

"Meet me tomorrow down at Scrubby Crook?"

Her pink face darkened to red.

"Three o'clock?"

Finally, a whisper. "Okay."

Mikey grinned and kissed her again. The Leprechaun inside him danced the jig and clicked its heels.

****

Scrubby Crook was a sandy bend in the creek that formed the back boundaries of the Kinane and Olsen farms, a favourite swimming hole with a wide sandy beach covered in lush couch grass. Kitty trembled with every step she took. She had spent an hour putting on makeup only to clean it off; she carefully styled her hair then brushed it out. She donned her favourite dress, gathered her courage, and set off, hair falling about her shoulders. Butterflies fluttered in the air and in her stomach as her feet slipped down the creek bank to where Mikey sat in the sand, tossing pebbles into the water. Concentric circles overlapped on the glassy surface. The thought crossed her mind that he might want to have sex with her and while that thought turned the butterflies to eagles, the notion of pregnancy terrified her. He got to his feet, arms akimbo.

"Look at you, Kitty-Kat, my little blonde bombshell." He pulled her into his arms; his lips possessed hers. She'd had one quick kiss during a party-game of hide-and-seek—a quick lip-smack that left her bewildered. Why all the fuss? With one kiss, Mikey had taught her the difference between boy and man. He dragged her into the deep end to drown in his fiery embrace. Mikey's kisses made her insides swirl like a tornado, winding an invisible clock-spring so tight it might snap an any moment and send her fleeing back to the safety of her mother's apron. She had never been so close to anyone outside her family, his body hard and muscular, strange and exciting—and scary. She liked his spicy scent with a subtle trace of sweat that signified his masculinity. Movement against her stomach made her look down, the front of his jeans bulged. His blue eyes watched hers as she looked up and drew her bottom lip between her teeth.

His voice had a hard edge as he whispered in her ear. "You're making me horny, but I can wait. You're too young."

****

Mikey spent many Sunday afternoons with Kitty on that sandy bend, cuddling, kissing, and making plans—their hearts beating with sweet torture. In the bark of an old gum tree, he carved a big heart skewered with an arrow, for weeks 'M loves K' oozed red sap. School ended for Mikey and he found a job. He went out on the town with his peers, to parties and to the pub but he kept Sunday afternoon for Kitty. Girls swarmed after him and he exploited them. Only a rare young man would knock back what they gave freely. He needed release and Kitty was underage. He reasoned she'd never find out and when she turned sixteen he would give up the other women.

Mikey bought a third-hand Harley Sportster with a rumbling 1000cc engine, in awe of his older brothers' motorcycles. It took him ten minutes to talk Kitty into climbing on behind him; she clung to him as they roared down the hill to the bitumen road and squealed as he accelerated towards the Bruce Highway.

4.

Paul Matthews 1973.

Paul Matthews' stomach rumbled. The night before his mother, Michelle, had gone out and forgot to make his dinner. The only food was a stale bread crust in a packet next to his mother's makeup on the kitchen table. There was no electricity; Michelle had spent all her money on a new outfit. Paul had laughed as she rushed in, bursting with excitement.

"Look what I bought for myself, Paul!"

A grin spread across the little boy's face as his mother donned the paisley print mini dress and pulled on the white knee high boots.

"Wow! Michelle—you look pretty!" Paul stroked the crisp fabric on the long flared sleeves.

"Don't touch!" she pushed his hand away, "you'll make it dirty. Ooh! I can't wait to wear it!" She swayed into the bedroom to admire herself in the mirror.

One week passed, and Michelle had taken her new dress out on the town every night. Paul sat up and watched TV until it went off the air; most night's he fell asleep on the lounge while he waited for Michelle to return. When they turned the power off, he lit a candle and sang all the songs he knew. His mother had run away from her fundamentalist Christian parents at fifteen; she gave birth to Paul at sixteen. It was 1964 and the matron of the hospital had announced they would put the baby up for adoption. Michelle snatched her baby and fled. She made it through Paul's baby years because Gwen, her elderly neighbour took her under her wing. Then she took a job as a cleaner and old Gwen cared for little Paul. Gwen died when Paul was six and Michelle got by, working during Paul's school hours. Through school holidays, Paul stayed home alone. He read comics and listened to the radio, taking in the DJ's banter.

****

"Michelle, I'm hungry." Paul opened the door to his mother's room. She didn't stir. "Michelle—"

A man sat up in the bed, scratched his armpit and cast a bleary gaze over the boy.

"Gidday, kid. Where's the dunny?"

Paul's eyes widened and he backed out the door. He pointed across the hall to the bathroom, the man staggered to his feet and farted, his erect penis waved from side to side as he passed. Paul stared after him, the man didn't close the door as he directed a yellowish brown stream into the toilet, finished with a couple of squirts and compressed another fart between the cheeks of his hairy arse.

Paul giggled. "You fart a lot!"

The pressure relieved, the man scratched his groin and returned to the bed, his penis had already gone back to sleep.

"Michelle, I'm hungry." Paul could hear her breathing, she wasn't dead. "Michelle—"

"What's your name, kid?" The man leaned over the side of the bed and picked up his trousers.

"Paul."

"My name's Pinkie, here go and buy something from the shop." The man passed him a two-dollar note.

"Pinkie—that's a funny name."

Pinkie reached under the sheet and scratched his genitals. "I'm a funny man, Paul. Go and buy some breakfast."

5.

Tom Kinane 1974.

Tom Kinane had inherited The Valley Star Hotel in Fortitude Valley from his father, a popular and profitable drinking hole. He bought the farm on the Sunshine Coast to get Mikey and the twins, Liam and Aiden, out of the city before they found themselves in real trouble. Tom was never serious about farming and greeted with relief when his eldest son, Jimmy, took to it with natural ease. He had worried he'd forced them into the tough, unpredictable life of a farmer. When Craig finished school, he helped his father manage the pub and urged his father to buy into the nightclub scene. Tom bought a dilapidated old club in Wickham Street and began renovations. On opening day, a bagman arrived with his hand out.

"Piss off!"

"Now, Tom, that kind of attitude is not going to get you what you want. If you want protection you have to pay what's due."

"You've got to be joking! This is Brisbane not New York!"

"It works the same all over the world—you pay your insurance and we'll see you're taken care of. You see, the nightclub scene can get rough, Tom."

"Do you think I don't know that? I've been running pubs all my life."

"But night clubs are different—if you're gonna play in the sandpit with the big kids you can expect to get some dirt in your eye."

"You'll get a fist in your eye if you don't fuck off!"

"Your attitude is regrettable, Mr Kinane."

"Get out, you slimy mongrel!"

The Pearl's doors opened to the public and night after night, crowds eager to see the revamped club flocked in. Craig proved popular with the public and excelled at management. After three months, Tom forgot about the bagman. The money poured in.

****

Fred Donnelly

From the opposition benches, Fred Donnelly got to his feet, licked his lips, and shuffled his papers. For months, he'd hammered the Minister for Police at every opportunity, trying to make him slip up and admit to the corruption in the police force. The State Parliament resumed sitting that day after a six-week break and Fred had returned, armed with a fresh scandal to throw at the government.

The Speaker's voice rang in the chamber. "I call the Honourable Member for Samson for a question without notice."

"Thank you, Mr Speaker. I have a question without notice for the Minister for Police." His voice drowned amid groans from the government benches. "Mr Speaker, recently a brothel opened its doors right across the street from where I live with my wife and—"

"That's convenient for ya!" The quip came from across the chamber amid gales of laughter.

The Speaker's bored voice cut in. "Order."

"…my children, Mr Speaker. My neighbours have to listen to the tawdry sounds of indecent acts for all hours of—"

"Close your window so they can't hear ya, ya dirty mongrel!"

Fred's voice faltered against the tide of laughter; the sight of Max Maxwell's beer belly bouncing with uncontrolled laughter made his throat constrict in frustration.

The speaker straightened in his chair and tugged at his collar. "Order! The member for Lowan Bay will cease interjections!"

"…can the Minister for Police confirm to the house that every step will be taken to shut these illegal brothels down?" Fred jabbed a finger at the police minister. "Or doesn't he care as long as they're not in his electorate?"

The cadaverous police minister got to his feet. "I'll look into it for you, Fred."

"Ya might need a ladder, Sid."

"Or some binoculars!"

"Order! The house will come to order!"

Fred resumed his seat and began searching for his notes on an illegal casino.

Tom Kinane polished glasses and set them in the fridge basket, preparing for the evening rush.

"Look at that little poonce." Margie, the cleaner placed freshly laundered runners on the bar top and watched the six o'clock news on channel nine. "Suppose 'e's got a point though—they need to do somethin' about prostitution."

Tom cocked his ear to the news report. "I can't see the harm in it if they're all consenting adults. They should just move them away from residential areas."

Margie edged closer and lowered her voice. "Me neighbour's daughter is a workin' girl and she reckons that some of the brothels 'round the place are runnin' kiddies as well as grown women and ya know what?"

Tom shook his head and waited.

"There's some cops in on it too."

"Yeah?" Tom hoped Margie's neighbour had lied.

"She did say a few names but I can't remember 'em."

"Jesus, if that's true it needs to stop."

"Sure does, Tom."

Fred Donnelly spent Sunday morning in church with his family. He nodded approval as the preacher sermonised about the sanctity of marriage and the need for chastity. After the ceremony, he took the time to shake the hands of his fellow parishioners and listened with a politician's satisfaction as many commended his parliamentary campaign. Tom Kinane and his wife Mary greeted him as they left.

Tom shook his hand and leaned closer. "If you're looking for more ammunition to fire at Sid, the other day, one of my staff told me a rather horrific story about some of the local brothels."

Fred's scandal radar homed in. "Really? I'd like to hear it."

"I'll get her to write down the names of the brothels that are hiring kids to perverts."

"Perv—er—really?" Fred's face tingled and his lips numbed. He regurgitated a bit of breakfast.

"Yeah, and she reckons the cops turn a blind eye."

"Oh, well yes. That is disgraceful! I must get details; bring them into my office as soon as you can."

"Maybe I should just take them to the papers or a TV station—the government is not going to do anything."

When Fred arrived home, he excused himself. "I'm sorry, my dear but I need to make some phone calls. I'll try not to be too long." In his office, his hand rattled the receiver as he picked up the phone and dialled the number from memory. "It's Fred. We have a problem…"

6.

1974.

Michelle began working for Pinkie; Paul stayed home and watched TV until they played 'God Save the Queen.' Then he'd fall asleep on the couch. In the morning, he'd put on the same dirty school uniform, eat a piece of toast and decide whether or not he went to school.

"Hey kid, ya wanna go to a party?" Pinkie emerged from Michelle's bedroom, scratched his arse and fumbled with the studs on his black silk shirt.

"Yeah!" Somewhere in his past, Paul had attended a party. Piles of cake, lollies, and a rainbow array of fizzy drinks. He remembered laughing a lot and playing games.

"Alright, be ready to go tonight when I come to pick up Michelle."

****

Pinkie took Paul in the back door of a place called Ruby's Wine Bar. A woman with curly blond hair and bright-red lips greeted them. Paul gazed open mouthed at her silver cigarette holder. Ruby Landers took Paul upstairs and told him to take a bath. She came in as he towelled himself dry and gave him some clothes to put on. Paul squeezed into the shorts and assumed Ruby would notice they were a bit small on him; she might have a bigger pair.

"Come on, put on the vest."

"But there's no shirt, and these shorts are too tight."

"They don't wear shirts at this party, just put on the vest." Ruby stuck her cigarette in her mouth, helped him on with the satin vest and combed his wet hair. When they emerged from the bathroom, there were two boys and a girl, all a few years older than Paul. The boys wore clothes like Paul's, tight black satin shorts and a vest. The girl wore a pink, baby-doll dress, pink high heels and more makeup than Michelle wore. The older kids didn't look at Paul; they stared straight ahead with lifeless eyes.

Maybe they don't like me.

"This is Paul." Ruby addressed the stony-faced trio. "Paul this is Shane, Ben, and Maria. They're coming to the party too."

"Hello." Paul smiled and waited for a response, but the three kept their eyes fixed on the wall.

"Here Darling, take this." Ruby gave him a little white pill and a glass of water.

"What is it?"

"It's a pill to make you happy."

Paul didn't think he would need it but shrugged and swallowed it.

****

The party wasn't what Paul expected. Although there were cakes, lollies, soft drinks, and a swimming pool, there were also four men. Ruby sat at a table with a woman, they talked quietly, smoking and tapping their feet to the music.

"Hello, what's your name?"

The man lifted Paul onto his lap and held him in place.

"Um, it's Paul." Paul squirmed, uneasy with sitting on a man's lap.

"My name is Billy."

Paul's head grew heavy and his limbs weak. His eyes opened wide as the man's mouth covered his—Paul pulled away, he wished Michelle had come to the party; he wanted to hide behind her. The man breathed hard, fumbled with his trousers and took Paul's wrist.

He guided Paul's hand to squeeze his rubbery genitals. "Feel that. Isn't it good?"

The evening blurred past, sweets and drinks, groping hands and tearing pain. Hushed and panicked voices woke Paul where he lay on a banana lounge. The grownups crowded around Maria, the man who called himself Bobby knelt beside her, pumping her chest and blowing into her mouth.

"Fuck! How many pills did you give her, Ruby?"

"Three. I've been warning you, she's getting too hard to handle."

"Well, I think we can safely assume she is dead."

The words jarred deep in Paul's conscience. He sat up and tried to focus on the girl. His head throbbed, his stomach ached, and his anus burned; the men's voices thrummed in his ears.

"Dead? What are we going to do with her? Does she have any family?"

"No. She's a nobody."

"And judging by that belly, I think she might be a pregnant nobody."

"Well it's not mine—I had the snip six months ago."

"This is terrible!"

"Calm down, Harold!"

"Strip her off and chuck her in the canal for the bull sharks."

"But you can't just—"

"Well what do you suggest?"

Harold wrung his hands. "I don't—oh God! This is awful."

The banana lounge pressed against his cheek; Paul's head weighed a ton. His eyelids drooped and closed.

****

Paul's life had never been especially happy. When Michelle chose to, she cared for him like a mother should but for much of his early childhood she lived for herself, her son little more than a burden. The day after his ninth birthday Paul copied Shane and Ben. He directed an aerosol nozzle into a paper bag, sprayed and inhaled his mother's hairspray. It helped him forget about the parties, it relieved the pain they caused. Paul watched as his mother too fell between the insidious claws of addiction.

25

7.

Michelle clenched her fist and swung it at Pinkie's face; the momentum propelled her against the wall. "You dirty, filthy, two faced fucking rat! You scummy bastard—arsehole!"

Pinkie took a mouthful of vodka and swallowed, backing away from the deranged hooker. "What are ya on about, ya stupid moll?"

"You know what I'm talking about!" Michelle bared her teeth, scarlet lipstick bled against the yellow. Her once pretty face framed by brittle blond hair; bloodshot eyes streaked black eyeliner down her hollow cheeks. "These fucking parties you send my boy to—you're hiring him out to rock spiders, aren't you?"

Pinkie dragged on his cigarette. "What did ya think he was doin'—goin' to Sunday school? Ya dumb cunt!" Smoke streamed from his nose.

"You've turned me into a tramp but I won't let you do it to my little boy!" Michelle's voice quaked; her hands shook as withdrawal gnawed. "He's a child! You—I won't have it—I'm going to the police!"

Pinkie chewed his lip as he watched Michelle stumble down the hall.

"This'll never do, Pinkie."

He had some cops in his pocket but not the Snow Whites. Pinkie feared the Snow Whites. The gulp of vodka stung his throat and Pinkie pulled his keys from his pocket. He crushed out his cigarette, scratched his forearm and trotted after Michelle; he slipped his arm around her waist.

"Come on, Lovie—I'll drive you home."

"Fuck off! I'll find my own way home!"

"Don't be stupid, girl! You're in no state—" Pinkie reeled back as Michelle grabbed a heavy glass vase and smashed it across his mouth. He spat out his front teeth and a mouthful of blood. "You fuckin' cunt! Now you've really pissed me off!"

Michelle's head whipped sideway at a punch and she sprawled on the carpet. He dragged her back to her room.

"Now Lovie, have a shot of smack. Come on, it'll make you feel better."

When the heroin had calmed Michelle, Pinkie led her to his car. It neared two a.m. when Pinkie U-turned onto the edge of the highway high in the Cunningham Ranges, and switched off the ignition. The motor ticked, cooling in the chilled mountain air. Above him a billion stars glittered in the black sky. The unconscious hooker weighed little as he hauled her from the car, dragged her to the edge of the road, wrung her neck and threw her into the pitch-black ravine.

****

Pinkie took Paul to live upstairs at Ruby's Wine Bar. He shared a room with Shane and Ben, his pervert party mates. Paul was ten, Shane and Ben eleven. Ruby's Wine Bar closed at one p.m. but the brothel upstairs opened all hours. Each night Paul fell asleep to the sounds of commercial copulation, grunts and moans—whores faking orgasms. The only thing about the place Paul liked was the food. The boys had three meals a day, something Paul had rarely had.

Sharing a room with Ben and Shane made life a little easier, the big brothers he never had. The older boys often discussed what happened to them, and for Paul, talking about it diminished the horror. Paul missed his mother and dreamed of the day she would return and take him out of Ruby's place. She had vanished. Paul didn't allow himself to grieve for her—that would be admitting to the world what he knew in his heart. The girl was dead. His mother no longer existed.

****

Shane flicked through a Phantom comic and Paul drifted into sleep when the door burst open, Ben hurried to the vanity basin and washed out his mouth.

"How was it?"

"Not so bad. Old Bouncy Harold again, he only wanted me to play with his noodle and then suck it."

"Better than having a sore arse for a week."

"I heard Ruby organising another pervert party for Saturday night." Ben wiped his face, closed the door and flopped on his bed.

Shane groaned and threw the Phantom comic. "Oh no—not again!"

Paul's eyes widened. He felt sick; he hated Ruby's parties. "I'd rather live on the riverbank with the bums than go to another one of those parties."

"Me too," said Ben. "I might get a job."

"Well let's go then."

"Wait—tonight when Ruby goes to bed, I'll sneak down and knock over her safe." Shane kept his voice to a whisper.

"How?"

"I know the combination."

"How?"

Remember that night after the last perv party, I was spewing up everywhere?"

Paul and Ben sat up.

"Ruby took me down to her office and fed me a slug of brandy. While I was drinking it, she opened the safe and put some money in it. Six, six, nine, three. I was sitting right there watching, she probably thought I was drunk or half asleep."

"How much do you reckon she has in there?"

"Dunno. Heaps."

The hours ticked by, Ben watched through the crack in the door. Finally, he gave Paul and Shane the thumbs up.

"Wait for a bit, let her go to sleep."

"That won't take long," said Ben, "she drank half a bottle of gin tonight."

The brothel fell quiet as usual on Monday night when the parade of horny johns inexplicably slowed. The three boys gathered their belongings, crept down the stairs and along the corridor to Ruby's office.

Ben pushed against the door. "Damn! It's locked!"

"Where's the key?"

"Ruby takes her keys with her to her room."

"Shit! How are we going to get them?"

"I'll get them." Paul hurried away and up the stairs before the others could argue. He excelled at sneaking around; he had often taken money while his mother had slept, both from her and her boyfriends. He slowed as he entered the hallway, praying the floor wouldn't squeak. He eased Ruby's door open and listened for a full minute. Soft snores emitted from the room. The door creaked a little as he pushed it wider, but the snores continued. He crept across to Ruby's bedside, the keys lay on the nightstand, his hand closed around them and he backed away. As he slipped through the door, a loud snort made Paul's heart bang against his ribs. He stood still and listened. A minute passed and the snoring resumed.

He sprinted soundlessly towards Ben and Shane. "Got 'em!"

"You beauty!"

The boys got away with one hundred and seventy dollars to split between them.

8.

Jack Walker

An hour past midnight and The Pearl's DJ, Jack Walker, noticed the boy peering from the backstage door watching the dance floor. While a song played, Jack crept over and grabbed the boy before he could run.

"What are you doing?"

"I'm just watching!"

"You're too young to be in here. Where are your parents?"

"I don't have any parents."

"Where do you live?"

"Nowhere."

"You must live somewhere."

"Just here and there."

"You live on the street?"

The boy lowered his gaze.

"You don't have a home, do you?"

The boy shook his head. "But I'm okay. I just want to listen to the music."

People occasionally wandered in the back door of The Pearl. When the bands finished playing after midnight they sometimes didn't latch the door properly. Jack often had to ask people to leave. This little boy looked about ten-years old and homeless.

"Look—ah—why don't you sleep in the dressing room at night? I'm sure Craig won't mind. You'll have to get out when the bands are here, there's a shower in there if you want to use it. Just don't make a mess, okay?"

The boy looked at Jack with disbelieving eyes.

"What's your name?" Jack hoped his generosity would not come back to bite him on the arse.

"It's Paul."

"Okay Paul. You must promise you won't go wandering around inside the club. Back stage only."

"Okay."

"You promise?"

"I promise."

"Okay, you can sit out here and listen to the music. Just stay out of sight."

****

As Tom went about his evening routine, serving beer and chatting with the regulars, Margie passed him a folded sheet of paper.

"That's those names ya wanted, Tom."

"Thanks, Margie." He slipped it into his top pocket.

"See ya tomorra, Tom."

In his office after closing time, Tom pulled the list from his pocket. His eyebrows shot up as he read it.

"Mother of God!" He stuffed the sheet of lined foolscap into his top drawer and locked it. Some of those names would rock the city of Brisbane to its foundations. He would quiz Margie in the morning about her source. He could be sued, big time if he went waving that information about town. He needed time to think about this.

****

Naz Van Nek

Naz listened from outside as his cousin argued with someone on the phone, anger throttling his voice. *Crash.* The receiver hit the cradle and the call ended. As he took a step towards Rick's office the phone rang again, the receiver rattled and Rick snarled, "What! Yes, it's done! Now get off my back!"

A thump told Naz another call had ended.

"Everything alright, Rick?"

"Yeah—fine. Why are you listening to my conversations?"

"Well, I was coming to see if you wanted to go and get some lunch, geez—sour!"

"It's just business, okay?"

"Maybe you should get Burt to sort a few of them out."

Rick shook his head; his eyes went to the window. "Yeah, come on. Lunch."

9

Vince and Eddie

Vince Wilkins and Eddie Holt set out to celebrate the launch of their security business, an exciting venture for the young men. Vince was a brawny, twenty-seven-year-old. Eddie's polio shortened leg slowed him a little, but at twenty-eight, he packed a powerful punch. Vince and Eddie met in prison. Vince had served time for aggravated assault and Eddie for armed robbery. They both intended to go straight—the security business their one chance at joining civilised society. They had a number of clients already signed—security patrols at several used car yards, bouncers and doormen to nightclubs and pubs, even walking with pimps and madams as they deposited their takings at the bank. As always on a Saturday night, Ruby's Wine Bar hummed with patrons and a piano tinkled an accompaniment to the banter. Ruby looked radiant in her lime-green flares, platform sandals and halter neck top. As always, she held a silver cigarette holder between her fingers, in her other hand a tall glass of amber liquid.

"Good evening, boys. I hear you're celebrating your new business. Let me buy you the next round."

"Sure, Ruby." Vince passed her a card. "Anytime you need help with your security, give me a call."

****

Vince woke the next morning in a strange room, dull pain pounded in his head, his body weak and sweaty. Someone had knocked on the door. He scrambled out of bed and found his pants, neatly folded over the back of the chair. He tried to recall the night before; he remembered coming into Ruby's to celebrate his new business venture. He remembered Ruby's toast to their success, a vague recollection of stairs, and bright flashes of light—a storm? The harder he tried to recall the quicker the memory slipped away.

"Vince?" Eddie's voice bore the hallmarks of a hard night out.

Vince pulled the door open.

"Oh thank Christ! Man what did we do last night?" Eddie rubbed his face and yawned, bloodshot eyes stark against his white face.

"I was going to ask you the same thing. Where are we?" Vince poked his head out and peered down the hallway. The place looked like an old-fashioned hotel.

"We're upstairs in Ruby's Wine Bar. Only it's nothing like a wine bar, it's a fucking whorehouse!"

"Let's get the fuck out of here."

****

Two days later, Vince sat at his desk and stared at photos that fell out of a manila envelope; his insides lurched. A wave of nausea crashed over him as he picked up a picture of himself and two little boys—naked. It was the room he'd woke in on Sunday morning. There could be no mistake; it was him in the photo, looking dazed but apparently awake. Vince could remember nothing of the scene. His hand shook as he rifled through the rest of the photos. He and Eddie both photographed naked with little boys. He examined the boys' faces, he'd never seen either of them before, but the evidence indisputable. The photos slipped from Vince's fingers as the phone jangled beside him; his hand shook as he lifted the receiver.

"Hello," he croaked.

The man's voice carried a lilt of amusement. "Do you like the photos?"

"Where—how did you get these photos?"

"Doesn't matter. I've got them. Ruby provides many services including family portraits."

"Why are you doing this?"

"Listen carefully. If you don't want those photos spread all over the city, to every newspaper, TV station, and to the police— listen carefully…"

10

Carla

Carla Creevey had a bad case of the whips and jangles; her last fix had happened around midnight. Heroin, the beautiful dream; the emotional levee that always broke and flooded her with emotions she'd rather ignore. As her liver eliminated the alcohol from her system, the rats of withdrawal woke and chewed at every nerve; an invisible hand punched her guts at irregular intervals. Her daughter slept on a mattress on the floor of the fleapit she called home. Little Jody—only three years old—father unknown. Carla shivered and wracked her brain; what had upset her the night before? Pinkie. She'd been drinking with Pinkie. He came around and shagged her, then produced a big bottle of Vat 69. Her pimp; but last night, as he often did, Pinkie sampled the goods he flogged to every man and his dog.

Carla reeled back from her reflection in a black-spotted mirror above an ancient dresser. At thirty, she looked and felt fifty. Her desire for the act she charged money to perform had faded in recent years.

"Youth's a mask but it don't last, Carla." She brushed her hair and redoubled her efforts to remember what Pinkie had said or done that disturbed her so. Then from the clouds of withdrawal, the memory hit her like the Sunlander on a downhill run. The Pearl—he said The Pearl would go up tonight. Carla thought it a pity; Craig Kinane was a nice bloke. A horse's hoof—poof—queer—fairy queen, whatever you liked to call them but he didn't deserve to have his club burned out. She'd have to write it down otherwise she would forget about it by lunchtime. She found a pen and looked around for something to write on—Carla didn't usually write anything. Her daughter's copy of Dr Zeus' The Cat in the Hat the only available paper. She wrote inside the back cover, *'Tonit eval peple are gon to burn the purl and valley star. Pinkie told me all ebout it. He nos who, I can't rember.'*

For good measure, Carla signed her name and peered at the calendar. It was definitely Saturday—Saturday the sixth—she wrote the date next to her signature.

"There, that makes it legal—doesn't it?" Carla had signed a number of police statements in her time.

The pages flapped a little as she picked the book up, shrugged and dropped it into her daughter's old cardboard school port with her doll and the clothes she took to the babysitter.

What are you going to do about it, Carla?

The effort of writing that statement nauseated her and Carla's mind returned to her own situation, she needed a fix—quickly. She searched through her drawers, under her cushions and in the freezer. Nothing. Concern over Pinkie's disclosure of the night before flickered and died in the shadows of a more pressing problem; she needed a fix.

****

Pinkie woke with a taste in his mouth like a gorilla's armpit and the scent of antique farts in his nose.

"What the fuck did you get up to last night, Pinkie?"

He vaguely remembered going to visit Carla on her night off. He had been feeling horny but because he'd recently had the rest of his front teeth knocked out, he was in no condition to try his luck at one of the clubs. He'd gone around and screwed old Carla. With enough booze in him, Pinkie would shag a brown snake; he thought he probably had at some point.

There might even be a few little snakettes out there with my face on them.

The conversation they'd had trickled back, a word here and laugh there...

"Pinkie, you fuckin' dickhead!" He leaped out of bed and the hangover jackhammered his forehead, he panted until his vision cleared. "You told a hooker something you were meant to tell no one. Old Carla's mouth is bigger than a hippo's cunt!"

He snatched up his car keys and his bag of gear. All the way to Carla's place, he justified his intentions to himself.

Carla's best years are behind her, she'll soon be too old to work in a brothel.

When women became too old to be hookers, they either found religion and became a born again pain in the arse, or took what remained of their feminine charms to the seedy back streets and along the dockside. The fix they had needed to sell their youthful bodies became the driving force that motivated their sleazy trade. With their best years behind them, the darkness was their only friend.

Pinkie would save Carla from that fate; she welcomed his arrival with a bag of smack.

"Pinkie, have you got some gear? I'm dying."

"Don't sweat it, Honey, of course I have." He tossed her the tourniquet. By the time he had it cooked up on the tarnished spoon, she had isolated a vein for him to inject an elephantine dose of pure heroin.

****

Paul welcomed a safe place to sleep, Shane and Ben moved in with him. Each night they slept in the dressing room and left before the cleaners came. Ben and Shane didn't return until the early hours, but Paul always came back when he saw Jack arrive for work. Sometimes another DJ took Jack's place, Paul kept himself well hidden; there hadn't been many adults in Paul's life the he had trusted, but he trusted Jack.

One morning in the dark before dawn, the boys awoke to the sound of hushed voices and footsteps. They cracked open the dressing room and watched two men lug a big plywood box into the backstage area. The floor shook as they set it down.

"Under here."

Paul's suspicion of men kept his attention to detail. The man had carrot coloured hair and a pronounced limp. His left leg had a

40

shrunken appearance. His companion brawny and square jawed with light brown hair.

They opened a low panel under the back of the stage and shoved the box in. The carrot top crawled in, pushing the box further under the stage. The other man shone a torch after him; Paul could see them clearly. The man came out feet first, pulled himself upright.

"Okay. We've done our bit."

The brawny man grabbed a broom to sweep the dust back under the stage.

"Come on, stop fucking around—let's get out of here."

"I've got to clean up all the dust you dragged out with you."

"Well fuckin' hurry up."

The hatched clicked shut. "Okay, let's go."

****

On Saturday night, an unfriendly DJ filled in for Jack. "Gorn—fuck off out of here!"

Paul scuttled out the backstage door and wandered towards Chinatown. He didn't know where Ben and Shane went but he knew a spot he could hide until it was safe to return to the Pearl's dressing room. After the band left, he could sneak in and he hoped the hostile DJ wouldn't see him.

****

Ten minutes to three on Sunday morning, Craig Kinane collected glasses and chatted to the stragglers as they downed their last drinks. Those who still had energy to burn swayed on the dance floor; young men ramped up efforts to lure girls to their beds. The DJ pumped out David Bowie at a volume unchecked, and a girl tried to drag Craig onto the dance floor. As he turned back towards the bar, an invisible force like a giant fiery fist hit him from behind and flung him like a ragdoll. Screaming patrons fled for the exits; some with their clothes alight. Flames climbed the stage curtains and licked the walls, acoustic tiles fell from the ceiling and the fire crawled into the roof. Intense heat buckled the Pearl's tin roof, the bright orange flames broke through and the updraft spurred the blaze high above Wickham Street. Around in Brunswick Street flames consumed the Valley Star Hotel. Upstairs, Tom and Mary Kinane slept; the lethal smoke crept into their room and claimed their lives minutes before the flames reached them. Dirty ash rained over Fortitude Valley, a light northerly carried black smoke, the acrid stink of burning paint, carpet, and human bodies across the Brisbane River.

****

Things didn't go to plan for Paul. As he wandered back towards Fortitude Valley, a gang of teenagers chased him. Paul had to take another route to evade his would-be attackers and in the early hours he emerged onto Wickham Street. The wail of sirens roused his curiosity and he quickened his pace; ahead, strobing red lights and the glow of flames drew his attention. In the distance the smoggy air glowed, a fire appliance roared past. Paul shook.

Is the city on fire?

He waited along the street until Ben and Shane returned. They debated whether to tell the police what they'd witnessed. They didn't know whether or not the men who put the box under the stage were responsible for the fire.

"I don't think we should tell the fuzz anything," said Ben. "If they find out we've been sleeping in the Pearl's dressing room, they might blame us for the fire."

"Yeah, I say we shut up and stay away."

"Okay." Paul trusted the judgment of his older companions.

11

Lester

In the following weeks, Detective Sergeant Lester Gainsford reflected on the oath he swore when he joined the Queensland Police Force. Something about swearing by almighty God without favour or affection, malice or ill will; something about discharging all the duties legally imposed upon him according to law. So help him, God.

As he often had done, Lester climbed out of bed at dawn after precious few hours of sleep and scratched his testicles. Another Sunday morning and the work roster demanded his presence. He opened the curtains to a hazy daybreak, the eastern horizon red and the sky dusty pink, fading to grey in the west.

"Bushfires are early this year by the looks of it."

His head turned to the empty bed; it was three weeks since his wife took their kids and left him to a steady diet of cigarettes and misery. Lester was forty-two and that morning, each of those years dragged on his shoulders and etched on his face. He stretched, joints popped and cracked. His yawn deteriorated into a moan. He fumbled for his cigarette packet and flipped the top. With a frown and grunt, he plied the lighter.

"Fuck, fuck, and fuck." He coughed out a cloud of smoke, stumbled to the bathroom, peed, showered, and shaved. Then to the kitchen for coffee and toast. His human male identity joined him as he cleaned his teeth and dressed. He arrived at Police Headquarters at six a.m. to a hive of activity.

"Gainsford, you're just in time—we're about to start." Inspector Wright held a manila folder in one hand and a mug of coffee in the other.

"Start what?"

"You haven't turned on a TV or listened to the radio this morning, have you?"

"Nuh."

"Just get in there."

Lester squinted; his boss looked on edge. He opened his mouth to enquire what had the Inspector looking like he'd slept with an echidna but shrugged and proceeded into the briefing room. As Lester yawned and took a seat beside detective constables Ray Sims, and Dave Cramb, he glanced around the room. His skin crawled; Lyle Furner and Charlie Doyle of the Licensing Branch sat in the corner, heads together; their lips framed a muttered conversation. He had spent three years in Licensing—about two years and eleven months too long.

Wright placed his coffee mug on the desk and looked around the room.

"Most of you know about the fires of last night," he paused to cast an accusatory glance at Lester. "For those whose minds were elsewhere, the Pearl nightclub and the Valley Star Hotel burned down in suspicious circumstances. We haven't confirmed how many died but I think the number will go above five including Tom and Mary Kinane, and their son, Craig.

"Senior Constable McCaffery was first on the scene at The Pearl. Constable?"

McCaffery pushed his blond hair back as he took his place beside Inspector Wright to read from his notebook. Lester's mind drifted to the Kinanes. The name carried respect in the city, god-fearing Irish Catholics—a part of Brisbane's history. Whom had they upset?

"Gainsford."

Lester snapped out of his gloomy reverie. Inspector Wright frowned at him.

"Yes, sorry—I was thinking."

"Good. Do a lot more thinking because I'm putting you in charge of this investigation." His eyes lingered on Lester before returning to those seated before him. "Those of you already working on cases stay on them but keep an ear open—someone out there will know who set those fires. If you hear anything, report it to Detective Sergeant Gainsford. Lester, you take Ray, Dave, and any available uniformed officers with you, get over to Fortitude Valley. See what you can dig up. Have a good day, people."

The room filled with scrapes of chairs, shuffling papers, and the rumble of voices as the officers on duty moved out for another day policing the city. Few of them knew what Lester knew, that the police force they had sworn to serve to the best of their ability had patches of rot. Cancerous corruption. He didn't know how far up the tree it went, but he was certain that one day the whole thing would come crashing down and prayed he'd come out with his integrity untarnished.

"Gainsford."

A chill skulked down Lester's spine as Detective Constable Charlie Doyle sidled up. Lester squinted at the hawkish features of Detective Sergeant Furner's lapdog—backstabber extraordinaire.

"Would you like a tip, Lester?"

"No, but I'm going to get one anyway so go on." Lester's scalp prickled—listening to Charlie Doyle's slippery utterance was akin to lifting the lid on a trapdoor spider. During his years in the Licensing Branch, Lester had often suspected Furner and Doyle received kickbacks, but instead of seeking evidence, he deemed it wise to stay the hell away. He wanted his career to carry him through to retirement.

"You'd be better to go to Sydney and ask questions. Those gangs down there are trying to muscle in on the local scene."

"I'll keep it in mind." Lester walked away, Dave and Ray followed.

My money is on someone closer to home.

****

As Lester drove towards the Valley, a column of smoke rose and curled; it spilled into the cooler air above the leaden waters of the Brisbane River. At the Pearl, firemen wound a hose back onto its reel; each turn forced a spurt of water from the nozzle like a retching python. Part of the building's façade remained black and forlorn against the dirty apricot sky. In the Sunday morning stillness, a distant ship's horn barged upriver from the Hamilton Docks.

Standing back watching the forensic officers sifting through the remains of the Pearl, Lester fretted about Queensland, his home state—the Sunshine State. This suburb, Fortitude Valley, was the locus of all the graft and corruption. By day the streets were all but empty, not many ordinary businesses remained. By night it came alive—the place to be if you sought entertainment. Alongside the legitimate clubs, restaurants, and hotels, illegal brothels and casinos operated in plain sight protected by the very people paid to prevent their existence. The illegal outfits paid for protection and as long as they made regular payments, they could operate with impunity. Even the legitimate clubs had to pay for protection; failure to do so brought gangs of thugs to start a brawl. No club owner wanted his place to gain a bad reputation.

The Pearl was one of the legitimate nightspots, a place where young people went to drink, socialise, and see a live band. The Apollo Nightclub next door showed signs of damage, both fire and water but it remained intact. The owner kept his business legal, though Lester had heard rumours of unpaid debts. He eyed the scorched paintwork and his thoughts meandered—Lyle Furner had expressed his interest in buying the Apollo when Lester had worked in the Licensing Branch. He brushed aside the memory of nearly two years before; nothing had come of it. Furner continued to serve in the police force.

"I'll have an interim report for you in about an hour." The head of the forensic team was a dour man in his late fifties, one who had scraped up too many dead bodies—world weary and worn by death and destruction.

When Lester's team moved on to what remained of the Valley Star, he caught sight of his most useful informant across the pile of burnt iron and smouldering timber. The old lagger made eye contact, limped across the pavement and disappeared between two buildings. Ross Young worked as a yardman around various pubs, a former stevedore; he'd left the port after an accident had shattered his leg.

"Wait for me, boys. I'll just go and have a word with Ross." As he followed, Lester checked his pockets for cash. A ten and two fives plus a handful of shrapnel. He found Ross sitting on a low brick wall at the end of the lane that ran behind the burned out pub. For a man with a crippled leg, he'd covered a fair distance in a short time.

"Had an idea I'd be seein' you sometime this mornin', Gainsford."

"You know me, Ross—anywhere there's murder and mayhem." Lester pulled out his cigarette packet, transferred one to his mouth and extended the pack to Ross. The old stevedore took one with a jittery hand. Lester lit their cigarettes and drew a lung full of smoke. "What have you got for me, Ross?"

"There's been a lot of talk going about." He looked both ways along the lane, coughed and spat a tobacco-stained glob. Lester waited for him to continue, Ross focused on dragging his cigarette down to the butt.

"What kind of talk?"

Ross stuck the cigarette between his lips and folded his arms. Smoke leaked out of his face. "I dunno—it might be all bullshit." The cigarette jiggled as he spoke.

"Tell me what you know and let me work out what is bullshit and what's not."

"I only know a tiny bit—me and old Pinkie was over at The Brekkie on Fridee and Daryl Reid and that young fella, Rusty Russell, was talkin' to Pinkie. I didn't 'ear all of it, but Pinkie was sayin' there was gonna be fireworks on Saddee night." He sucked on the cigarette and plucked it from his mouth. "I think they wanted to sound like they was in league with the big boys. Stupid bastards, all of 'em. That young Daryl—he's a bit..." Ross circled his ear with his cigarette hand.

Lester had heard of Daryl and Rusty. They'd started out as two wide-eyed boys, a little too enthralled by the city's underbelly. They'd been arrested for a number of offences from robbing a TAB to car theft.

"Did you happen to hear why?"

"The talk was it's all about drivin' down the price of The Apollo next door to the Pearl. Some crooked bastard wants to buy it cheap."

Lester frowned; murdering innocent people was a brutal way to get your hands on some cheap real estate.

"But I dunno—I reckon one of t'other club owners 'ad the shits on Tom and his boy. They was makin' heaps of dough. Rick Campbell and his half-wit cousin was bitchin' about the Kinanes last time I was in Rick's joint—I wouldn't put it past Rick to do somethin' like this. It's bloody awful, Lester, I hope you catch the bastards who dunnit."

Lester pulled a ten out of his pocket, tucked it into the cigarette packet and passed it to Ross. "Thanks, Ross. I'll see if I can find Reid and Russell. I might be able to squeeze the truth out of them."

****

Vince and Eddie laid low that Sunday morning and waited for the police to come an arrest them. They'd been instructed, *Just plant the bombs and shutup.'* Their blackmailer had assured them no one would die, the bombs would go off inside empty buildings to scare the Kinanes.

Eight a.m. and Eddie drained his second glass of bourbon, the ice rattled as he set it on the table.

Vince slumped on the lounge; his hands obscured his face. "We shoulda known—there is no safe way to burn down a building."

"They said they would go off well after closing time—maybe we shoulda gone to the cops."

"Do you really think the cops woulda believed we'd been set up that night at Ruby's?"

“I dunno.”

Vince rose and clicked on the TV. “We’re ex-cons. You know we couldn’t have taken that chance.”

“So whadda we do?”

“Wait and see. What else can we do? We don’t have enough money to leave the state, let alone leave the country.”

Eddie nodded. “Yeah. Yeah you’re right. I say we carry on as normal—we’re legit businessmen now. The last thing I wanna do is walk away just when we’re getting established.”

“I fuckin’ feel sorry for the Kinane family. Tom and Mary Kinane lived upstairs at the Valley Star, that arsehole said the building would be empty. Now they’re dead! We shoulda checked.”

“It’s done now, there’s nothin’ we can do.”

“Fuckin’ nothin’!”

<h1 style="text-align:center">12</h1>

Jack Walker never knew his heart could hurt this much and not kill him. Craig was dead. The love of Jack's life, a love they shared behind closed doors. The kind of love that could see them imprisoned. Until he met Craig, Jack's life had proceeded like that of many gays who, through no fault of their own, found themselves living outside the law. Many tried and inevitably failed to live a heterosexual life. Meeting Craig hadn't brought Jack within the boundaries of society's notion of normality but it brought security, someone to come home to—someone to share his life in the shadows.

Jack's tears fell on the silver framed photograph of Craig; he brushed them off and hugged it to his breast.

"I'll get them, Craig. If it takes me the rest of my life, I'll get them."

He grieved alone; at the funeral he sat in the back row. He didn't approach Craig's brothers and sisters—what would he say to them? He sat in a state of detachment as he listened to the preacher, but as the Kinanes bore Craig's casket on their shoulders, Jack's tears returned. When they lowered him into the earth, Jack turned away. He locked himself in his car and cried alone, without

Craig there remained no reason to exist. Craig's smile lingered but the warmth of his touch had moved beyond Jack's reach.

****

The funerals came and went in a haze of blackest grief. The remaining Kinanes clung together, trusting the police to find those responsible for the death of their parents and brother. The three eldest Kinanes, Jimmy, Nola, and Fiona, tried to step into their parents' shoes as they watched the youngest three closely; the loss of the middle child, Craig, opened an unforeseen divide. On compassionate leave from the ADF, the twins had arrived home for the funeral in a murderous rage, and it rubbed off on Mikey. They talked late into the night of revenge, amid angry tears they devised abstract plans to annihilate those who had torn their family apart.

"Boys," said Nola, "please stop talking like that. The police will find who is responsible and they'll be sent to prison."

"Not if I get hold of them first." Of all the Kinanes, Mikey stood the tallest—blessed with the best and worst of Irish blood, intelligent, handsome, and charming. Rarely showing his dangerous side—when wronged he could plumb the depths of malice. Any who crossed Mikey Kinane had better prepare for the fight of their lives.

"Mikey, please." His sister sat beside him, her arm around his shoulders. "Mum would have told us to pray. To ask Jesus—"

"Pray?"

"Like Mum used to, remember the pictures she had of Jesus?"

"Yeah, I remember. Sad Jesus. Healing hands Jesus. Nailed by the hands and feet Jesus. The keeper of my greatest sins Jesus. The knower. The forgiver. The man who gives me a break. The man who gives a shit. The man who let my family burn! Or maybe the man who isn't there at all, dammit!"

"Mikey—"

"Sure, Nola. Let's pray. Pray to Jesus to curse those men to burn in hellfire and send them his wrath, pain, and pestilence—curse them to die of disease or drown or suffocate! You can pray all you like." Mikey's face tingled as he sucked in air. "Or if we really want results, why don't I handle it? Let them die with my bullet in their head."

Mikey threw off his sister's arm and sprang out of the chair.

Nola fell to the floor.

"Mikey!" Jimmy's face paled.

Mikey's anger spiralled to guilt as he helped his eldest sister up and hugged her. "Nola, I'm sorry. I didn't mean to hurt you."

"I'm okay, Mikey. Just stop all this wild talk, please. Let the police handle it."

"But what if they don't?"

"Then we'll reassess our options." Jimmy patted his back. "Remember what Dad used to say? 'Don't bid the Devil good day until you meet him.'"

Mikey scowled, nothing could obviate his fury. "I'll do more than bid him good day, I'll waltz the bastard right across Brisbane." He strode from the house into the solitude of darkness.

I'll waltz the bastard straight to the door of those who took my kin.

Angry tears fell as Craig's laughing face floated before him. He screamed inside at the time he'd wasted wanting his brother to be like him. He was a Kinane; nothing else mattered.

Visions of flames and explosions tormented him.

Nobody should die like that, especially a Kinane.

Mikey had grown up believing his family name meant something. The Kinanes had owned pubs in the Brisbane area for over a century, generations of proud tradition and before that, his great-grandfather owned a pub in Belfast. Their Irish blood filled him with fierce pride. Black Irish—not the carrot topped variety. Wild and tough and invincible.

Why did you let this happen, Dad? What was all that shit you used to say about Irish luck?

He climbed onto the tractor beside the shed and watched a sliver of moon sink into the tree line—absorbing the picture for his parents and brother, a vision they would never again see. As he watched, he sought stillness in the white-water torrent of his youth. The deaths of those who bore him conveyed Mikey to the edge of mortality, to gaze into the dark chasm that waited for him. The outline of the Olsen's farmhouse a dark shape in the distance drew him back; thoughts of a future with Kitty calmed him. He'd find a way to rebuild his family's business.

I'll show those bastards they can't fuck with the Kinanes.

His father's voice rang in his head, laughing and sprouting his Irish wisdom. *'You can't build a barrel around a bunghole, Mikey.'*

13

The search for Daryl Reid and Rusty Russell led Lester and his team into the rattiest rat holes in Brisbane. While he drove across the Story Bridge for the fourth time that morning, chatter on the police radio carried news of the death of a prostitute named Carla Creevy, found dead of a suspected overdose. Carla had worked for Pinkie Pinchester for eighteen years.

Dave Cramb grunted from the backseat. "Well that was always gonna happen."

Detective Constable Ray Sims nodded from the front seat beside Lester. "Got her hands on some pure heroin."

Lester pitied working girls; many started and promised themselves they would stop as soon as they got some money together. Many never got it together and too many of them had their lives destroyed. Only the smart and the lucky walked away with money to begin a new life. "Poor girl—what a shit life to lead."

Ray was unsympathetic. "She could have got a job as a checkout chic at Woolies or somewhere."

Lester ignored Ray's censorious statement. "I might also ask Pinkie about Carla's death while I've got him."

"You reckon he might've done it?"

"Nah. Probably not. He's a sleazy little cunt but when it comes to violence, I doubt Pinkie's balls travel too well."

Dave leaned forward. "Hey, Carla had a kid, didn't she? Get on the radio and ask what happened to him—or her."

Ray lifted the microphone out of its cradle, asked the question and waited. Minutes passed—Ray repeated the question. Finally the radio operator replied. "According to the guys who investigated her death, an aunt has taken the child."

Lester parked the car half a block from Pinkie's cathouse in West End. He waited, his colleague's heads, one bald, one blond, bobbed along a brick wall and disappeared around the back of the old cottage. Lester entered the frowsy foyer without ringing the bell. Long years of foot traffic had flattened the grubby shagpile. A fly speckled bunch of plastic roses gathered dust on the nest of tables in the corner. The brooding eyes of a nude invited him into her grimy frame, its tarnished gold befit the shabby room. The reek of mould and incense reigned in the brothel's Monday morning silence.

The floor creaked and a woman poked her head into the room. "Can I help you?" The woman's gimcrack dress resembled a string bag overstuffed with onions, around her neck hung a fox fur that might have had its head slammed in a car door at some point.

"I'm looking for Des Pinchester. He's not at his house, so I'm guessing he's here."

"Pinkie has gone interstate, he won't be back for about a month."

"Where did he go to?"

"Dunno. Interstate."

"Do you mind if I take a look inside?"

"Sure. Perhaps I can introduce you to our new girl, beautiful young thing—only four—sixteen—you'll love her."

"Fourteen eh?"

"No—no, that was just a slip of the tongue."

"Well you're in the right place for that, hey."

Her screech of mirth rattled his eardrums. "Oh! You're a cheeky one aren't you?"

Lester massaged his ear canal. "That's me. So let me take a look inside."

Lester, Dave, and Ray combed the brothel amid complaints from the girls trying to sleep in.

"Like I toldya, he ain't here."

Lester passed the madam his card. "Well if you see him, give me a cooee—we would like to ask him some questions."

Pinkie was nowhere Lester searched that morning and he refused to believe the interstate story.

Gone to ground like a typical rat.

They abandoned the search for Pinkie and concentrated on finding Daryl Reid and Rusty Russell. Two days passed and they caught Daryl hiding at his girlfriend's house.

"Daryl Reid, we like to ask you a few questions regarding the firebombing of the Pearl and the Valley Star Hotel." Lester failed to dodge as Daryl swung a stinging punch; he grabbed the alleged felon's wrist and threw him on the floor. "You want me to bring you in for assaulting a police officer?"

"Fuck off! I don't know nuthin'."

"Let me decide how much you know, eh?"

"This is police brutality—"

"Yeah, and it hurts, hey?" Lester tweaked Daryl's arm higher up his back and ground his face into the filthy carpet that moulted in patches like a mangy dog.

"Now, where is your mate, Rusty Russell?"

"Fuck Rusty."

"I don't want to hear about your love life, I just want to know where I can find him."

"I haven't seen him for days—he disappeared."

"What's his address?"

"I dunno."

"You need to cooperate or maybe you'll find yourself taking the rap for the whole thing. Eight counts of murder plus a few counts we haven't thought of yet."

"Okay—okay, he lives out at Wavell Heights. I'll tell you— but don't tell him I told you. He hangs about with some dangerous people these days."

"Right, I'm going to release you, but you better not try to hit me again. Okay?"

Daryl nodded, his cheek rubbed on the carpet.

"Now, tell me what you know about the firebombing."

"I said I don't know nuthin!"

"Well I've heard different. I've heard you know all about it."

Several hours of questions yielded nothing. Lester suspected Daryl knew plenty but someone had put the frighteners on him. He released him and began compiling notes. The next day he would chase up Rusty Russell. Nightfall approached when he decided to quit and go home.

"Lester," the telephonist called as he passed. "I just put a call through to your desk; Daryl Reid wants to talk to you."

Lester sprinted back to the office, skidded to a halt beside his desk and snatched up the receiver.

"Daryl—"

"Sergeant Gainsford! I've changed my mind—I'll tell you everything—but you have to come and get me now!"

"Where are you?"

"You have to promise I'll be protected!"

"We can hide you, yes—I promise—now where are you?" Lester heard noises in the background—a crash of breaking glass?

"I'm at my place—please hurry!"

His colleagues, Ray and Dave had already clocked off. Lester checked Daryl's address on his notes; ran to the rack and grabbed the keys for his work car. Down in the car park, he discovered he had the wrong keys and ran back upstairs, cursing. His hands shook as he checked a dozen keys before he found the correct set; someone had muddled the key rack. Snarled traffic on the Victoria Bridge halted his progress. Lester grabbed the microphone; the radio was dead.

"What the fucking hell?" He crashed the handpiece back into its holder and turned on the siren. Even with the flashers on it took him close to forty-five minutes to reach Reid's house. He sprinted across the front porch and banged on the front door; he couldn't see any lights inside. He hammered the door again and called out. The door opened and Lester's heart dropped to his boots.

"Detective Sergeant Gainsford, returning to the scene of the crime are we?" Lyle Furner's dead snake eyes shifted from Gainsford to the street and back.

"What crime? What are you doing here?"

"Attending a murder scene—why did you come back?"

"Come back?"

"Charlie and I got a call from Reid saying you were trying to break into his house. When we got here, Reid was dead, stabbed with his own kitchen knife—but don't worry, Lester—we've sanitised the scene. No one will be able to pin it on you."

"What are you talking about? I just got here!"

"Of course you did! Stick with that story, Lester. Charlie and I will back you up. You did the city a favour really, Reid was just a petty thug. We're all better off without him."

True to his word, Lyle and Charlie attributed the mysterious death of Daryl Reid to a person unknown. Lester told his side of the story so many time's he worried it had begun to sound rehearsed. The whispers of the CIB's entrenched corridor assassins left Lester looking as bent as Uri Geller's practice spoon.

14

A crash and a tinkle of shattered glass woke Rusty Russell as he wrestled with a dream—the sheets tangled and soaked with sweat. He sat up, eyes agog in the dark. The black space of open door lightened as a big fair-haired man appeared; Rusty's bowels loosened.

"Get dressed, Rusty. We're going cruising"

"Who are you?"

"Your worst nightmare. Hurry up!"

"What do you want? I didn't do anything!"

A knife pricked the skin of Rusty's jaw. "Nah, but you're going to. Hurry up and get dressed or I might slit your throat instead."

Rusty pulled on his jeans and t-shirt; as he leaned down to put on his shoes, something thumped the back of his neck. Rusty slumped to the floor. Rope pinched his wrists and jolted him back to awareness; he tried to kick free but his feet and hands shared tethers.

The carpet chaffed his cheek as he twisted his head towards the ceiling. "Please don't hurt me!"

"Shut up." A piece of sticky cloth taped stretch across his mouth.

A brawny arm encircled his waist and Rusty watched the hall carpet roll by under his face. Out the door, down the steps, across the pavement his captor puffed with exertion. A car door squeaked and the man threw him on the backseat. Rusty tried to sit up but rolled onto his back on the floor as the car accelerated around the corner. Snaking through the streets, the car stopped and started as it negotiated traffic lights across the city. The speed increased and the city lights gave way to black sky with glimpses of headlights reflected in the canopy of tall trees. Rusty made pleading sounds to no avail—a cassette clicked into the stereo and the sound of sixties Euro-pop rattled the reedy speakers; the driver added his flat voice to the jangle. The car slowed and meandered along a rough track, uphill and down; gravel spattered in the wheel arches. Rusty's fear rose with the sour taste in his mouth, his stomach cramped in terror. He rolled against the back of the driver's seat as the road sloped downwards; the car halted, the engine turned off and the handbrake creaked on. The cab light flared and died as the driver opened and closed the door. The crunch of footsteps faded to the irregular ticks of cooling metal.

The man returned, hauled him from the car and dragged him down a grassy riverbank; with an ape-like grunt, he threw Rusty into a dinghy. The little boat pitched as his captor climbed in and started a small outboard motor. Minutes later the boat nosed onto land and stopped.

The man ripped the gag and a small patch of skin from Rusty's mouth. "Welcome to my private graveyard."

The stalk in his jeans stiffened as he dragged Rusty Russell from the boat, up the sand bank to his shack, and left him lying in the sand. Time to feed the hellish beast dormant in his heart. His torch beam found the skeletal figure of his other prisoner; his sunken eyes blinked into the beam.

"Still alive? You must be just about out of rations by now."

The stench of the hut filled him with loathing and quiet pride. A flashback to his boyhood, when his father locked him in the feed shed for a week at a time. On that isolated farm, no one could hear his cries for help. The old man tormented his son—tortured and raped him but the boy had survived and triumphed; he'd grown into a strong man—a somebody.

The chains clinked as the emaciated prisoner cowered. "Please, let me go! I'll pay my dues, I just need time."

He smirked and shook his head. "Nuh, time's up. I've come to make an example of you—I have a young fella here who needs to learn a lesson in the ways of the world and you're gonna be teacher's little helper." He grabbed the chain and jerked it. "Up—come on! You can take a bath in the creek first. I don't like fucking filth."

Rusty recognised him. He watched in abject terror as the big detective grunted and moaned, his hips lunged with a final thrust into the prisoner's scrawny arse. He withdrew and his erection subsided, but when he picked up his knife, his penis swelled again. An arc of arterial blood sprayed, intestines trailed across the nightmare stage; the sight of butchered flesh would haunt Rusty for the rest of his life. As the blond haired detective ejaculated over the dying man, Rusty fouled his pants and vomited.

15

Lester scratched his head and listened with astonishment as Rusty confessed to the firebombing of the Pearl and the Valley Star. In interview room number three, he confessed to everything though he couldn't give details—*'I was high—I can't remember...'* Lester could have cleaned up every unsolved crime committed in the city for the past five years with Rusty's willingness to stick his head in a noose.

With this confession, fresh rumours circulated that somehow Lester must have intimidated him into pleading guilty. Lester was certain coercion had taken place but from where, and by whom, he couldn't prove. Rusty had had a watertight alibi but now he insisted he'd lied in spite of evidence to the contrary. Lester and his team searched Rusty's flat and found a homemade detonator and a ten-gallon drum of Shellite; Rusty's fingerprints coated both.

The forensic examiner had scratched his head as he showed Lester the evidence. "Mate, rows of hand prints over the surface of the drum might be a detective's dream but this is ridiculous! It's too good to be true. What was he doing? Groping the drum?"

"Are there any other prints?"

"Yeah, there's a partial set on the bottom of the drum but they don't match any that we have on record. They're probably from someone who sold it to him."

In the Chief Superintendent's office, Lester expressed his concerns. As he listened, he watched his boss steeple his fingertips under his nose. Lester's narration faltered as the man visibly inhaled.

Are you sniffing your fingers?

"Don't let it bother you, Lester. The public wants a conviction. You've got a confession; you've got evidence—get it over with. The Kinane family will be relieved to see their loved ones' killer behind bars."

Gainsford dropped a brick,' was the word around the station—rumours that he had planted evidence.

As the media speculated about intimidation, Rusty pleaded guilty, citing a newfound fear of god. *'RUMOURS OF COERCION HAVE EMERGED DURING THE TRIAL OF RUSTY RUSSELL. Once again allegations of corruption in the Police Force have come to light.'*

The internal investigation into the death of Daryl Reid was a whitewash insofar as it didn't find a guilty party. Lester supposed he should be grateful they believed his account of events. Furner and Doyle's account was a fine old work of fiction but only Lester knew that. Their names bore respect in the ranks, two diligent cops that sometimes bent the rules a little but they would never let their colleagues down, would they? Lester feared to challenge their evidence. Meanwhile, a water cooler inquisition raked over his account—why had he taken so long to get to Reid's house? Why had he attended the scene alone? Who had cleaned the fingerprints from the crime scene? Reid's phone records showed he had received a call from a public phone less than a minute before he had made the call to Lester. Who had made that call?

Suspicion marred his career and Lester had no alternative but transfer to Rockhampton, seven-hundred kilometres up the coast. There, alone in his unit, Lester switched on the TV to the news of Rusty Russell's apparent accidental death in Boggo Road.

'Just hours ago prison staff found Russell deceased in the shower block. He is reported to have died of a head injury. The Minister for Police has not yet made any comment…'

The screws reported he had slipped and hit his head. Lester drowned the newsreader's voice with a groan and cupped his face in his hands.

And that poor little bastard thought he'd be safe inside prison.

Lester's last hope of proving who actually committed the crime died with Rusty Russell. Pinkie had yet to resurface. The investigation over, crime solved. Life in the Sunshine State cruised on.

16

When Kitty read the Sunday Sun's report of the court case, she hurried to find Mikey grieving alone. His siblings had gone to church but he vowed he'd never step inside one again. He met her at the door and led her to his room.

"Hold me, Kitty." Mikey sat on his bed; his eyes brimmed with tears. Kitty sat beside him, her arm across his shoulders. "Whoever killed my brother and my parents has gotten away with it—the papers reckon the cops got the wrong man; he was one skinny kid, he couldn't have done it alone. I swear I'll find out who's behind it, Kitty. One day—somehow I'll find them."

Kitty got to her feet to hug him, his body tensed—his strength overwhelmed her as he drew her between his thighs.

"I'm so sorry, Mikey." Kitty's tears fell into his hair as he laid his cheek against her chest; folded together they wept. His hands shifted, his mouth found hers. Her dress loosened and slid to the floor.

"Mikey—"

He wasn't listening; he removed her bra and cupped her breast. Holding her against him, he nuzzled and sucked her nipples.

"Mikey, please—we said we wouldn't!" Kitty trembled as she pushed against his shoulders.

"Don't fight me, Kitty!" The anger in his voice scared her, "I need you, now!" He pulled her panties down.

"But we said—"

Kitty had never seen him so angry, white-faced and shaking, his heartbroken grief had morphed into rage.

"Don't!"

He laid her on the bed and moved over her. She pushed against him as he forced her legs apart. His breath ragged as he fumbled with his fly. Kitty felt him against her leg, warm and hard as he pushed into her.

"No! Mikey—it hurts! Stop!" Kitty sobbed against his chest as he thrust fast, she had wanted their first time to be an act of love, not this brutal assault. Pleasure—not searing pain.

"I love you, Kitty," he breathed. She felt him pulse and warmth flooded inside her. He moved to kiss her and Kitty turned away, the pain too raw.

"Kitty, please let me kiss you—"

"No—let me go, Mikey!"

****

The orgasm calmed Mikey's blinding rage. When he opened his eyes to Kitty's distress, his tears returned. The sight of blood brought home his crime. This was his Kitty; the idea that any man might treat her this way had always roused his protective instinct. Now he had done the unthinkable. He'd always had an explosive temper but he never imagined himself taking it out on the girl he loved.

"Oh god, Kitty. I'm so sorry. What have I done?"

"You raped me, Mikey. That's what you've done."

"I'm sorry, please Kitty, I love you."

Kitty got to her feet and sobbed as blood flowed from her. Mikey picked her up and carried her to the shower. When the water ran warm, he helped her in, removed his clothes and stepped in with her. His heart hurt as she pulled away.

"Kitty, please forgive me."

She shook her head and hugged herself, standing under the stream of water she wept. It hurt to see the face he loved contorted in pain. He drew her in his arms and held her against him.

"I was angry, Kitty—I lost control. Please, let me make it up to you? Please? I love you. I can't live without you."

Her arms slipped around him, his cue to lift her face to his.

"I swear I'll never hurt you again, Kitty. Please, forgive me."

Her blue eyes looked into his; he saw in them a mixture of sadness and love.

"Please don't stop loving me, Kitty."

She shook her head. "I'll always love you, Mikey."

****

Mikey bundled up his bloody towels and bed covers and took them to the laundry. As he sprayed them, Jimmy entered the back door and the bloodstains drew his gaze.

"Jeeze Mikey. Had an accident?"

Jimmy caught Mikey by surprised and he tried to stuff a bloodied sheet into the washing machine, he tried to speak but too late, Jimmy saw his guilt.

"Mikey?" Jimmy glanced out the back door, "is that Kitty's blood?"

Kitty had left a few minutes before to walk home. He opened his mouth to speak but words evaded him.

"You didn't."

Mikey leaned against the wall and covered his face. "I was so angry, I just lost it. She was there—she's so beautiful—Jimmy, she forgave me. Jimmy—she—"

"She's fifteen!"

"I love her, Jimmy. She's been my girl for two years."

"Not like that I hope!" Jimmy indicated the sheets.

"No—of course not."

Mikey waited for a reply, his brother's gaze like a spotlight.

Finally, Jimmy inhaled and shifted his feet. "I know telling you to leave her alone is pointless, so I will tell you this; use a condom if you really must have her like that, and be super careful. She's jailbait, Mikey. Sixteen is the age of consent but I'll bet her parents would have plenty to say about it even if she was sixteen."

Mikey nodded, sadness all he had in the face of his brother's anger. He shut his eyes on the tears, Jimmy's arm wrapped around his shoulders and Mikey sobbed.

"I can't deal with it, Jimmy."

"I know. It's hard for all of us."

The media had shouted down the verdict on Rusty Russell and greeted his imprisonment with suspicion. They condemned the internal enquiry into the death of Daryl Reid, reporting it had had all the hallmarks of a cover up. Mikey had listened as Jimmy called the police headquarters in Brisbane and asked for an explanation—an air beating exercise at best: they had transferred the detective who had led the investigation and they wouldn't say where to.

"I'm going to find who did it—"

"Please, Mikey. Calm down—you must."

Mikey wanted to pull himself together—he needed to pull himself together—but the anger raged on. The Leprechaun inside had turned into a monster—a cold heartless brute.

"Mikey, I know it's tough but we have to pull together the best we can. Mum and Dad wouldn't have wanted you to take your anger out on Kitty, they wouldn't want to see any of us fall from our standing among decent people."

"Decent people? I thought that was what the police were. They got the wrong man—"

"We need to calm down and plan what we're going to do, Mikey. If we rush down there now and start a blue, they'll kick our arses all the way home. Besides, we wouldn't know where to start—we don't know why and we don't know who. We have to plan this carefully, take our time—"

"So you're going to help me find them?" Mikey looked into his brother's blue eyes; Jimmy's eyes were gentle, kind eyes—like their father's. He nodded and a weight lifted from Mikey's shoulders. With his brothers behind him, he could win. If one Kinane brother went off, they all went off. The surviving Kinane brothers were set to explode.

17

1975

They'd crossed the line; Mikey made love to Kitty every Sunday afternoon. At first she refused, fearful of the pain and the danger of pregnancy. When he produced a condom from his wallet, she relented. She longed to please him. Life floated by in a bubble of joy until Kitty's father caught Mikey kissing her behind the shed after rifle practice.

"What the hell are you doing, boy?"

Mikey let go of Kitty as if she were a venomous spider. Kitty's father grabbed him by the shirtfront.

"Dad! Stop it!"

"You get home, girl—I'll deal with you later!"

"Dad, we weren't doing anything—"

Her father's face purpled and he roared, "Get home! Now!"

"Go on, Kitty." Mikey's pasty face puzzled Kitty. He towered over her father yet he shrank under the older man's rage.

Kitty ran home in a flood of angry tears. She railed against her parents for hours. She threw things, refused to eat and for several days, she refused to talk.

She tried pleading. "But I love him, Dad."

"You're too young to know what love is, Kitty."

"He loves me, we want to be together."

"He's a grown man, Kitty—you're a girl. Not only is it wrong—it's illegal."

Angry words spilled from her to suffocate under her parents' adult wisdom. They grounded her so she couldn't go find Mikey. For a week, she seethed and plotted. She would run away, find Mikey and they would leave the district. On Sunday night, she hid her bag under the bed. She had packed all her favourite clothes and would sneak out in the dead of night.

As she waited with her door open, listening, life crashed down around her. Her parents and older brother, Eric, gossiped in the kitchen and her body heat rose at the mention of Mikey.

"Did Jimmy tell you about Mikey?"

The sink cupboard clunked. "No, what—"

"He's getting married."

"Really? Who to?"

"Barbara Matheson, Bill Matheson's daughter. Shotgun wedding, apparently."

Her father growled, "Why doesn't that surprise me?"

"I didn't know she was his girlfriend."

"She wasn't, but she's up the duff and it's Mikey's."

"Mikey's been headed for trouble ever since he left school. Hopefully married life will settle him down."

Eric chuckled. "Poor bugger, she'll be a handful that one. Daddy's a politician, so she'll expect Mikey to become high-classed overnight."

Kitty shut her door and fell into bed. As her tears soaked the pillow, she turned and tossed, trying to understand what she had done wrong. Mikey said he loved her—how could he get another girl pregnant? It was only two weeks since she had last been with Mikey—she knew enough to know he must have been seeing Barbara Matherson for the same time. The whole world had turned on her. Wallowing in self-pity, she sobbed the night away, her mind in turmoil. Exhaustion claimed her as dawn lit the east.

She woke to a knock on the door and her mother's voice telling her to get up for school. The door opened and her mother looked in.

"Darling, you look terrible! Are you sick?"

Kitty nodded and closed her eyes. She told no lie—her head ached and her stomach hurt. Her throat sore, even her ears buzzed with the volume of a thousand crickets.

"You better stay home, Kitty. Do you want some breakfast?"

Kitty shook her head, her lip trembled and tears prickled her eyes. Did her mother think she had forgotten Mikey already?

"I'll bring you a cup of tea, Sweetheart."

Kitty nodded, tea sounded appealing.

Kitty had the rest of the week off school; her mother took her to the doctor in an effort to cure her daughter's mysterious lurgy. Why couldn't they understand? Shattered at fifteen, betrayed by everyone she loved. Red-hot anger alternated with icy-cold loneliness. She couldn't talk to anyone; Mikey had been her closest friend, or so she had thought. Her relationship with Mikey had been grown up—her school friends were too immature to understand.

****

Mikey longed to see Kitty, to hold her one last time and explain his predicament but even if her father allowed it, how could he tell her that through the three years of their relationship, he had lived the life of Lothario? A modern day Casanova. Mikey could, and did, charm his way into the pants of any girl who took his fancy. It was 1975, sex free and pretty girls everywhere. Pretty girls, but none came close to his beautiful Kitty, and now, fate had torn them apart. The thought of her moving on to find someone else sickened him; Kitty was his. Was. When other men came sniffing around Kitty he had chased them away, but Mikey could not raise a hand to the one man with the power to remove her from his life—her father. He might have waited until Kitty was older but the planets had aligned themselves against him. Barbara Matherson, a girl he hardly knew, expected his child.

At his engagement party, his face ached from the forced smile and feigned happiness; listening to Barbara's soft breathy voice irritated the shit out of him, he tried not to compare her to Kitty. Slim, blonde with beautiful cornflower blue eyes and clear, pale golden skin; at fifteen, Kitty showed promise of physical perfection. He knew no girl who compared in either looks or demeanour—Barbara paled before Kitty's radiance. His future loomed bleak, the carefree days of youth poised on the edge of an abyss of adult obligation. At twenty years old, the last thing he wanted was a wife, but he'd have to make the best of the situation.

You had a skin full, Mikey, and you got her pregnant. Tough.

Even if by some miracle he could pull a stunned rabbit out of the hat and avoid marriage to Barbara, he still couldn't have Kitty. He resigned himself to a loveless marriage; this was the seventies, civilised society demanded a child be born within the security of wedlock. Even Mikey believed he must do right by the baby. What he couldn't do was love Barbara.

The impending marriage made him rethink the course of his life. After the death of his brother and parents, his greatest ambition was to rebuild the family business—and above all, destroy those who had torn his family apart. A dream he would not abandon. The Mathesons had their own plans for Mikey. Bill Matheson neared retirement and he fully expected his charismatic son-in-law-to-be would replace him in parliament. The party saw a star recruit in the youngest Kinane. In the meantime, Mikey would take over management of the Matheson's farm. He'd never considered a farming career, or politics, and in the hours before the wedding ceremony he had a thought-provoking conversation with his brothers, Aiden and Liam. Their career in the Australian Defence Force had ended. Both trained-up SAS *Chicken Stranglers,* they'd had enough of superiors breathing down their necks. The Kinane brothers all shared a natural born hatred for authority. Mikey bemoaned his fate—a farmer had little chance of making money and if he wanted to avenge the deaths of their loved ones, he would need money—a lot of it. They had sold the pub licence but the family still owned the licence for the nightclub and they intended to use it.

Liam squinted into the mirror and fiddled with his tie. "What makes you think you can't make money farming?"

"What makes you think I can?"

"You don't have to raise cattle or grow pineapples and sugar cane only. There's big money to be made from growing other things."

"Like what?"

"The old Bob Hope."

"Dope?"

"We can get good quality seed, if you can find somewhere to grow it."

"Bill Matheson has spent the last thirty years clearing his farm, there's nowhere I could grow and hide a crop." The Kinane brothers' attitude to authority was so entrenched, the only thing that might prevent them breaking the law was finding somewhere to break it.

"Build a new machinery shed. Bill's old shed is ready to fall down."

"But you can't grow it in shade."

"Grow lights."

"But—"

"Build a shed with an invisible attic."

"But what about getting the soil—"

"Hydroponics."

Mikey frowned from one twin to the other, chewing his lip; they had obviously thought this through. He was clever with his hands and could easily construct a shed. With a bit of planning he could do it.

"We'll help." The twins spoke in unison—their siblings had come to expect it.

Mikey looked at the clock. The time of his doom had arrived. The Olsen family, friends of both the Mathesons and the Kinanes, were invited but he hoped Kitty had found an excuse to stay away—he could not imagine exchanging vows with Barbara while Kitty listened.

****

With everyday farming activity to hinder them, it took the Kinane brothers months to construct the steel framed shed. Thirty metres square and ten metres in height, from the outside it looked like a normal flat roofed machinery shed, time would tell whether it would bear closer scrutiny. Inside the outer walls, they built a hidden second floor just over two metres below the roof disguised with a ceiling of roofing iron underneath and supported by hefty steel beams. On each end, they built a double wall; one concealed a staircase to the upper floor and the other, drying racks. The invisible doors were a sheet of tin secreted behind tool racks that unclipped and swung out to allow access. A buzzer upstairs alerted them when someone entered the shed below. A hidden electric pump piped water up to a small holding tank. Months later, they harvested a first class crop and began supplying dealers all along the coast but avoided Brisbane and The Gold Coast; they weren't yet ready to tread on the enemy's toes. When they did, they anticipated a right old barney, and for Mikey, it couldn't come soon enough.

18

Kitty's school friends could almost make Mikey fade into the background but her thoughts rarely left him for long. She lived in a state of detachment for months without crossing his path, but in a small community, to avoid anyone was impossible. An unexpected encounter with the one she had loved since childhood cut like jagged ice. Her school's annual fete was a major social event in the town. As she wandered gossiping and laughing with her friends, Kitty's eyes found Mikey in conversation with a group of farmers. He looked every bit the happily married man. She guessed his wife must have given birth because he held a small baby in the crook of his arm. Before she could look away, Mikey locked eyes with her and smiled. Kitty had no smile back; her insides froze as his gaze raked her body. She fled to lock herself in a toilet cubicle and surrender to a flood of tears. Her bewildered friends checked on her but she sent them away.

Kitty learned the art of distraction; she loved to shoot and thanks to the patient coaching Mikey had given in happier times, she could hit a target within a hand span of the bullseye. She practiced every weekend with her father's Winchester .243. The big rifle kicked like a mule but she learned to control it. To take her mind off Mikey she joined the local taekwondo centre. She excelled at the discipline and amazed her brother, Eric, a pupil of some years. She needed the therapeutic kicking and grappling with her peers.

****

Mikey cherished a secret dream that he and Kitty might reunite at some future point. Once she was of age, once he had extricated himself from his marriage, once the world got out of the way they could be together. Even her father could not stand between them, could he? A love that strong would withstand the ravages of life, wouldn't it? After seeing the hurt and anger in her eyes as she passed, he feared he might be wrong; he feared his hoped-for reunion was a long shot. Instead of torturing himself with memories—agonising over what he had lost, like a man possessed, Mikey threw himself into making money. Lots of it. Cash from the attic crops flowed in, he and his siblings laundered it by hiding the profits among the proceeds of farming and his sisters' fashion boutique. They deposited it into a family trust; someday soon, they'd be ready to stare down their enemies.

****

Barbara.

Barbara had fallen in love with Mikey at high school. He'd stood for the position of school captain, and she his deputy. She had assured her success by threatening to strike any who didn't vote for her from the guest list for her seventeenth birthday party—exclusion from which guaranteed social ruin. Her minions made a note of any who didn't raise their hand in support. Victory fell to her but she might well have not existed in the eyes of Mikey Kinane.

Four years later on the night of the local B and S Ball, she had dragged him, drunk and stumbling onto the dance floor. He leaned on her as she waltzed him for the last dance.

"Think I mazeswell fuck you, Margaret." He hiccoughed in her ear.

She steered him around the floor like a shopping trolley. "Barbara."

"'Eh? Who's 'e?"

"I'm Barbara, not Margaret."

He pulled back and surveyed her with dead mackerel eyes.

"Really? Well bugger me, I thought you were Mar—hic—Margaret."

She pulled her foot from under his. "No, I'm not—"

He leaned heavily on her shoulder. "Well, who's Margaret?"

Barbara eased his tall frame upright. "I've no idea."

"Nah—hic—nuh!" He shook his head, nonplussed.

He had screwed her and fallen asleep on the back seat of her car. Barbara broadcasted the news during the recovery breakfast; she had captured Mikey Kinane. Every girl in town wanted Mikey and Barbara rejoiced when he agreed to marry her. The unplanned pregnancy foreshadowed a major embarrassment for the

Matherson family, but as good luck would have it, it landed her the man she had wanted since age fifteen.

Sunday morning she woke to him sleeping beside her. The baby, Danielle, had begun to fuss; soon she would be bawling for her morning feed. Barbara sighed and got up. Mikey wouldn't do it; he made little effort to help with their daughter. As she pulled on her dressing gown she paused to gaze at her husband's striking features, relaxed and contented in sleep. As soon as he woke, lines of discontent would reclaim his face—worse today, she expected. He had spent last night with his brothers and cousins sitting around a backyard bonfire—drinking, smoking, and laughing. She had gone to bed early and until she closed the window on their noisy repartee, she had listened as lewd jokes and four-letter-words drifted in. Barbara worried she would never make a gentleman of her husband, she played only a minor role in his life. He had sex with her several times a week and insisted on wearing a condom. It was just a physical thing for him, there was no love, and he took no interest in her satisfaction. Some mornings he rose early, ate breakfast, and left the house before she woke. His brothers, Aiden and Liam, often arrived on their motorcycles to help with chores. Barbara didn't like the twins—they weren't as tall or as handsome as their younger brother. They lived in battered army fatigues, leather jackets, and bikie boots. When they stomped into the kitchen with Mikey, Barbara would find an excuse to leave the room. The twins had a hard-bitten look about them—sharp featured with flinty grey eyes. Mikey's face was pretty in comparison; though Barbara knew inside he was as hard as his brothers.

As she fed Danielle, Mikey slouched past and into the kitchen. Barbara listened as he filled the kettle and switched it on. Footsteps sounded on the veranda; Barbara saw his reflection in the glass as he jogged down the road to the farm gate and collected the morning paper. He returned and set about making coffee and toast.

She wiped Danielle's face, draped a towel over Mikey's shoulder and handed him the baby.

"She needs burping."

He scowled, laid the newspaper on the table and set his coffee cup down. He took the baby without speaking and returned his attention to the paper; Barbara once again found herself looking at his eyelids. He rarely looked at her for more than a few seconds.

Barbara tapped an advertisement sprawled across the bottom of the page. "The Show Ball is on next Saturday night. Mum has booked a table. I've told her we will be there."

"Righto."

"Don't forget."

"I won't."

Barbara poured her coffee, sat opposite her husband and resumed watching his eyelids. She had just swallowed the second mouthful of coffee when Mikey rose and thrust the baby at her.

"She burped and puked a bit and I think she might have shit herself." He turned and strode out the door.

19

Late Saturday afternoon and Barbara dressed for the Show Ball, the social event of the year. Mikey emerged from the shower with a towel around him and padded barefoot across the bedroom.

"Mikey, can you zip me up?"

He frowned. "Why are you all dolled up?"

"We're going to the Show Ball, what do you think we're doing?"

"I can't go to the Show Ball. I've got errands to run."

"Errands? Can't they wait until tomorrow? Mikey, I told you last week the ball was tonight. Mum and Dad are expecting you to be there. Members of the party will be there, they expect—"

"Well they can expect away, I've got work to do."

"What work?"

His eyes narrowed. "Just work, okay?"

"Mikey, where do you go when you take off with your brothers?"

"Ask no questions, Barbara and I'll tell you no lies."

"Is there someone else?"

His laugh stung like a slap in the face. "I should be so lucky."

Barbara looked on in dismay as he dressed in jeans, T shirt, and a black leather jacket. "Mikey, why won't you come to the ball?"

"I'll come when I get home." He towelled his hair. "I'll be back in about three hours, then I'll put on my suit and come to the ball like the good boy I am."

"Why can't you run your errands tomorrow?"

"Business is business. I can't leave it until tomorrow."

"Just once—"

"No!"

"But Mum and Dad—"

"I don't give a rat's hairy arse what your parents expect! I'll get there when I get there! Okay?" The towel flopped in a wet heap before her.

"You only ever think about yourself! You don't care—" Barbara stopped at the dangerous set of his mouth and his narrowed eyes.

"No. I don't care, actually."

Barbara folded her arms. "Who is she? The woman you mumble to in your sleep?"

The anger in his eyes softened. The dark fringe of his lashes fluttered and shielded the pain she glimpsed in the deep blue.

"Well? You're always thrashing about and mumbling to her."

His face whitened and he made a fist. He inhaled, shoved her onto the bed and walked out. The back door crashed and a minute later, his Harley roared away.

The only child of well-to-do parents, Barbara had not often heard the word 'no.' Things had always gone her way; the big handsome man she married was the first person who dared defy her.

Three hours had turned into five. It was 11.45 p.m. when Mikey arrived at the ball and his wife in the shittiest of all shitty moods.

"Would you like to dance?" He thought he should ask.

"No—go and dance with your dream girl." Barbara's lips thinned to a fine line, her arms and legs entwined so tight she resembled an octopus stuffed into a beer glass.

Mikey looked around, he couldn't see Kitty in the crowd and his mouth was dry as a buzzard's crotch. He beelined for the bar, distant from the loud music and ordered a double Bundy and Coke. Propped against the bar, he had an intriguing conversation with Max Maxwell, a state government minister and friend of his father-in-law. A fifty-something man with a large, florid head and bags under his eyes big enough to fetch the groceries.

"So young Kinane, how long before you bring your family name back to Brisbane?" Alcohol fumes clouded the air around Max like methane around a night-cart. His elbow propped on the bar and his belly protruded from his jacket towards Mikey.

"What makes you think I intend to?"

"You Kinanes aren't the kind to roll over and—*hic*—piss on your guts. You still own that liquor license." He belched and squinted a pouchy eye.

"Someday I will—when I can form a small army. I'm going to need it; it'll be hard enough to fight those bastards who murdered my kin, but I'm going to have to take on bent cops and politicians as well."

"You wound me, boy. I'm not bent." Max's elbow slipped off the bar top, Mikey put a hand out to stop him sliding face first against his chest.

"Maybe not, but how many crooked cops and pollies are there?"

"Sadly, I can't tell you that. I'm—*urg*—tipping we'll have a new police commissioner soon and things could go either way—maybe better, maybe worse. But with Bill Matheson as your father-in-law, you're in with a chance. Bill's as pure as the—*urp*—driven snow Mikey, and the party listens to him." His voice curdled with beer and phlegm. "They listen to him. Beautiful man is Bill. He holds a lot of gout—*hic*—clout."

His father-in-law did wield considerable power in the State Government but Mikey knew at home his domineering wife henpecked him mercilessly; marriage to Bill's daughter doomed Mikey to a lifetime of similar treatment. Not long before his parents died, Mikey had discussed women with them and recalled his mother's wisdom: *'As the mother honours the father, so shall the daughter honour her husband.'* He preferred his father's version: *'As the hen cackles, the pullet learns.'*

Mikey returned to provoking Max. "So why don't you two do something to stop the gangs that have taken over The Valley? Weed out the crooked cops?"

"It's so bloody secretive, Mikey—*hic*—us good guys haven't a clue where to start."

"So all I can do is go in there and start a war—is that it?"

"Beat them at their own game, Mikey. If your enemy is paying a hundred for his per-tection, you pay one-fifty. Lay some bait for the bent cops and—*urgh*—grab the bastards by their clods. Bend them to your *wir—hic—*will."

Mikey stared, Max instructed him to bribe the police.

"See, if you pay more than your enemy," Max's eyes went out of focus as he counted on his pudgy fingers, "he'll have to pay more again because the fucking cops will look after the guy who pays the most. And what's more, Mickey—Mikey *(ur-rup)* you'll have the advantage of being the new guy in town, you'll have the newest nightclub and it'll be rakin' in the dosh. Old Rick won't be able to afford to cough up more than you."

"Rick?"

Or any of those fellas—" Max coughed, waved a loose hand and lowered his gaze.

"Just how many enemies am I likely to encounter?"

"Dunno—maybe none, Mikey—maybe none."

Mikey surveyed Max with narrowed eyes. "We've got to get approval first—that'll be the hard part."

"Leave that to me and Bill, Mikey. We'll get it approved for you."

And you said you weren't corrupt.

Mikey eyed the crowd as he turned over Max's words. His gut clenched; Barbara approached with dudgeon aloft, a face to curdle milk at fifty paces.

"Mikey! I'm going home now!"

"Yeah, righto."

"Well? Aren't you coming with me?"

"Piss off—I only just got here." Mikey's plan was get pissed, begin here, and go home to finish the job.

"Don't you dare take that tone with me!"

"Go home, Barbara. I'll come when I'm finished talking to Max."

"You might find yourself locked out."

"Just try it." Mikey held her gaze as he took a long drink of rum and Coke.

He grimaced at the stiff lines of her back as she stalked away.

"She has a voice like a little bird, dun-she?" Max's eyes didn't quite make it all the way to Mikey's.

"It's like having a fucking mozzie stuck in my ear. Just a high pitch whining—day in, day out. It's the greatest boner-killer you'll ever hear."

"Kick her to the curb and *(hic)* get a bird with big tits and no voice, Mikey—" Max closed one eye, it seemed to help his coherence, "—and a throat of Linda Lovelace pop—proportions."

"I might do that one day, Max."

20

Rick Campbell

Rick watched Bev emerge from the ensuite, she was a beautiful woman, and after seven years of marriage, they had settled into a routine—she had affairs and he turned a blind eye as long as she kept it discreet.

"So where did you go?"

"To the Apollo, then Poppy's, and then on to Rubies."

"You didn't go to The Capital?"

"Well I knew you weren't going to be there so I just went along with the girls. If you had been there I wouldn't have been able to keep the girls away, you know what they're like."

"Yeah, I know." Rick smiled—women loved him. The Capital was his nightclub but tonight he'd stayed at home with their son. The endless lazy Susan of Bev's social life took her out at least four times a week and Rick stayed home with his boy—unless Bev's mother volunteered to baby-sit. They'd maintained the pretence of a happily married couple, Rick loved her but he had a problem. He was grateful his wife wasn't one for confiding her troubles with her high society friends. Everyone assumed Rick a loving and faithful husband—plenty of women tried to lure him but he rejected their advances.

"Well, I'm stuffed. Goodnight." She leaned over and pecked his cheek. He caught a glimpse of her amphetamine eyes before her lashes covered them.

"Goodnight." Rick closed his eyes hoping to fall back to sleep.

This isn't the life you planned, Rick. Why can't you be happy with a beautiful wife and a son?

Rick Campbell was thirty-six, classically handsome and filthy rich. He and Bev shared an enormous and expensive house in the leafy suburb of Clayfield in Brisbane's northeast. A businessman, he had fingers in multiple pies; a string of nightclubs up the coast, an illegal casino in Fortitude Valley, an illegal brothel in Chermside and as a sideline he imported and supplied drugs to dealers all over Queensland and Northern New South Wales. Popular, Rick had few close friends but a multitude of acquaintances. He'd also earned a reputation as a dangerous man; getting on his wrong side could prove fatal. The most powerful gangster cop in Queensland had his hand in Rick's pocket, once a week a bagman called to collect on behalf of the Lark, a corrupt syndicate embedded in the Queensland Police Force. He paid and they stayed away.

21

The starched collar pinched Mikey's throat. The starched company grated his nerves. The last place he wanted to be was here in a CWA hall in the heart of the Bible belt; Barbara had dragged him along for a political fundraiser. The dinner ended and a grinning organist strove vainly to impersonate Liberace. Country entertainment in mid-seventies-Queensland style. On the dance floor, a handful of couples danced the dance of confusion—was it a waltz or was it a tango? The ladies suffered the crush of oversized feet; sweaty hands squeezed their flesh as half-tanked farmers skidded them across the Pops. Mikey sipped a watery scotch and dry, and listened as his father-in-law pitched the idea of building another bridge across the Brisbane River, a bleary-eyed Max Maxwell, and the teetotal Premier nodded. Mikey's scrotum shrivelled as his eyes found Barbara across heads of the crowd, tittering with a group of party wives. A cold shudder quaked his existence, clear to his future grave; since giving birth, she'd begun to resemble her mother—the same eyes, mouth, and nose—the same body. An embryonic version of the old nag and even divorce would not eradicate her from his life. The child they shared bound them forever. He grimaced and shifted his gaze to Max Maxwell's daughter where she leaned against the wall nearby, looking bored. She seemed to sense his eyes on her and locked on. Her eyes smiled before her mouth, Mikey's pulse increased tempo. His gaze travelled down to witness her nipples harden through the skin-tight jersey dress. He excused himself and made for the bar, he needed to distract the rapidly growing hard-on. It wouldn't do to crack a major fat in such pious company. He downed the last of the scotch—ice cubes and all, hoping a brain-freeze would put a stop to the testosterone rush. He ordered a double, belched and looked down, she moved up beside him and he could see down her cleavage into the pale valley between those melons. The thin fabric of her dress failed to stop them bouncing like twin jellies. His cock began to throb as he speculated whether she wore anything under that dress.

"I think I'll pop outside for some fresh air." She fanned herself with a handkerchief and set the jellies in motion again.

"I've forgotten—what was your name?"

"Carissa." She had a slight overbite and Mikey imagined sliding his cock past it. His breath caught in his throat as she leaned closer.

"Five minutes, Mikey—behind the hall."

As he watched her arse disappear out a side door, Mikey had a brief moment of married man scruples but his rogue hormones demanded he let them loose. With a rush of fire to his loins, he cast a glance at Barbara; she huddled in a tight circle of gossip with her matronly cohorts. Mikey followed Carissa outside. He caught sight of her standing outside the circle of light cast by a bulb above the door. She glided into the dark; Mikey loosened his tie and took a different direction until the darkness hid him. He lost her for a moment then saw her standing beside a car ahead of him.

His legs shook as he slipped his arms around her perfumed body, a handful on the side of plump; their mouths met, he bit and she sucked, their tongues probed. His hands groped for her breast, hot and firm, the nipples taut under his fingers. She pulled her dress off over her head.

"Jesus! You really were wearing nothing under that dress."

"I never wear underwear."

"Even out here in the bible belt?"

"Especially out here in the Bible belt, you'd be surprised…"

He lifted her, his lips devouring hers. A slick of fluid wet her inner thighs. She wriggled from his grasp, opened the back door of the car and reached inside to kill the cab light. She turned to help Mikey strip and pulled him into the back seat, her mouth descended on his cock. She cupped his balls and teased him. He moaned as she stopped and moved to straddle his lap. She slid onto him, tight and satiny; she squealed as an orgasm took her. He panted and grabbed her arse, bouncing her on his cock—the pressure increased, her nipples brush his lips.

"Mikey!"

Her tongue pushed into his mouth and the throb of another orgasm pulsed.

"Mikey—oh god!"

He spurted into her, his heart jackhammered in his chest. "Oh Jesus! I needed that!"

"Mikey! What are you doing?"

Barbara.

He puffed. "Getting my leg over. What does it look like?"

This didn't bode well for the drive home.

Barbara marched away to the car and warned Mikey to be there in two minutes or she would leave him behind. With Carissa's phone number in his pocket, shirt untucked, and his tie draped around his shoulders, he slid in behind the wheel and turned the key. The poisonous atmosphere enveloped him. Barbara alternately sobbed and raged, shrieked and clammed up. Mikey sighed. Any half-alive young man could not have said no to Carissa, the best fuck he'd had since the last time he'd had Kitty.

Kitty. As he drove, his imagination created scenarios that might reunite them—each more improbable than the last.

****

Danielle cooed at Mikey from her highchair, her cheeks pink from Barbara's vigorous wiping with a face cloth. He concentrated on finishing his breakfast as his wife stomped to the kitchen. Sunday morning, Barbara wanted Mikey to attend church and his refusal had soured the mood. Mikey planned a delivery run to Bribie Island; one of his best dealers was low on stock. After, he planned a quick trip to Brisbane to spend a few hours with Carissa. Barbara didn't know of his affair; he'd convinced her the night in the back seat was an isolated incident—bored and drunk. A mistake. He'd even made a small gain—Barbara had stopped nagging. Temporarily. Over the previous week, the flaw, ingrained in her by nature and nurture, resurfaced. Worse, for she had added ammunition—he'd been caught in *flagrante delicto*.

Danielle cooed louder and he smiled. "What do you want, kid?"

The baby laughed, bounced and held out her chubby arms. Sadness settled over Mikey as he lifted his baby daughter over his head and jiggled her. She giggled and pedalled her legs; he set her on his lap and pushed his hot coffee out of her reach.

"Why can't you leave your so called errand until this afternoon?" A crash of crockery underlined Barbara's niggle from the kitchen.

Danielle snuggled against him, Mikey lifted her to his chest and one tiny arm tried but failed to encircle his neck. He pressed his lips to her silken hair.

Barbara's voice shrilled again. "Well?"

His eyes shut and his mood darkened. Danielle had only come into the world because of his carelessness, a perfect little human, innocent and trusting. Too often it happened, a couple people with nothing more on their minds than sexual gratification found themselves encumbered with a baby. He marvelled a moment that two people who might never succeed at anything else could produce, without conscious effort, a flawless child. Generations of humanity marched on across time while people blundered through life, making plans, grand and trivial—triumph and failure—laughter and tears.

Danielle grew still, savouring their nearness, silent except for the wet sound as she sucked her fist. Mikey laid his cheek against her downy hair and inhaled her scent. A visceral emotion seized him—affection morphed into a solid bond, Mikey had to stop himself weeping at a love frightening in its power. This tiny baby's innocent trust crystalized his paternal instinct. Since his marriage to Barbara, he'd grown self-absorbed, and angry with himself for his stupidity. He'd loved but resented his daughter for the role she'd played in his predicament.

Another crash from the kitchen made him wince. "Mikey! Answer me!"

He hugged his daughter closer. He couldn't love her mother no matter how he tried, but he loved the baby they had made. He accepted Danielle was destined to grow up with estranged parents and he would move mountains to ensure this precious baby didn't suffer for that. To be a good father to his child didn't require he remain with her mother.

Barbara's voice cracked. "Well?"

Those moments spent with his daughter eased the grief that had embittered and shaped his life. His child; his anchor. The death of his parents and brother would remain an open wound. The loss of Kitty a constant ache in his breast; his love for her resilient, as impervious as diamonds to the ravages of time. Kitty was his past and he hoped—his future. Carissa a luscious bridge over the chasm of misery.

"Mikey!" Barbara stood beside him, hands on her hips and a tea towel slung over her shoulder. "Are you listening?"

Mikey rose and passed Danielle to his wife.

"I went to your church for our daughter's Christening, I'm not a churchgoer, and if I was it would be to the Catholic Church. If you don't like that, Barbara, then you shouldn't have married a Mick. However—" he cut her off as she filled her lungs for another onslaught. "—when you do sit in that church this morning, instead of looking around to see who isn't there and worrying about making a good impression, I recommend you listen to what the preacher says—you might learn something. I'll be back this afternoon."

****

Mikey dove head first into his affair with Carissa. His favourite thing about her was the penchant for zero underwear; that and she might easily suck the chrome off an MGB—that Linda Lovelace throat her father had suggested. Her physical attributes outshone the shortcomings. Selfish, spoiled and dim-witted, but in a way, a good thing. All he need do to keep her happy was buy a few trinkets and laud her beauty. She had terrible taste; she proudly redecorated her apartment in shades of dogshit-brown and turd-green with splashes of grasshopper-guts yellow on the curtains and cushions. Mikey made deceitful noises of approval and dragged her to the bedroom. It became routine for her three-legged dachshund, Barkley, to leap from the bed and bay at Mikey. That two-foot-long tube of piss and wind hated his mistress's boyfriend. Mikey dealt with him by seizing the scruff of his neck and relocating him to the balcony when he sat and snarled through the glass, baleful eyes watching as Mikey shagged his mistress.

22

Ben 1976

Crestly Park was one that city hall forgot about until something bad enough brought it to their attention. Over grown grass, broken bottles, broken benches and dirty, graffiti coated public toilets that attracted the wrong kind of visitors. A man could run through this park with an axe in his skull and nobody would pay him any attention.

"Get your laughing gear around that, pretty boy." The man waved a twenty-dollar note. His erect penis swayed like a baby bird in a nest of black hair. To Ben, the man before him looked at least two steps down the evolutionary ladder from modern humanity.

"Give me the money first." Ben tasted bile in his throat. Thirteen years old and living on his wits; already done with life, this was his nightly routine but it beat eating out of bins. Unwanted and unwished for, rag-dolled by Pinkie and Ruby and the world in general; Ben had intelligence enough to wonder what a different life he might have had with different parents. He couldn't recall his mother and had never known a father.

"Nuh! Suck my cock then I'll pay up." The man took a footballer's grip on Ben's head and forced him to his knees. A cane toad bunny-hopped into the overgrown grass. "Suck it!"

The man groaned and Ben vomited. Pain exploded in his head. He came to with a man kneeling over him—not the hairy john. This man was younger, handsome and well dressed. And familiar.

"Are you okay? Can I call you an ambulance?"

Ben shook his head. "No. I'll be alright." His hand flew to his pocket. His wallet was gone. "I've been robbed."

"What's your name?"

"Ben."

"I'm Billy. Come on. Let's get you out of here."

That night, Ben became what other street boys referred to as a himbo—the male equivalent of a bimbo. Billy installed him in a little unit, gave him money for nice clothes and everything else a thirteen-year-old boy could ask for. In return, Billy made frequent visits and Ben gave him everything a thirty-something-year-old rock-spider could want.

23

The last two years of high school crawled. Graduation night arrived and Mikey's name on the program set Kitty's stomach roiling. As a former school captain and son-in-law of the local Member of Parliament, he'd make a speech and present the awards. Kitty kicked herself for working hard; one of those awards was hers. She craved invisibility as he spoke and cast repeated glances in her direction. Kitty's throat burned and tears stung—her mind could not absorb his words. Mikey finished, applause broke the singular voice, and the time had arrived for awards. When Kitty's turn came, she dream walked, heart drubbing in her ears, and faced him for the first time in nearly two years, Mikey had shook the hands of previous recipients but Kitty received a hug and a kiss on the cheek.

His voice in her ear set her insides ablaze. "Can I see you on Sunday?"

She met his gaze and breathed his scent; so close but the throng seated before them kept their distance wide. Kitty lifted her shoulder an inch.

"Please?"

Kitty shut her eyes, dipped her chin and left the stage.

****

Mikey started the car and cringed. Barbara's sharp intake of air augured an imminent pizzling. He inhaled and forced himself to think of fluffy clouds and rainbows.

"Why the special treatment for the Olsen girl?"

"Why not?"

"I'm asking you why?"

Because I love her, you carping trout!

Mikey chewed his lip as he navigated the congested street. He could feel a major fight coming on and he needed a good row to take out his sadness on Barbara, for what had happened to his life. He had to get away; he could no longer bear to be in the same room as her, which presented a problem; he loved his daughter with a strength he never knew he possessed. At some point soon, he would walk away from Barbara and being close to Kitty that night had brought his dilemma into sharp focus.

"Well?"

Barbara's ridiculous baby doll voice grated on his last lonely nerve. As he moved out of the traffic and onto the road out of town, he slouched behind the wheel and sighed. His anger boiled up and exploded.

"Well-the-fuck-what?"

"Don't use that language at me! I'm asking what you said to the Olsen girl?"

"I asked who she thought would win the cricket!"

"Don't lie to me!"

Mikey opened his mouth to tell the truth but snapped it shut. Barbara was a dreadful gossip and devious as buggery, the last thing Kitty needed was to fall victim to her spite.

"She was my neighbour growing up. She was the only person I presented an award to that I knew. I congratulated her."

"Her face didn't look like a girl being congratulated—"

"She's a teenager! How the fuck do I know what goes on inside their heads! Now will you just shut up bitching?"

"Don't shout at me!"

"Just leave it, please—" Mikey's voice fell away, he knew shouting at her never got him anywhere. Nothing did. Her body language led him to hope she'd given up; legs entwined and arms folded, she went quiet for the rest of the drive but as he pulled into the garage, she returned to the attack.

"She's the one you talk about in your sleep, isn't she?"

His scrotum tightened and the hair on the back of his neck bristled. "I wouldn't know—I'm asleep when I talk in my sleep."

"Don't be smart!"

"If I was smart I wouldn't have—oh forget it!"

Mikey pushed past her and into the kitchen, a bottle of Bundy sat in the cupboard and he planned to drown himself in it.

"She's a little young, don't you think?"

"There's nothing going on, Barbara." His clenched jaw muffled his words.

Isn't it funny how I can lie to you without a shred of guilt?

"Don't lie to me! I saw—"

His icy stare exhorted her to silence.

If only you knew how close you're cruising for a good smack across the mouth.

If he didn't get away from his wife, he would explode.

"Go to bed!" He took the rum from the cupboard, collected a glass and a tray of ice cubes and walked out. Mikey wanted somewhere quiet to get drunk and lose himself thinking of Kitty. He went to the shed, through the hidden door and climbed the stairs. Sitting amongst his seedling crop, he wasted himself with an oversized doobie and washed it down with rum.

****

Kitty fought with herself, she wanted to be with Mikey but her seventeen-year-old's maturity told her to stay away. Her parents had gone away for the day so there was nothing to stop her; she set off for Scrubby Crook at three o'clock on Sunday afternoon. He got to his feet as she approached; they stepped into each other's arms, the unhappy void they'd endured for two years filled and overflowed. Tears and kisses choked their words as they clung together.

Mikey held her away from him; sadness clouded his eyes.

"Kitty—I'm so sorry."

"I'm sorry too—my father—"

He shook his head. "Your father was right—I was too old— too irresponsible. I hate what I did to you." His lips devoured hers, feverish lips soft on her face and neck. "You've grown—you're taller."

Kitty laughed through her tears. "I'm also old enough to be with you. If only I could."

"You can—we can be together—just like we used to."

"No, Mikey. You're married—I can't be with you." She sobbed. "I can't—it's wrong."

"I'm not happy with my wife, Kitty. I can't bear her to touch me. I'm close to hating her."

"She's still your wife."

"Not for much longer."

"I'm leaving town. I'm moving to Brisbane in January."

"I wish you wouldn't—"

"I'm going to college for a year and then I'm joining the police force."

"Kitty? Jesus—be careful. The police force is no place for a beautiful girl. Girls have been raped—" His back muscles tensed, arms tightened. His voice shook. She fancied she read his thoughts. "Kitty—be careful." He tilted her face; his eyes brimmed. "And be happy. I'll always be there if you need me. Always."

Kitty nodded as her tears increased. Love used to be a joyful thing, now all it gave was pain beyond endurance. She sobbed against his shoulder; minutes passed and they calmed. Mikey took her hand a led her to the patch of grass where they had lain in happier times. She knew she shouldn't but his kisses slowly stripped her resolve; since their last time together, his touch was all she had craved. The hands she loved wove their spell, peeling away her clothes. His mouth closed over one nipple; he nudged her legs apart and caressed her with his fingers, tongue and lips.

****

Mikey needed the silky smoothness of Kitty against him, if only for one last time. She had grown taller; her breasts had filled out, round and firm. Carissa could not compare—no woman could compare to Kitty. He used his tongue on her and roused her to fever pitch. He slid into her and with each thrust, her breasts bounced, watching her body heightened his yearning. Eyes closed, lips parted and her long pale hair fell across her face. Her orgasm pulsed and he thrust harder until his own shattering climax.

He kissed and nuzzled, savouring the sensation of her skin against his. Their heartbeats raced as one, their sweat mingled and whispers of love separated by kisses.

When they parted, they made no promises. Life had created a rift that neither could bridge and only time would reveal their destiny.

****

Mikey stared at Bill Matheson. His father-in-law had just offered to sell him the farm at a good price. He guessed Barbara hadn't told her parents about Mikey's indiscretion. His departure from their marriage would present Mikey with a problem: the shed. While he controlled the farm, he could steer people away from the shed, to walk away might open an economy-sized can of worms.

"Sure, I'll buy it. Give me time to get the finance." Mikey already had the kind of money Bill asked but he didn't want to draw attention to his mysterious wealth.

"There's no hurry, Mikey. I intend to stay in parliament for at least another two terms but after that, I won't resume farming."

Mikey knew Bill still cherished the hope that he'd replace him in parliament and he would let him live with that delusion a few more years. By the time Mikey had finished what he soon intended to start, the party would bar its doors against him—that's if they discovered who was behind it.

24

1978

In the years before Kitty joined the Queensland Police Force, they'd recruited women at double the rate of other states, but the year she entered, a new regime had taken the reins and Kitty was one of a handful of female recruits to slip through.

"So, Katrina. Why do you want to be a police officer?" The interviewer's tongue seemed too large for his mouth and it flobbered behind his thick lips as he spoke.

"I want to work with disadvantaged and abused young people. I'm also interested in helping women who are victims of domestic violence."

"Aren't you interested in fighting real crime?"

"Child abuse and domestic violence are crimes, aren't they?"

"In most cases it's necessary discipline." That sentence presented a linguistic challenge and his tongue lolled.

Kitty stared. That wasn't what her parents taught her about human decency and kindness.

"Do you live in a de facto relationship?"

His question caught Kitty off balance. "N—No."

"Do you have a boyfriend?"

"No—"

"Why not? Are you a lesbian?"

"No!"

"You're a bit of a harpy, aren't you?"

"What?"

Fortunately, the interview ended shortly after or Kitty feared she might have to kick his fat mouth.

She found herself at the mercy of her male fellow recruits and the training officers. Compelled to wear a skirt, heels, and stockings, she and her fellow female officers had to share facilities with the male officers. She often found herself avoiding the groping hands of her male counterparts and called a lesbian when she smacked them across the ear. A fellow rooky, Barry Bridger, was particularly antagonistic towards the girls and singled Kitty out for special treatment.

"Make me a coffee, Constable."

"Make it yourself, Constable." Kitty continued typing a witness statement for Detective Sergeant McCaffery of the Licensing Branch.

"Hey, Princess Katrina—how does it feel to look like a playboy bunny?"

"You ought to know."

She sensed cogs grinding and processing her words; he recovered and ventured a riposte. "I am a bit of a rabbit in the sack."

Kitty shook her head, this guy begged annihilation. "In size more than prowess I would imagine."

"Constable Olsen, haven't you got work to do?" She looked up. Senior Constable Smith loomed over her. "If I hear you gossiping again, you'll be on report."

As soon as Smithy moved out of earshot, Barry resumed his harassment. "Make me a coffee, Constable Olsen."

Later that day, she found a fellow female recruit weeping in the staffroom.

"Shannon, what's wrong?"

"I'm on report."

"What happened?"

"Sarg found out that I live with my boyfriend."

"But this is 1978; plenty of unmarried people live together."

"He says they can't have that kind of immorality in the police force."

It dismayed Kitty when a few days later, Shannon left the force. It seemed a trivial thing to discipline an officer over; Kitty knew of several male plain-clothes officers frequented a brothel in the city and they weren't there for friendly chit-chat. She suspected they were there for freebies in exchange for indemnity. In the coming week, Kitty would discover the hypocrisy that existed at a management level. When Detective Sergeant McCaffery brought in a pimp who operated a dirty little brothel in South Brisbane, Kitty witnessed his shouting match with the Detective Inspector.

"You did what?"

The Detective Inspector sounded bored. "I've dropped the charges."

"Why? That bastard is prostituting girls as young as fifteen and feeding them heroin."

"Rubbish, there's no heroin in Brisbane."

McCaffery's voice cracked with astonishment. "How can you say that?"

"Look, Chris, drugs and pros are everywhere, you can't fight it. They're just girls trying to make a living, there's no point in us being righteous about it. It's not up to us to enforce our morality on those women."

"A few weeks ago, you lot drummed a girl out of the force for being in a de facto relationship and you reckon you can't enforce morality—what—and you just let a pimp go!" Kitty swore she saw flecks of foam spray from McCaffery's mouth.

"Go and do your job, McCaffery." Kitty watched the inspector swipe the file off his desk and into the bin.

"I thought that was what I was doing!" Red-faced, Chris McCaffery slammed out of the inspector's office. "Come on, Constable Olsen. Let's go looking for couples who are living in sin."

****

Chris McCaffery

Thirty-five year old Chris McCaffery had joined the police force in the 1960s and had worked his way up to Detective Sergeant. He married Wendy, a registered nurse for six years but things hadn't gone to plan. They had both wanted children but it wasn't to be and after years of failure the strain had proved too much. Chris had walked out on Wendy but they'd never divorced. Love wasn't their problem; they still loved each other but couldn't live under the same roof without fighting. Both busy with their careers, neither could make time to talk about their differences and so they snatched an evening here or an afternoon there to spend together. His career had stagnated when he'd refused to join 'The Lark.' He couldn't bring himself to cast aside everything he valued about his job to join their corrupt system and that resulted in his becoming increasingly marginalised—pissing into a headwind. If he joined The Lark, he'd lose his usefulness as a police officer. He played it straight and the only convictions he clocked up were small players—junkies and hookers or punters taking a bet with an SP Bookie, the true villains out of his reach. There had always been a culture of bullying, sexism and corruption in the Queensland Police Force, but lately, things had deteriorated.

Sitting across the table from him, sipping an orange juice, Kitty Olsen looked bewildered. He chastised himself for thinking her too beautiful to be a cop. She was on report for kicking Constable Barry Bridger's arse all along the corridor; Barry had stuck his hand up her skirt as she took a drink from the cold-water fountain. Chris' team of 'snow-whites' heard the ruckus and came out to find Bridger of the floor in a shoulder lock and Constable Olsen's knee pressed into his back, her face pink and hair dishevelled.

"Don't give up, Kitty. You're going to be a hell of a good cop."

"I only got off desk duty two weeks ago and now I'm back on it."

"Chin up, little one." Chris laughed. "I wish I could have seen you in action. That weasel's face when you let him up was priceless!"

"Yeah, then he went sooking to Smithy."

"Don't worry; my team will corner him when he's on night shift next week. A host of pain is coming Bazza's way; he's going to be the guest of honour at a world class sock party."

****

Kitty took a sip of her drink; her career as a police officer hadn't worked out as she had hoped. Her life had taken her from one unhappy place to another. Since she and Mikey first became a twosome, she'd lived on the periphery of happiness, they'd loved one another but had to keep it hidden—then he'd destroyed everything. Kitty sighed; what he'd done lay in the past and best it remained in the past. Her love for Mikey would endure, but if they had a future, it remained ahead somewhere unseen. At this point of her life she lived one day at a time; wishes and regrets only brought misery.

"I never expected it would be so difficult to do my job. I've never been treated so badly for no other reason than I'm a woman. You, Dave, and Simsey, and a few others are the only ones who treat me like a human."

"The new hierarchy are the problem, so much so, I'm thinking of getting out."

"What will you do?"

"I might set up a private detective and security agency. There's a market for it here in Brisbane."

"I might come and work for you." Kitty smiled, half joking but in her heart she could see a career change on the horizon. She no longer viewed her job as a lifelong career.

25

1980

Mikey smiled, Danielle laughed as the old man pulled a coin from behind his ear and made a show of presenting it to her. She loved magic tricks and this old Albert Einstein look-alike seemed full of them. Eli Meyer spoke with a faint German accent. His son, Greg Meyer, and a little Frenchman Fabian Guerin, accompanied him. The men had arrived mid-morning and asked for a few moments of his time. Mikey set the tray down, passed the drinks to his guests, and pulled up a chair.

He had recently begun divorce proceedings. When Barbara had found the scarlet imprint of Carissa's lips on his jocks, he threw his hands in the air and confessed all. Finally accepting she would never win Mikey's love, Barbara had flounced and now demanded he buy out her share of the farm. He intended to grant her wish but in doing so, he would have to delay the renovations of the old cinema on Wickham Street in Fortitude Valley by six months.

Danielle, who spent most weekends with him, climbed onto his lap and took her glass of Strawberry Quik.

"So, what can I do for you, gentlemen?"

"We have a proposal to put to you, but first I will have you know who we are." Around forty, Greg Meyer was big and could easily be the twin of Elvis Presley, except he spoke like a Shakespearean actor.

"I'm the manager of Ellie and the Wolfmen, Fabbs here is the manager of Screaming Sally—"

"Wow!" Mikey mentally kicked himself for sounding like a star struck school kid.

"—and Eli, my father, is the manager of the Scullion Theatre in Kelvin Grove."

"And I'm just a busted arse farmer, but I'm pleased to meet you." Mikey smiled. Screaming Sally had stormed to the top of the Australian music industry around three years before and remained there. Ellie and the Wolfmen was a theatre rock band—new on the scene but already, you couldn't pick up a women's magazine without seeing little Ellie's face on the cover. A tiny blonde with big blue eyes and a voice to put a horn on a jellyfish, she played her red Stratocaster like a bloke. She had the body of an Olympic gymnast—nice legs, nice tits, nice arse—a living Barbie doll.

"We've heard a whisper that you're intending to open a new club in The Valley but don't have all the finance."

"Who told you that?"

"My old chum, Max Maxwell. So, is my information correct?"

Mikey smiled and nodded. "Bang on."

"We'd like to offer a proposal. Between myself, Fabbs and Eli we'll put up forty-nine percent of the finance and when our bands perform in Brisbane, it will be in your club. There'll be a few provisos, dress and behavioural standards—the place must be above the law."

"You see we are not impressed with The Capital." Fabbs spoke for the first time and Greg Meyer laughed.

"The Sallies ran amok there a few weeks ago and Rick vowed he won't have them back. Rick is a dodgy prick—The Capital is a front for prostitution and upstairs is an illegal casino. It's true! I've seen it firsthand. If you go there on Wednesday night, they have strippers. Which is fine—I'm no prude—but it's disturbing that the girls are then expected to service the clients. Eli and I don't want Ellie anywhere near the place. None of the other places suit, they either don't have big enough stages or they attract the wrong kind of clientele."

"Does Screaming Sally often run amok? I don't want my brand new club busted up by a bunch of rampaging rock stars."

"Occasionally they do—you know—artistic personalities. But Rick—he pissed them off—badly." Fabian Guerin smiled and splayed his hands. "I am employing a road manager and I hope he will keep them in line."

"Are you blokes for real? You're not taking the piss?"

"We're for real."

"Great! Where do I sign?"

Mikey glanced in the direction of the shed and hoped they'd never find out how he'd come by his money.

26

Creating the Phoenix Pearl from a dilapidated cinema to a classy entertainment venue took months. Mikey, Liam, Aiden, and their cousin Stanley McClurg, armed with a couple of his overfed, fart filled Dobermans, took turns to camp in the building each night. During the early stages of the renovations, several attempted burglaries happened. Mikey caught a couple of teenagers pouring petrol on the front doors and sent them on their way with matching bruised ears, Doberman teeth marks on their arse cheeks, and a warning ringing in their ears that next time he'd set them alight.

Mikey no sooner had approval to apply his family's liquor license to the new nightclub and a bagman arrived. John Yarrow sat across his desk and complimented Mikey on his coffee making ability.

"Well thank you, John. What can I do for you?"

I've taken an instant dislike to you, arsehole—may as well save time and hate you straight up.

Yarrow or his predecessor almost certainly had a hand in the events that led to the deaths of his parents and brother. Mikey tightened the lid on his hatred; it served his best interests to keep the man onside.

"Well it's like this, Mikey boy. In the city, we have ways of doing things."

"What? Different to how we do them up on the Sunshine Coast?" Mikey resisted batting his eyelashes.

"Quite possibly—yes. Ha-ha."

Ha—fucking—ha!

Mikey leaned back in his chair, folded his arms and set his frown in place. He knew what the man wanted but he'd make him work harder to get it.

"You see, the nightclub scene in this city can be perilous when you're just starting out—"

"Sounds daunting."

"It is—it can be." Yarrow nodded, pleased Mikey caught on so quickly. "But there are people who can help you."

"I haven't met any of those yet—do I have to call someone?"

"No—no! That's why I'm here; to sign you up for protection."

"I have bouncers."

"No—no, not protection from the punters, ha-ha."

"Who else do I need protection from?"

"You see, it's like this, Mikey boy. Not all the other nightclubs are prospering and they don't like it when a new place starts up, especially one as big and classy as yours."

Piss in the other pocket, arsehole, it's waterproof.

"Yeah?"

"You'll do them harm, put some of them out of business, even."

"Gee, will I?"

"Quite possibly."

"So what do I have to do?"

"Pay insurance, Mikey boy."

"I've already done that."

"Perhaps I should make myself clear."

Finally! He slithers up to what he really wants.

"Perhaps you should." Mikey open his desk drawer, pulled out a hunting knife and began scraping imaginary filth from under his nails.

Yarrow's eyes flicked to the knife and back. "You have to pay protection money, Mikey boy—it's as simple as that."

"Took you long enough to cough it up, and now I'll tell you what I want." Mikey unfolded himself from the chair, strode around and sat on the edge of his desk, closer to Yarrow than courtesy dictated. He held a loose grip on the knife and paddled the blade between his thumb and middle finger. Yarrow's tongue circled his lips, he watched the knife but he held his ground. "One, if you call me Mikey boy once more I'll cut your tongue out." He kept his voice even. "Two, I'll pay you fifty percent more than your best payers pay and no more. I want total protection, from the other clubs and from the cops. This place will be completely legal, the wallopers will have no cause to raid it, but I don't fucking-well trust the bastards. So yeah, I'll pay for protection and if I don't get it—well let's just say—I always get what I pay for, one way or the other." Mikey extended the knife and shaved a stray whisker off Yarrow's face.

Yarrow leaned away. "That will cost you a grand a week."

You have balls the size of a gorilla's—I'll give you that.

"It'll cost seven-fifty. You see I know how much the other's pay."

"How?"

Mikey's smile didn't reach his eyes. "I'm very resourceful, Mr Yarrow."

"I see."

"You'll also see that I'm not as nice as my father was." Mikey lurched to his feet and Yarrow flinched.

Go outside and shake the shit out of your undies, cunt.

He opened a hand towards the door. "See yourself out."

Mikey's threat hadn't gone over well with Yarrow but greed had lit a fire in those shifty eyes; the man was aboard with his ticket punched. A dog kicked in the guts would always return if offered steak. He'd be watching closely over the coming months, if Yarrow double crossed him, he'd receive a lesson in ruthlessness.

****

After Craig's death, Jack Walker had given away the DJ game and concentrated on his bank job. When he heard the Kinane brothers were opening a nightclub, Jack decided he would apply for the position of resident DJ. He didn't need the money; his day job paid well but six years after losing Craig, Jack was no closer to finding those responsible. No one believed Rusty Russell's guilt—no one cared either. Certain the Kinanes would care, Jack wanted to get close enough to gain insider knowledge of any clue that might have come their way. The rage that had burn inside had forged into something cold and hard.

A carpet layer pointed him to a door beside the bar when Jack inquired where he'd find the manager. The odour of paint and new carpet stung his eyes as he pushed the door and entered a narrow corridor. At the end, he found the office and tapped on the open door. The man who looked up from the desk was so like Craig, it hurt Jack to look. Mikey Kinane stood taller and heavier than Craig but otherwise might be his twin.

****

Mikey estimated Jack Walker in his mid-thirties; his light brown hair showed slivers of silver and early age lines marred his face.

"What can I do for you, Jack?"

"I'm hoping you're looking for a resident DJ."

"I will be—are you a DJ?"

"Yes—well I was, and I'm looking to get back into it."

"Do you have a reference?"

Jeez mate you might be a little old for the job.

"If your brother was here, I'm sure he would vouch for me."

"Which brother?"

Jack didn't answer for a moment; a flash of pain crossed his face.

"Craig. I was the DJ at The Pearl. I—I was on a night off when—" He stopped, grimaced and shut his eyes. "Craig and I were close—friends."

Jack's eyes sparkled.

"I see. More than just close friends?"

Jack Walker looked up with a veiled expression; gauging Mikey's mood.

"It's okay. We knew our brother was gay."

Jack's lips trembled and a tear spilled onto his cheek, he swiped it away and sniffed. "I still miss him, every day."

"We do too, Jack."

"Have you found out who—?"

"Not yet, but we will never stop trying. When we do find out—"

"I'll help you."

The cold, dead expression that stole across Jack's face Mikey had seen many times in the mirror.

"We'll start with getting your advice on the in-house sound system." Mikey extended his hand. "Welcome aboard."

27

1981

Kitty read the memo again and shrugged.

Could be worse. It could be Mt Isa.

Her impending transfer to Longreach in Western Queensland didn't faze her; the hierarchy's latest attempt to oust her came as no surprise.

Chris McCaffery lounged with fingers laced across his midriff and feet on the desk. "You could appeal it, Kitty. Sending a girl way out there could be seen as extreme punishment."

Kitty smirked. "Nah! I'll handle it."

"Are you sure?"

"How much worse could it be than here?"

After a two-day drive from Brisbane, Kitty caught her first glimpse of Longreach across the black soil plains, a hot westerly wind flattened the dry grass of the open country, roly-polys tumbled across the parched landscape. Miles of telephone lines looped rhythmically between poles that tracked the fence line beside the highway. She slowed at the edge of town; a bustard stepped to the side of the road and turned a sinister eye in her direction.

She grinned. "Welcome to the outback, Constable Olsen."

Senior Sergeant Laurie Miles stalked into the smoko room and kicked a chair aside.

As the offending chair knocked a dent in the fridge door, Lester Gainsford looked up from his magazine. "Burr under your saddle, Laurie?"

"Have you had a look at the new recruit from Brisbane?"

"Nuh. What's wrong with him?"

"Her. Lester, those cunts sent me a Vogue model. I sent back a perfectly good constable in return for a horny blonde."

Lester grinned. "If she can ride a horse, I'll have her."

"Don't fucking joke, Lester. Take a look at her; she's at the front desk—if she can ride a horse I'll eat my fucking hat—badge and all!"

"You never know, she might be a good cop."

"Every young buck for miles around is going to be committing misdemeanours just to get arrested by her."

Lester tossed the magazine on the table. "That good, huh?"

"Mate…"

Lester pushed past his boss and made for the front office.

28

Up the stairs at the Capital, Rick Campbell leaned on the plush bar rail and sipped a glass of port. Pendulum lights over the tables illuminated the room. The click of chips, soft voices, and laughter—the money rolled in. The pianist dripped soft notes of a familiar melody over the room; the bass thud of the disco downstairs vibrated through the thick red carpet.

Rick scowled as a champagne sipping blonde sidled up to him all lush lips, long nails, and brimming cleavage.

"Hello, Rick, I haven't seen you in ages."

Rick cast a calculating eye over her. Tammy, or maybe Tanya; the gold-digger girlfriend of a business associate. Her boyfriend had escaped his wife tonight and brought Tammy out on the town. Rick looked around for the boyfriend and spotted him standing at the roulette table. He resembled a carpet python that had swallowed a wallaby. Round-shouldered, long, thin, and reptilian with a bump of a gut at the middle. His gargantuan wallet the main attraction, not his looks.

Tammy tried again. "Rick—how have you been?"

"Just fine."

"Why don't we get out of here and go somewhere quiet for a drink?"

"What about old Coatsie?"

Her big round eyes rolled from Wally Coates to Rick. "What about him—you're much more interesting."

"No I'm not."

"I think you are. I've always fancied you, Rick." Her manicured hand brushed his forearm.

"Jesus! I've met some cunts in my time but you, lady, take the biscuit."

"What? What's your problem?"

"Old Coatsie has a wife at home—she's a good woman. I don't know what he sees in a bloodsucking moll like you, take your fake tits and get out of my club…"

Tammy's stricken faced turned pale under Rick's invective.

"…women like you. Coatsie has kids at home but why would you care? As long as he lets your fingers in his wallet—"

"Rick—enough already." His cousin Naz grasped his elbow and dragged him away.

"Fuck off, Naz." Rick was just getting into his stride. "Bitch, move your fat arse—"

"That's a bit unkind, Rick—come on. Let's get a drink and talk."

Tammy scampered off to join Wally; she tucked herself into his side and shot reproachful glances at Rick.

Naz drew him to the end of the bar and forced him into a barstool. "There, that's better."

"I get sick of women doing that, especially when they know I'm married."

"Yeah, fuck 'em—you're a good bloke, Rick. I don't often say that to your face but—"

"Ah shuddup, Naz, you're pissed."

"Doesn't matter. I know what I'm talking about."

"Yeah?"

"Yeah. You're the pick of your whole family, Rick. Did you know that?"

Rick lifted his glass to his mouth. "Well, in my family, that doesn't make me all that great, does it?"

29

"Ready to go, Constable Olsen?" Lester picked up his duffle bag and smiled at the girl standing in the door of his office. She gave a new rhythm to his pulse. His fellow senior officers had scoffed when he'd recruited the new constable into the stock squad in the first week after she arrived in Longreach. She could ride a horse or motorbike as well as any of the men she worked with and knew a lot about livestock. She wasn't precious about the lack of a shower every night when they had to camp out in the line of duty. Shortly after she arrived in town, a fellow constable had tried to grope her, and she dislocated his finger before kicking him in the crotch. A veteran of twenty-six years, Lester hated how some of his workmates treated female officers. They wouldn't like to see their mothers or sisters treated that way.

"I am."

"What do you drink?"

"Fourex, but I don't drink much."

"Good girl. We have an esky full of Fourex."

"Is that all? I'll have to discipline myself not to drink it all in one sitting."

Lester's skin tingled at her smile. Dressed in a plain blue shirt, jeans and RM Williams boots, the girl seemed unaware of her male colleagues' appreciative glances. She switched her hold on her duffle bag from her left to right and turned to leave.

"Olsen, wait." Lester stepped over and closed the door; it irked him to see trepidation steal over her fine Nordic features. "Are you enjoying working in the squad?"

She nodded, her eyes wary.

"Hey, I'm not going to grab you girl. You got your hat?"

"Yes."

"You're too pretty to be a cop, you know that?"

"What should I do? Pick a few fights and get my face busted up?"

Lester grinned and gently tweaked her nose. "Please don't. I like your face the way it is." He wished he'd kept his mouth shut when he saw the wariness return to her eyes. He was forty-seven; Kitty Olsen around twenty-three. "You'll ride in my cruiser with me, okay?"

She dipped her gaze. "Thanks."

****

The horse supplied by the cocky was a little skittish, not used to the light touch of a woman on his back. Kitty had kept the reins held short for most of the morning. She stood at his head, sharing her sandwich with him and gently coaxing him to relax. That morning they had followed the tracks of forty-five cattle driven by two riders. The cocky had noticed them missing the day before and called the stock squad. The trail was a couple of days old but all they had to go on at this stage of the investigation.

"You're spoiling that horse."

Kitty looked around; Lester Gainsford made himself comfortable on a log, sandwich in one hand and a mug of coffee in the other.

"I'm trying to make friends with him; he's been threatening to throw me off all morning."

Lester smiled and carefully set his mug on the log beside him. A handsome man, well-built and tough looking. With brown eyes and premature grey hair, Kitty thought he'd be around her father's age. His eyes slid down her body like Mikey used to do. When she thought of Mikey, a pang of sadness stung her heart. She hadn't seen Mikey since that Sunday afternoon after graduation and the familiar craving ached inside.

Somehow, you must get over him, Kitty.

The horse settled, tractable and placid. Late that afternoon they emerged from the timbered country onto a wide expanse of grassland. They camped near a bore tank on a fence line. When the Landcruisers arrived with their equipment, Lester told the men to turn their backs while Kitty took a wash under the flowing water.

"Feel free to take a bath under the bore pipe, Constable Olsen; we'll keep our eyes to ourselves. The water should be nice and warm."

The sulphurous artesian water was almost too hot for Kitty but she felt better for washing the dust and sweat from her hair and body. Clean and dressed, she took a seat with the men.

"I enjoyed that little strip-tease, Olsen." Constable Lehman grinned and raised his stubby; a hairy brute of a man a few years older, Kitty could find little to like.

"Is your nose broken, Lehman?" Lester took a beer from the esky and passed it to Kitty.

"No—" Lehman's brow creased.

"No it's not—but if I had seen you perving on Constable Olsen, it would be, so shut up and go take a bath yourself. You stink."

While the men went to wash themselves. Kitty sat alone and waited. Ten minutes and Lester returned wearing jeans and T shirt.

"That feels better." He took another beer and resumed his seat, his wet hair untidy. "Let me know if Lehman is giving you the creeps, Kitty. I'm looking for an excuse to get rid of him."

"Can't you just do it anyway?"

"Unfortunately not without a good reason, he's experienced with horses and knows a bit about livestock—people like that are not common in the force. It's his attitude to his colleagues and to the public I don't like."

"He doesn't bother me much." Kitty lied; she didn't want Lester to think her timid. Lehman was a big man and she didn't like her chances of holding him off if he tried anything.

In the morning, mounted and ready to go, Kitty waited for her colleagues. Far above, a jet tore a white line across the blue Queensland sky. She gazed at the downs country, its wide flat grassland in stark contrast to the lush coastal farm where she grew up. Laughter punctured the silence; Kitty looked around in time to see Lehman toss a small goanna under the hooves of her horse; he reared, spun and bucked. With no time to react, Kitty could only pull her feet from the stirrups and let go. The horse bounded away with the stirrups tapping his flanks and the fleeing goanna at his heels.

"You dopey bastard! Go catch the fucking horse and don't come back until you've got him!" Lester knelt beside her. "Kitty, are you okay?"

"I think so." Her arse cheek hurt where she landed on it and apart from that, a burning pain in her wrist all she could feel. Humiliated, she held her wrist out, it swelled rapidly.

"Ah Christ, Kitty! If that's broken, I'll break Lehman's neck for him." Lester helped her to her feet and dusted her off. His brawny arms pulled her to him; Kitty thought he might have kissed the top of her head.

Sergeant Crichton approached. "Take her back to town, Lester. I'll take care of things here."

30

Gary Snelling was both lucky and unlucky. As far as taking a punt with SP bookies was concerned, he was unlucky. Owing four-hundred dollars to Naz Van Nek with no way of paying proved more bad management than bad luck, but when Naz sold the debt to German Burt, Gary's luck took a nose dive—with Burt's interest rates, the debt doubled overnight and Burt was no mathematician—whatever he said you owed, you owed. Burt had no PNS system, he gave you twenty-four hours to cough up or he'd beat the shit out of you; he made violence an art form. Then if you still didn't come up with the money—well—rumours abounded of Burt's private graveyard. So how was Gary lucky? Five days after the first warning, he still survived. Severe concussion, a punctured lung, both eyes swollen shut, face sliced from cheek to chin, front teeth knocked out, and his arm broken twice with a pick handle.

Chris McCaffery accompanied Dave Cramb and Ray Sims to interview Gary Snelling in his hospital bed.

"This bloke's not going to tell us anything," said Ray.

"I'm betting the hillbilly hitman, German Burt, is behind this; it's his style." Dave pushed the door open and strolled into the ward.

Sims grunted. "Could be. I don't think Burt's all that dangerous, it's the rumours. That's what scares people."

"Betting is what got old Gary into the shit in the first place." Chris grinned at the older detective and coughed, disinfectant hit him like a slap in the face. His wife often came home with that scent on her clothes and in her hair. He'd not long moved back in with her and so had to get used to it again.

"Figure of speech, Chris. You take your life into your hands defaulting on a debt with the SP bookies around Brisbane."

"Wake up, Gary," Ray Sims slapped the bed. "The doctor said you're fit enough to talk to us."

"I am awake." Gary turned his dog's-breakfast of a face towards him.

"Oh, so you are. So what happened, Gary?"

"I got in a fight"

"What with? A jackhammer?"

"Ha ha. Just a fight—I don't need you blokes."

"Let us be the judge of that. So come on, tell us who did this."

"I might be stupid but I'm not crazy."

Chris took a chair beside the bed. "We can take the guy off the streets, Gary. Just tell us who to arrest."

"I've said all I'm going to say. Forget it, fellas. That's what I'm going to do."

"So you've paid the debt then?"

"How do you know I owed money?"

"Sophia Thomas made a statement. She's given us some very credible information."

"She's a hooker."

"So? Hookers see many things that the rest of us don't. If you still owe money then you're still in danger."

"And if I talk I'll be in even worse danger."

"We can hide you, Gary."

"Bullshit. You might hide me from Burt but you won't hide me from—" Gary stopped and shifted in the bed.

"So, Burt did this did he? German Burt?"

"I'm not sayin' nothin'."

"So who else are you afraid of other than Burt?"

"I'm not sayin' nothin'."

"Come on, Gary—we can help you."

"Help me get killed, yeah. I'm not sayin' nothin'."

****

Dave Cramb eased his bulk behind the wheel of the unmarked Falcon sedan.

"Well that was a waste of time and energy."

"We know German Burt is our man, let's bring him in and see what we can get out of him."

Sims slammed the back door and rolled down the window. "You can bet Burt won't tell us anything."

"Who else do you reckon Gary is scared of?"

"Dunno. But if they scared him more than Burt, they must be pretty dangerous."

****

German Burt, born Burton William Campbell was the younger half-brother of Rick Campbell. He had earned his nickname from his fascination with everything German. For years, he'd driven a Volkswagen Beetle with a Porsche sticker on the rear windscreen. Then he bought himself a wheezy old 1962 Mercedes 220S. The twenty-year-old car blew a cloud of black diesel smoke when he started it and the motor ran like a chaff cutter but few dared laugh. Burt hulked at six feet, three inches, pale blond hair and pale green eyes—one of which mostly looked at the wall—Burt weighed around nineteen stone and some who dared risk a bit of levity at his expense, estimated a good percentage of that weight was his head. A thug for hire, Burt earned the bulk of his living buying outstanding debts off the SP bookies and loan sharks. Such men never had time to chase errant clients so they commissioned the debts to German Burt. The money they loaned with a smile, Burt recouped with a pick handle. The interest rate he charged would make an American Express executive salivate.

****

German Burt sat with arms folded and legs akimbo, sneering at the detectives. He paid the bagman good money for indemnity, but these blokes were known as 'snow whites'—the incorruptibles. They managed to put away enough of his ilk to make Burt nervous, but he wasn't going to let them see they had him rattled. McCaffery and Cramb sat across the table like a pair of tombstones, undaunted; they had even taken his lucky pick handle. They could interrogate the paint off the walls but Burt had a good lawyer who had performed more saves in the last five minutes than an A-grade goalkeeper during a ninety-minute soccer match. Finally, McCaffery rose and left the room. Cramb lounged, arms folded and waited, Burt thought the detective might fall asleep. Twenty minutes later, McCaffery returned.

"Well, Burtie boy, you'll be held in custody. Aggravated assault is a serious crime; you're looking at a lag in Boggo Road."

Burt blenched. Furner had better get him out of this or he might cop a flogging with a pick handle as well.

"I never assaulted no one."

"We have a victim who seems to think you did."

"He'll soon change his—"

"Burt, don't speak." His lawyer dived to the rescue again. "My client will exercise his right to silence."

****

Sophia Thomas licked her glossy red lips, squirmed in her chair, and swung a long leg over the other, her nipples beckoned under the transparent chiffon. The mini skirt left little to the imagination and Constable Peter Joyce blushed like a schoolgirl—his imagination in overdrive.

"So what do you boys want from me?" Her eyes slithered down Peter's front, fixed on his crotch then flicked back to his face.

Dave Cramb's frown glanced off his bashful colleague and back to Sophia. "Cut the act, Sophia. Tell us what you know about German Burt's assault on Gary Snelling."

"Maybe I've changed my mind. Maybe I don't want to tell you anything."

Cramb leaned across the desk. "And maybe I'll get a subpoena."

Sophia's black eyes sparkled as she folded her arms; her cleavage bulged out of her top.

"I'm scared." She pouted at Peter, the big man's heart melted in the face of her Gig Puppy eyes.

"Don't feed me that shit," growled Cramb, "what are you scared of? Burt's in jail."

"Those jacks."

"Which jacks?" Cramb's frown lines deepened.

"Lyle Furner and Charlie Doyle."

"What have they got to do with this?"

"Everything."

"Can you be more specific?"

"German Burt is their man, he doesn't only do beatings for himself; he bashes anyone who won't—or can't pay the bagman and he bashes anyone who crosses Furner."

"Who is this bagman?" Cramb had heard of the bagman, a shadowy figure rumoured to liaise with the licensing branch—an emissary for the proprietors of brothels, illegal casinos, porn shops, SP bookmakers and even legitimate licensees.

"I don't know—John somebody—all the houses pay him and he passes it on to Furner and Doyle and the other boys in on the Lark."

"Bullshit. Furner and Doyle are honest detectives, working in the licensing branch."

"They come in to my workplace at least once a week, looking for favours."

"What kind—"

"Head job. Hand job. The works." Sophia's tongue flicked across her lips, her eyes stared into Peter's then dipped demurely; the long legs swapped positions. "We have to give it to them or they'll bust us and they keep raising the payoff; Ruby threatened to go to the papers and Furner did something to her—" Sophia shrugged a shoulder. "He really put the wind up her. I don't know what exactly, but she was too scared to take it any further. When I asked her about it, she told me to shut my mouth and never mention it again."

"Would you be prepared to make an official statement?"

"Not until you guarantee my safety—I can tell you other things too." She pouted at Cramb. When he failed to respond, she redirected it at Constable Joyce.

"What other things?"

"Big things." Sophia checked her cleavage and adjusted her arms.

"Stop playing games, Sophia!" Cramb folded his arms and leaned back in his chair, he glanced at his colleague. Joyce's expression was that of a begging dog.

"The biggest event that ever happened in the Valley."

"The fires?"

Sophia dramatically lifted her shoulder and rolled her eyes to the ceiling.

"Would you be prepared to make a statement? Would you be prepared to give evidence in court?"

"If I knew they'd never find out who I am, sure; Craig Kinane was a nice guy, so yeah. I'll give evidence if you can hide me."

Cramb feared this whole case could see him ridiculed or banished to Birdsville or Doomadgee. A hooker's word over two of the state's most revered detectives. Could he put such a case together and then prosecute it? He had to try.

"I'm sure that can be arranged, your identity can be changed. In the meantime we can take you to a safe-house."

31

The pack bore down on Paul, his legs buckled and he fell exhausted to the ground. Wet and cold, it eased the fever that burned his body from the inside. His head spun, and the distant streetlight faded, Paul blacked out.

He came around as someone pulled him to his feet.

"Answer me, you fuckin' poofter!" The man shoved Paul and he landed back on the wet grass. Weeks of cold weather had worn him down and he had caught a cold. He'd become too ill to get himself to a doctor. He hadn't seen Ben and Shane for more than a month. Paul imagined when he could get himself back to his job as a trolley boy at K Mart, his boss would tell him to piss off.

"Let's give him a bit of what he likes, boys!"

Hands pulled at his jeans and Paul coughed, his lungs burned. The feverish black claimed him once again. He came to; jeers and laughter rang in his ears. An elbow pressed the back of his neck, squashing his face into the mud. Pain burned and the man on him thrust hard, grunting.

"You like it up the arse? I'll give it to you up the arse!"

Paul blacked out; when he came to, he opened his eyes, one of the men stood before him, a switchblade knife held loosely as he zipped his fly. Anger surged in Paul's feverish body; he rose to his knees and lunged, grabbed the knife and plunged it into the man's stomach. On his feet, he ran for his life pulling up his bloodied jeans as he went.

****

Jack often took a walk in the early hours. Daylight, but the sun had yet to rise when he parked on Alice Street next to The City Botanic Gardens. By day, families, joggers, and people enjoying the fresh air frequented the gardens, but at night, the perverts, drug addicts, and weirdos roamed—derelicts sipped methylated spirits from the bottle. The cold damp air invigorated him as he strode along the path. Only a minute into his walk, he heard a dreadful cough; someone struggled for breath. Following the sound towards an amenity block, he found a young man. His face battered and pale, his blond hair caked with mud. He leaned down and shook his bony shoulder.

"Hello? Can you hear me?"

Stertorous breathing of a serious condition lifted up from a boy. Apart from his physical injuries, he was gravely ill and underweight for his height.

"Come on, mate." Jack gathered him into his arms and carried him back to his car. He estimated the boy to be in his late teens though given the facial injuries it was difficult to say. He sat him in the back seat of his car, buckled him in and drove him to the Princess Alexander Hospital.

****

Jack returned to visit every day, in the absence of any identification, the hospital tag said name unknown.

"What happened to him, Doctor?"

The doctor frowned at Jack. "You're not related to him are you?"

"No, I found him in the City Botanic Gardens."

The doctor sighed as he hung the chart back on the end of the bed.

"I guess it can't hurt to tell you as nobody seems to be searching for him. He's had that nasty flu that is going around and still has a severe chest infection. The horrifying thing is, he was gang raped and I'm guessing the same people beat him up. Judging by the condition of him, I'd say he is homeless. We've been checking for any missing male persons and there haven't been any for quite some time. He has no fillings in his teeth so we can't even search for dental records."

"Is he going to be okay?"

"It'll take time. He needs a lot of TLC but he's young, he'll recover. We estimate him to be between fifteen and eighteen."

"Doctor, if he comes around and I'm not here, can you call me? I don't want to see him wander off back out onto the streets.

"I can do that. I should warn you, I think he may be an addict."

"Heroin?"

"No. Inhalants."

"He's a glue sniffer?"

"I think so."

"How can you tell?"

The doctor shrugged. "There was a tube of Araldite in his pocket, inside a plastic bag that has had the glue squeezed into it."

32

McCaffery and Peter Joyce drove Sophia up the range to a safe house in Toowoomba. On the trip up, they talked about the case; investigations into allegations of misconduct in the licensing branch had always fallen flat. Chris used careful words—saying the wrong thing to the wrong officer could land him in strife. No one knew whom they could trust. The bagman never identified different members of the Lark to one another. He kept them isolated. He kept them guessing. Chris noticed Peter's frequent glances at the girl in the back of the car. Olive skinned, black eyes, black haired and pretty but Chris didn't trust her. He wished Cramb or Sims had accompanied him for this trip but both men were busy on another case. Peter Joyce was single, in his mid-twenties and strangely shy for a police officer; Sophia's come-on looks got to him. Chris thought it a terrible idea to post Peter in the safe house with Sophia, he could see trouble coming like a swarm of locust backlit by the morning sun.

****

At the safe house, Chris saw Sophia settled. Peter Joyce took the room next door to be close by in case of trouble.

"Are you going to be okay here, Peter?"

"Of course, Sarg. Helen seems to know what she's on about." Peter nodded toward the caretaker of the safe house. "We'll watch TV and I'll send Sophia off to bed early."

"Look, Peter. If you need assistance, call the local station. Sophia is a hooker—be very careful."

"I'm sure I can handle her, don't worry."

Chris's alarm bells jangled as he drove back to Brisbane. Peter Joyce had assisted Chris with the Gary Snelling case and volunteered to sit guard on Sophia if she agreed to testify. Chris hadn't been concerned about German Burt; he wasn't that bright—an original idea would die of loneliness inside his vast skull—it wouldn't be hard to hide a witness from him.

Burt wouldn't recognise a lead if it climbed out of the gutter and pissed on his foot.

Now, with Sophia's revelation about Furner and Doyle, Chris worried. He didn't share Cramb and Sims' confidence in the pair from the licensing branch. He had heard whispers about Furner, the investigation into The Pearl bombing had a bad smell about it; Lester Gainsford had not had time to kill Daryl Reid, let alone a motive. The hierarchy transferred him out of Brisbane faster than Chris could say 'dodgy.'

Sophia spelled trouble. Though an experienced police constable, Peter seemed to have little resistance to Sophia's feminine wiles.

****

153

Helen Robinson, the caretaker, announced herself off to bed. The safe house usually had one or two women and a few kids, domestic violence victims the police hid from abusive spouses. Tonight she had none of that kind. Tonight's guests were Constable Peter Joyce and a prostitute called Sophia. Sometime after nine p.m., the pair retired to their respective rooms; Helen cleaned the kitchen and retired to her end of the house.

****

It took Peter Joyce around an hour to switch off his brain and fall asleep. He dreamed of soft lips on his and warm hands peeling away his shorts.

"Sophia!" he sat up, "what are you doing?"

"Just lie back and relax, big man."

"Sophia! This is—no! You'll get me shot, girl! Stop—"

She straddled his lap, her lips on his. Her tongue wriggled into his mouth and he lay back on the pillows, his hands on her shoulders should have pushed her away but instead they found her breasts and drew them to his mouth.

"You like my tits, don't you?"

"Yes."

"And you want them in your face, don't you?"

"Yes—"

Her wet genitals brushed against his stomach as he rubbed her breasts across his lips, sucking, first one nipple then the other. Peter had a girlfriend back in Brisbane but she never made him

154

feel like this. Raised in strict Christianity, he'd met his girlfriend at church. He had straight, missionary position sex with her once a week, except at 'that time of the month.' Peter's cue to go to the pub.

He moaned as Sophia moved down and took him in her mouth, working him into her throat and Peter cummed hard, panting—he wept a little. She shifted up the bed and straddled his face; he sucked and nibbled as she grasped the bedhead. Peter slid down the bed and lifted her arse, mounted her from behind, they made so much noise he worried Helen might hear them from the other end of the house. The bed squeaked as Peter lost control, his hips lunged hard, in and out; she had a way of hanging on as he pulled back for the next thrust. The orgasm took him; one last push and he collapsed on top of her, trembling and sweating.

****

Lurking in the dark, Lyle Furner's cold-heart was immune to other people's sex scenes, Charlie Doyle stood beside him sweating and rubbing the front of his trousers. He wrongly presumed Lyle couldn't see him wringing his knob in the dark. Constable Joyce collapsed on top of the hooker and Lyle's nostrils whitened as he grabbed his offsider's shoulder and shook some sense into him— now wasn't a good time for Charlie to cum in his pants. Then he pressed the gun into the back of Joyce's head and grinned.

"Enjoyed rooting a prostitute, Peter? They do it so much better than the average woman, don't they?" He looked over as

Charlie snapped his silencer onto Peter Joyce's service revolver and aimed it at Sophia's head.

Her eyes grew large in the darkened room.

"No! I don't—" Her hands spread in front of her face. The pistol cracked, a bullet punched a bloody hole through her hand and lodged in her face; the second shot silenced her.

"On your feet, Joyce."

Constable Joyce stood bigger and taller than Furner but the rogue cop kept the gun pressed to his head and he obeyed. Charlie Doyle removed the silencer from Joyce's gun, held it against his temple and pulled the trigger. Joyce dropped to the floor, Charlie positioned the gun loosely in his dead hand with the index finger poked through the trigger guard.

"Well that was easier than I expected. I didn't fancy dragging that hooker, kicking a screaming all the way to Joyce's room"

"Okay, let's go."

****

"Bullshit!"

Dave Cramb and Ray Sims exchanged glances; Cramb shook his head. He and Sims believed the forensic officer's evidence.

"I'm sorry, Chris. I know you liked Constable Joyce, but all the evidence points to a murder suicide. They'd had sex, there was a sign of a struggle, Sophia died from two bullets, shot from Joyce's service revolver and then Joyce used it to shoot himself."

Chris buried his face in his hands. "Fuck it! Just fucking—fuck it! I don't fucking believe it!" He didn't care how many of his colleagues heard his anger.

"There will be an official enquiry, of course."

"Of—fucking—course!" Chris leapt to his feet and the chair rolled away. "Of course there'll be a fucking enquiry; I hope they have a full bucket of whitewash because they're going to need it for this one!" Chris stomped off along the corridor. He needed to get out of the station and distance himself from his profession.

****

German Burt smirked at the 'snow whites' as they released him from the watch house. Nothing stuck, despite the shadows and whispers. Gary Snelling refused to give evidence against him.

"Well boys, I think I might take a little fishing trip this week, I know of a good spot up near Somerset Dam."

"Just shut up and piss off, Burt." The night blew in as Sims shoved him out the door.

"See ya round like a wheel, Simsie." Burt grinned and strode away.

"Behave yourself, Burt," Sims called, "or I'll be feeling your collar again."

The day after they released Gary Snelling from hospital, his wife reported him missing.

33

Jack Walker hurried across the hospital foyer and into the lift. He'd been in every day for the past week, with each visit the patient grew stronger. An hour before, the doctor called him to say the young man had woken. Jack didn't quite understand why he cared, but something told him if he didn't, the youth would be back on the streets and next time he might not be lucky enough to have someone like Jack save him. Jack carried the bag of clothes he'd bought; the youth would need more than hospital pyjamas when they discharged him. As he walked past the nurse's station the doctor beckoned him inside.

"Jack, I'm glad to see you. Our boy has told us his name; he is Paul Matthews. He is seventeen and has lived on the streets since he was ten, which was when his mother went missing. He's ready to go home—only—"

"He can come home with me. I live alone and have a spare room."

Suspicion crept across the doctor's face.

"It's okay, doctor, I'm not a predator. He needs somewhere to stay while he gets on his feet and I can give him a room."

"We've discussed his substance habit and he wants to stop. We have booked him in for rehab. It would be good if there was someone there to make sure he attends each week."

"I'll see he does."

"He's a victim of child sex abuse although he refused to discuss it other than to say that was why he took up glue sniffing. I have given him the name of a counsellor, he says he'll be okay but maybe you can talk him into seeing someone. His self-confidence is at rock bottom—he needs to talk to a professional."

Jack nodded. "I'll see what I can do."

"Perhaps if he is happy with his life, it will make it easier for him."

"I'll do my best, I promise."

****

Paul's limbs weighed a ton; he wanted to stay in bed and sleep for a month. The only other time he'd ever slept in a bed with clean sheets was at Ruby's. Worry gnawed at him, a nurse said they would discharge him that afternoon. He guessed he'd go back to the City Botanic Gardens and find somewhere he could sleep. He had nothing, his attackers had stolen his wallet, and the only clothes were those he'd been found in. The hospital had laundered them. He closed his eyes and listened to the piped music coming from the plastic tube that hung from the bed-head. Music was the one thing he had missed while he lived on the streets; occasionally he had caught snatches of songs as he walked past shops and houses.

He opened his eyes at the sound of a chair shifting on the floor, a man sat beside the bed.

"Hello, Paul. You're feeling better today?"

Paul nodded; the man looked familiar.

"My name's Jack. I found you in the gardens and brought you here."

"Jack! You used to be at The Pearl."

"Have we met?"

"I was the kid who used to sneak in there."

"So you are; I didn't recognise you."

Paul couldn't believe his luck when Jack took him home and installed him in his spare room. Nobody could call him a himbo; unlike Ben's living arrangement, Jack's only wish was for Paul's good health and happiness. As his strength returned so did his desire to inhale chemicals. He did as the doctor had instructed and attended rehab. Jack talked to Paul's boss at K Mart and convinced him to give Paul his job back. He also got Paul a job at the Phoenix Pearl as a trainee drink waiter.

Day by day, week by week, he scaled the rehab mountain, sometimes with barely a toehold. He had one session with a counsellor and quit. Talking to Jack acted as the best therapy. Jack kept him busy, learning to read above his grade two level, learning to add and subtract, multiply and divide. Paul recovered a little more each day—improving in health and confidence.

34

Late Friday afternoon, Kitty answered a knock on her door. Lester Gainsford had arrived with a bottle of wine and a parcel of fish and chips.

"I hope you're hungry, Kiddo. I've come to see how you're doing and I'm using that as an excuse to have dinner with you—if you can give fish and chips such a grand title."

Kitty smiled and let him in. She hoped no one from the station knew he visited, she'd never hear the end of it.

"How is your wrist going?"

"Getting better I think." Her wrist wasn't broken but sprained. The doctor ordered her to have two weeks off work. Twelve-hundred kilometres was too far to drive home to her family so she had bought a stack of books to read.

Kitty began to lift plates out of the cupboard but Lester pulled them from her hands and put them back.

"A couple of glasses are all we need." He set the parcel on the table and unrolled it. "A candle wouldn't go astray either."

She smiled as she searched for her candle supply; something about Lester made Kitty warm inside. Since she had joined the police force, she'd had a sense of vulnerability; it reassured her to know a senior officer cared. She fêted her ability to look after herself but a woman was always at a disadvantage in the face of male aggression and superior strength. She used the element of surprise to great effect; when a man gropes a woman, he doesn't expect her to retaliate. Tall and strong for a girl, Kitty excelled at rapid response; she used those initial few seconds to take down her adversary. She endeavoured to give policing her best shot but actions such as Lehman's were all too common and it worried her what such a prank might cost. A experienced rider might have tried to stay on the animal's back but Kitty's father had taught her she wasn't a rodeo rider and when a horse bucked, it was easiest to abandon ship. Many inexperienced riders found themselves hung up by a stirrup and dragged, trampled, or even rolled on by a panicking horse.

"Now this is romantic," Lester smiled as he filled her glass, "it's not every day an old hack cop like me gets to dine with a beautiful young woman."

Several layers of paper piled with fish and chips lay spread on the table between them. The Beatles played on the stereo and two candles, the only light.

"Here's to my commanding officer buying me fish and chips." Kitty raised her glass to his.

"Here's to old Lester having a date with the best looking cop in Queensland." His smiled faded as he held her gaze. "Anytime you want me to leave, Kitty, just say so. I shouldn't be here."

"Why not? What else is there for us to do way out here?"

"Nothing that I want to do."

"So let's enjoy ourselves."

"Do you have a boyfriend?"

Kitty sipped her wine and shook her head.

"The detective in me thinks you do."

"Not anymore."

"You're too young to have already had your heart broken. Tell me about him."

Stilted and stammered, the words came slowly at first then flowed as she told him about the boy next door.

"He isn't the first young man who made a stupid mistake and gave up his freedom to pay for it."

Kitty watched Lester's eyes as he gazed at the candle flame and blinked, trying to erase the after-image scorched in his retinas. She waited for him to continue but he picked up a chip and pushed it at her.

"This last one has your name on it."

Kitty laughed and took the proffered chip between her teeth, as she pulled it in with her lips and tongue she caught his eyes on her mouth and swallowed.

****

The grains of salt stuck to Kitty's top lip drew Lester's eyes. Those lips. He rose, leaned across the table and covered them in his own; he took in the taste of salt, lemon and wine. The brief kiss kick-started his heart. Her eyes widened, her lips parted and her chest lifted.

"Lester!"

"Sorry, I shouldn't have done that. I'd better go—"

"No—don't go." She shot out of her chair and gained her feet, skirted the table and leaned down. Their lips met in a long and tender kiss. Lester held her away from himself, for his own sake and hers, he needed to give them space—time to come to their senses. Her arms tightened around his neck as Lester got to his feet. He knew he should leave but his feet would no more walk out the door than would his arms grow feathers and fly him out. He drew her against his chest and kissed the scented skin below her ear.

"Kitty—"

"Shh." Her fingers light and warm across his lips, her smile didn't reach the sadness in her blue of her eyes. Lester watched as she extinguished one of the candles, a thin plume of smoke rose straight, spiralled and dispersed. She picked up the other, retrieved her wine and motioned for him to follow.

Lester, you're about to get luckier than you could ever have hoped for.

As consent left her lips, he possessed them, pulling them between his. He stripped away her clothes, impatient to see her naked. He'd caught a glimpse of her naked silhouette in the rear-view mirror of the Landcruiser as she'd emerged from that bore; the late afternoon sun only allowed him the vaguest peep of her shining, wet curves. His obsessed brain had tormented him as it replayed that image on a continuous loop. Her dress parachuted to the floor, Lester shivered, he could see through the white lace of her bra and his hands fumbled as she helped him remove it.

"Just beautiful." Her breast warm and firm, her skin smooth and golden beneath his rough hands as they slid down her body to remove her flimsy lace knickers. Lester had always been cocksure but as he undressed, painful awareness of his age plagued him. In good shape for an old bloke, he wasn't what he used to be. If Kitty noticed, she was undeterred and pulled him onto the bed with her. She pressed herself against him, her breath hot on his neck.

"Hey slow down, Kiddo."

Lester had enough experience with women to recognise the symptoms of ovulation and Kitty displayed all the signs. He rejoiced he'd had the snip around ten years before—he could take advantage of a horny girl without the risk. Flushed-face and feverish, she responded to his touch with a fiery ardour. As he lowered his head between her legs, his mind drifted to the man who had broken her heart.

You're a fool, Mikey Kinane. Hang on a second…

He stopped. Kinane; he knew that name.

"Lester! Don't stop—"

What are you thinking, Lester? Worry about it later.

He returned to his task, his tongue teased. When he moved over her, she pushed him back onto the pillows and climbed on, she slid onto him, tight and slippery. She moved slowly and her hair fell across his face; her nipples brushed his lips. He caught one in his mouth and sucked it hard. Her orgasm encircled him and he rolled her onto her back, thrust harder, and faster until she cried out again and he came like the proverbial freight train.

When his breath returned he rolled off her and pulled her against him.

"What have we started, Constable Olsen?"

"Call me Kitty."

"Kitty. Please don't tell me this is a one night stand."

"I hope not."

Silence fell in the candle light as they basked in the afterglow, idly exploring each other's bodies. As he nuzzled her neck, his earlier distraction returned.

"Mikey Kinane."

Her body tensed. "What about him?"

"The Valley Star Kinanes?"

"Yes, Craig Kinane was his older brother."

"And Tom and Mary were his parents."

"Did you know them?"

"I was in homicide at the time; I led the investigation into the murders."

"Was that guy really responsible? I remember the papers had a lot to say about it."

"We sent someone to prison, but I'm almost certain he didn't do it. I think he'd been scared into confessing—he was bloody terrified, I never saw someone so eager to get inside a cell, poor bastard would rather spend life inside than face whoever was responsible. He died in prison a few weeks later..." He told Kitty about the death of Daryl Reid and about the events that followed. "...so I came out of it with a shadow hanging over my integrity. The honest cops thought I was in on the Lark—and the Lark was having a good old laugh at my expense. Someone was being protected but I don't know who. Furner is a scary bastard—

everyone up the chain of command is terrified of him. He's climbed a long way since then and I reckon it's by intimidation."

"Lester, that's terrible."

"I felt sorry for the Kinane family and for the families of the other people who died in that fire. Those arseholes made me look as dodgy as they are. I dunno—fuck it." Lester tried to empty his mind of the anger the memory brought back. "When I got to Rockhampton, I decided I'd move on, concentrate on doing my job as best as I could. My team and I found a big old crop of dope growing north of Yeppoon. We watched it for weeks and lo and behold, it was Rick Campbell's operation. Rick runs a dodgy nightclub-come-casino in Fortitude Valley—The Capital—and pays out heaps in kickbacks to the jacks in the Licensing Branch. Anyway, we'd also discovered they were bringing in shipments of heroin via a remote boat ramp up there. They'd put their boat in the water and meet a fishing boat a couple of kilometres out to sea—" Lester had to stop and catch his breath. He swallowed and filled the room with his sigh. "The fucking government is always banging on about bio-security, you know—illegally importing seeds and stuff can bring in diseases that could wipe out our horticultural industry. But the powers that be in the police force— they turn a blind eye to people like Rick bringing in Christ only knows what."

"What happened?"

"We were about to move in a start arresting a few people but we were told to leave it alone. Once again, I was shat on from a great height. All our paper work disappeared." Lester ground his teeth. "We camped out up there for weeks, Kitty, getting eaten by mosquitoes. The mozzies up in that country are so big they could stand flat-footed and fuck a turkey."

He smiled at Kitty's fit of laughter, muffled against his shoulder, her body shook.

"Us old cops tell each other NRMA."

"NRMA, what's the NRMA got to do—hey, that was written on the wall above the water cooler in the Brisbane HQ."

"Yes it was. Nothing Really Matters Anymore. We go into the force swearing to uphold the law—thinking we're going to make a difference. But unless you're a traffic cop, booking people for speeding you can't make a difference. I know the drug laws are probably wrong but when you have the likes of Rick Campbell supplying heroin to dealers who push it to kids—getting them hooked. No, it's all bloody wrong. So—now here I am in the outback, chasing cattle duffers through the brigalows."

Kitty arms tightened around him and her lips, warm and soft on his neck.

"Don't mind me, Kitty—hopefully one day the honest cops will believe my side of the story—believe I'm not in on The Lark. In the meantime, I'm just trying to get on with my job."

"And you're doing a great job."

Lester moaned and moved over her.

****

Kitty's affair with Lester raised eyebrows, in and out of the force. She expected it would. They had hoped to keep it secret but in a small town it was nigh on impossible. The matrons of the town relished the scandal, tut-tutting the Queensland Police Force for thinking they could recruit women and expect the male officers not to succumb to carnal temptation. All blamed Kitty—young and beautiful—of course she took advantage of Lester Gainsford's loneliness. More than twice her age, divorced and living away from his family—*that Jezebel knows what she's doing.'* Her fellow (male) police officers both derided and envied Lester.

"The older the buck, the harder the horn, eh Kitty?" Constable Lehman almost earned a smack across the ear from Lester, but Kitty rebuked him.

"You can only hope that is the case, Constable Lehman; something you can look forward to in your old age because I doubt it applies to you at this stage of your life."

Kitty didn't mind taking the blame; it was her fault. Lester wouldn't have touched her but for her encouragement and for the duration of their time at Longreach, they kept one another happy knowing it couldn't last.

****

"Well, Kitty, this has been the time of my life but now we must say good-bye." Lester's eyes mirrored her pain.

"Only until we meet again."

"No, Kitty. We might see each other again but it will be as friends."

"Lester, why?"

"I can't compete with Mikey Kinane, Kitty."

"But it's over—"

"I've managed to steal you for a while, Kiddo." Lester laid his hand on Kitty's shoulder. "I've never met Mikey Kinane but he owns you; his name is written all over you."

Tears brimmed in Kitty's eyes. He spoke the truth. The moment she saw Mikey again, her childhood sweetheart would overwhelm her. Another world, another life, her romance with Lester might have endured for eternity. Head office sent him to Cunnamulla in the wide yellow grasslands and mulga scrub of South West Queensland. Kitty went to Rockhampton.

35

1982

Mikey had never encountered a woman as tough-looking as the one who stood before him.

"Me name's Margie and this is me sister, Bessie."

Margie's voice had a flat, nasal quality and she spoke with an Australian accent, but with a nuance Mikey hadn't heard before.

"We're lookin' for a cleanin' job. We work at The Capital but Rick don't pay much." The woman had no top teeth and her narrow face a roadmap of wrinkles. She was small and thin but Mikey sensed an underlying strength.

"Nah!" Bessie underlined her sister's words. Bessie too, was small and thin with fewer wrinkles and still possessed a smattering of teeth. Both sisters had grey hair and dressed in T Boots, khaki drill pants, and shirts.

"We used t' work for ya dad, Mikey."

"You did?"

"Yeah—'e was a lovely man. I miss 'im."

"I miss him too, Margie."

"We been with Rick for a couple of years. We don't like 'im much. Fact is, Rick's a dog. 'e's got the cops in his pocket and spends all 'is time plottin' to take some poor bugger down."

"Yair!"

"Me and Bessie can 'ear 'im from in the cleaners cupboard. There's an air vent Rick dunno about."

"You can hear what he's talking about?"

"Clear as a bell, 'ay Bess."

"Yair!" Bessie's voice had a birdlike quality; she nodded and kept her eyes fixed on the floor. Mikey's gaze shifted from Bessie to Margie, he'd seize this rare opportunity.

"I've already employed some cleaners but I'll make a deal with you. I'll top up what Rick pays you to above the award—"

"Ya will?"

"But I want something in return."

"Ya do?"

"I'll pay you for information. When you hear him plotting something that you think might hurt someone or something you think I might be interested in, come and tell me. I'll give you a bonus on top of what I pay you."

"Whaddya reckon 'bout that, Bess?" Margie's eyes never left Mikey's face.

"Eh! You wouldn't read about it!" Bessie bobbed in her chair, her eyes glued to the floor.

"So when can we start?"

"Right away."

"Well, Mr Kinane, I can give you a piece of information straight up."

"Go on."

"Rick's payin' Kev Dallas to stick a bullet in one of that band that pissed on 'is curtains. Them cheeky buggers, they're 'ear on Fridee night, ay—what are they called?"

"Screaming Sally?"

"Yair."

A shiver danced down Mikey's spine. "Tell me more."

"Well Kev is gunna shimmie up the fire escape to the roof of Poppy's across the lane and wait for the band to arrive, then 'e'll pick one off—like shootin' roos. Rick tol' Kev one of 'em will do, 'e reckons that'll be enough to finish the band."

"Eh! Ya wouldn't read about it!"

"Rick's been stewin' ever since last time they was in town."

"Jesus! Thanks, Margie." Mikey pulled a roll of money out of his pocket and peeled off a pair of fifties.

"A hundred bucks! Nah—I can't take that much!"

"Just take it, if Kev takes out one of that band, the music industry in this country will never recover." Mikey thought that might be a bit hysterical but the boys in Screaming Sally had become friends of the Kinane brothers.

"Thanks, Mikey. That Kev, 'e's a dangerous mungrel, so look out for 'im."

"I'm a bit of a pussy, myself." Mikey grinned. "But I reckon I might pull his hair and scratch his eyes out—what do think? That'll do the trick?"

Margie bared her gums, her faced crinkled like brown leather.

"Hah!" chirped Bessie.

****

Paul had lived under Jack's roof for a year and gradually came to see him as more than a friend. In the years he had lived on the streets, he'd scraped by working menial jobs and living cheaply. Unlike Ben, Paul and Shane had refused to prostitute themselves. When he was fourteen, Paul began dating girls until the realization hit him. He wasn't into girls. As a gay teenager, Paul was often a victim of poofter bashing gangs that roamed the parks at night. Meeting Jack changed everything. He had drawn Paul out of the morass to show him kindness and respect; from rescuer to parent, to mentor and finally, friend. As Paul went about his job as a drink waiter at the Phoenix Pearl, he often paused to watch Jack working the crowd, spinning records, beat mixing, joking and entertaining. Handsome and gregarious, the clientele loved him. Paul's admiration and affection grew.

Paul ran the cloth over the kitchen benches, inhaled and voiced the thought twirling in his head. "Jack, I think I feel something for you."

Jack turned from loading the dishwasher. "Like—what? Say that again?"

"I think—no, I know I love you. I want to stay with you."

"Well of course you can stay with me. It's nice having you around."

"But—I mean—I love you, you saved my life and I want to make you happy." The words tripped and stumbled of his tongue.

174

"You owe me nothing, Paul. You have to choose the life that is best for you. You know that I'm gay? You've worked that out by now, haven't you?"

"Yeah. I'm gay too and I love you."

"You must be sure of that, Paul. It's not the easiest life to choose."

"I didn't choose it. I just am and I love you." Paul advanced on Jack. The older man backed away.

"Paul, wait." He turned away, his breathing uneven. "I want you to be sure, you're very young."

"I'll be eighteen soon."

"I have to give you time to think about it. I want you to be sure. You must find who you are and be true to yourself."

Paul rinsed the cloth and dried his hands. "I have found myself. I'm gay. What happened to me as a kid didn't make me this way. I'm sure of it. Don't you feel anything for me?"

"Paul—just give it time, hey? Give me time."

"Okay but I won't wait forever." Paul smiled, rubbed Jack's arm and left the kitchen.

On the day of his eighteenth birthday, Jack invited Paul to blow out the candles on his first birthday cake. Emboldened by happiness, Paul's lips lingered on Jack's cheek and the thank-you kiss changed everything.

36

Rick wandered along the lane, searching for the greasy haired dealer who had grown from a splinter to a thorn in his side. Les Jones had showed up in Fortitude Valley around ten days ago and Rick's dealers reported a big drop in sales. He spotted Les propped against a brick wall; a cast iron downpipe stopped him sliding into the drain.

Rick stopped and lit a cigarette, watching Les finalise a sale, he waited until the customer moved on before he approached.

"Hello, Les. I'm Rick Campbell, I thought I'd come and introduce myself."

"Far out." Les wiped his nasal drip with the back of his hand then held it out for Rick to shake.

Rick eyed the shaking extremity, a snail-trail of snot glistened in the streetlight; he didn't move.

"You're infringing on my neighbourhood, Les, your presence here is not appreciated; my dealers are getting pissed off. Don't be here tomorrow night, am I making myself clear?"

"Groovy." He sniffed

"Groovy. I'll be checking." Rick turned to leave.

"You're Bouncy Harold's mate, 'ay?" Another rattling sniff.

Rick stopped and turned; Les Jones eyed him shrewdly, perhaps he wasn't as stoned as he looked. "How do you know Bouncy Harold?"

"I don't know him, 'ay—just know of him. He's a bit—" A drip fell onto his shirt as Les splayed his hand, palm down and waggled it.

Rick eyed Les a moment then strode back the way he'd come.

****

Everyone said Les Jones was harmless, he even said that himself. Les' mind and habits still coasted along in the sixties hippy era and hadn't yet come to grips with the eighties.

The eighties! Far out!

Skinny with long greasy hair, his nasal drip a permanent reminder of years spent snorting cocaine. Like many junkies, Les supported his habit by selling drugs. The lane off Vulture Street from which he sold his wares became a temporary no-go zone while the city council dug up the sewer and Les had to ply his trade elsewhere. Rather than tread on the toes of his South Brisbane mates he decided he'd move over to Fortitude Valley.

Far out!

He was glad he'd made the switch; he sold twice as much on this side of the river and he cruised along, rolling in the brass. It was after midnight; Les had sold most of his pills, bags and tabs. He had decided to call it a night when Rick Campbell turned up and leaned on him.

177

Crazy man—far out.

Campbell seem like a nice guy, Les appreciated his given him a warning. Other big suppliers would just beat the crap out of you. As he made his way back towards China Town, a bronze Kingswood pulled up beside him.

"You want a lift mate?"

Les looked in the window, a couple of hours before he'd sold some speed to the young man behind the wheel.

"I'm goin' all the way to West End, 'ay." He sucked in mucus.

"That's where we're going."

"Groovy." Les didn't feel like walking so he hopped in the backseat and the driver put his foot down. "Far out!"

****

Alan and Dale Ward were brothers—in both blood, crime, and mullets; Dale watched Les while his older brother steered the car left towards the Story Bridge and they cruised along the freeway towards Rocklea.

"Hey man, you missed the turn—" Les snorted back a drip "—West End's that way—"

"Hang loose, Les," said Dale, "we're taking the scenic route."

"Far out…"

As they continued on Ipswich Road through the Moorooka Magic Mile, Les grew agitated. "Fucken 'ay? Are you blokes gonna rob me?"

"Just shut up, dickhead and sit still."

When the Alan stopped at the lights, Les pulled at the door handle but they had the child locks engaged. "Fucken 'ay? I don't like this—"

Dale reached over the back of the seat and pointed a gun at Les' face. Les raised his shaking hands.

"Where are we going, man?"

"On a magical mystery tour, Les, so just shut up and enjoy it."

Alan pulled into the driveway of the old house that Rick's men used as an emergency hideout. In a dilapidated industrial complex at Rocklea with no power but the water was connected and for good reason. They used the garden hose on the sink tap to remove evidence.

"Hey boys, just take my stash and be done with it 'ay?"

Dale opened the door. "Come on, Les. Follow my brother there and don't try anything." He poked the gun into the back of Les' neck and the scrawny dealer obeyed.

"Just don't shoot me, 'ay? I'm harmless—*tuh*—and—*tuh*—"

Alan looked around just in time for Les to sneeze twenty minutes of un-sneezed snot—Les towered over Alan and the glob unfurled across his forehead.

"Ah you dirty fuckin' bastard!"

"'scuse me, 'ay. Got a bit of a problem with me snoot." A drip fell from his nose.

Dale staggered and hooted with laughter; he almost dropped the gun.

"A bit—" Alan plucked at the sheet of mucus sliding down his face. "Get him inside!" Alan screamed at his brother and Dale composed himself. Rick's orders were to dispose of Les in a way that would let others know they couldn't muscle in on his domain without retribution. Dale shook his head. Rick was pissed off with Les. Now he'd pissed Alan off too—that guaranteed he'd suffer.

37

Kev Dallas' mouth was as dry as a bat's arse from speed. He always popped a pill before a hit; it gave him confidence and energy. When fancy took him, Kev fancied himself a handful and tonight, fancy descended from on high. He'd welcomed Rick's order to take out one of Screaming Sally. He hated the bastards and that night he'd finally have his revenge. The last time the band performed at The Capital, Kev had taken his girlfriend Cheryl to see them. Cheryl was a fan and Kev found out the extent of her adulation when she opened her shirt and flashed her knockers at Frankie Swift. Later, Kev tried to impress Cheryl and engage Swift in intelligent conversation. He took a hard forearm across the chest and Frankie's signature response, "Fuck off!"

Kev took offence and called in three of his mates to help teach Screaming Sally a lesson. Longhaired and pretty-faced, Frankie Swift didn't look like a scrapper but assisted by Dave, the enormous, dreadlocked bassist, and Jeff, the drummer—he wiped the floor with Kev and his mates. Gerry Romano, the tall, skinny guitarist had the onlookers in stitches as he perched on the bar and described the action like a veteran sports commentator. That lairy fucker, Mickie Parker, the purple haired keyboardist took advantage of the distraction, stole Cheryl backstage and screwed her against the wall. Rick took the cost of damages off the band's fee. Their response was to piss on the backdrop, disconnect the power to the stage then superglue and screw the backstage doors closed. The next night, the DJ had a major bitch-fit when five minutes before start-up he found all the fuses removed from his bank of power amps. Rick had wanted revenge ever since, but he'd had to wait, Screaming Sally were a touring band, they spent months at a time away from Brisbane.

Kev was handsome; he worked hard in the gym and boasted he had muscles in his shit. He claimed the title of the best marksman in Brisbane though he had never put it up for contention. He floated through life in an overinflated, rose-coloured bubble of self-esteem. Dressed in black from head to toe, he climbed the fire escape to the roof of Poppy's Nightclub and waited for Screaming Sally to arrive for their gig at The Phoenix Pearl across the lane.

****

Mikey could have instructed one of the twins to do this; they had spent years training for this kind of task. However, he would never ask someone else to do his dirty work and so insisted he'd take care of it. Aiden and Liam had coached him how to prepare for a kill; he emptied his mind of emotion. The chill of the impending murder quieted his thudding heart. He crept across the roof and waited, a silent spectre lurking in the dark, close behind the sniper. Screaming Sally's limo stopped in the lane below and the band spilled out like stuffing from a split beanbag. The sniper watched, gun held relaxed. The lead guitarist, Frankie Swift weaved over to the wall and unzipped his fly; Mickie Parker, the keyboardist hitched his junk and feigned taking Swift up the arse. Swift's "Fuck off or I'll piss on your foot!" echoed between the buildings. Laughter drifted up to Mikey's ears. The rest of Screaming Sally and their road manager straggled up the stairs and through the back stage door, leaving Frankie to strain his potatoes against the bricks.

Kev pushed his beanie up his forehead and adjusted his grip on the rifle. "Go on, take one last piss, you smart arse cunt."

Mikey almost laughed as Frankie Swift swayed on the spot then pretended to shake the drips from an oversized appendage.

Fuck off, Frankie—it's not that big. Then again…

A legend among groupies, Swift stood almost as tall as Mikey.

The sniper raised the rifle and Mikey edged closer. Kev loosed a short yell as Mikey's hand clamped under his chin, the stubbled jaw prickled; a tilt of his head, a sideward jerk and twist; Mikey heard the spine snap and the man went limp. One shove and the body toppled to the laneway below. As Mikey kicked the rifle after its owner, he caught a glimpse of Frankie Swift disappearing through the back stage door.

His blood ran hot as he tiptoed across the roof, pulled on boots and a pair of cotton gloves, climbed down the ladder to the first landing and through an unlocked door. He crossed a deserted room and down the narrow stairs, he stopped and stuffed the cotton gloves in his jacket pocket and peered into the passage between the men's and ladies' restrooms. He inhaled to calm the shivers; he had enjoyed that moment of violence too much; it made him question everything about himself. The passage empty, Mikey strolled back into the clubroom. The throb of the disco had increased in volume by around twenty decibels in the forty minutes since he'd slipped out to watch for the sniper. Mikey watched the clientele, an assortment of white-collar workers, theatre types, gays and drag queens gradually filling Poppy's Nightclub. He leaned on the bar and talked to the owner, Pop Francesco. Pop paid the licensing branch (via John the Bagman) a hefty bribe; homosexuality was still illegal in Queensland and in return for the hush money, the bagman warned him when a shakedown was imminent.

"Well, I'll talk to you later, Pop. I have a club to run. The Sallies are about to start their set."

"Nice talking to you Mikey, have a good night."

"You too, Pop."

A crowd gathered on the sidewalk, mainly girls hoping to catch a glimpse of Screaming Sally. The Phoenix Pearl would be packed to the gills by now and the doors closed. Mikey caught sight of Greg Meyer climbing out of a stretched limo with a brunette on his arm, followed by a gay couple, Patrick and Sebastian, finally, Harriet Harry, a drag queen Mikey knew, and her date tumbled out.

How many more do you have in there, Greg?

"Mikey!" Meyer saw him and strode over to shake his hand. "Good to see you, old boy."

Mikey opened his mouth to reply when a strident howl split the air. Everyone turned to watch as Billi Sands burst from the laneway as fast as a six-foot tall man in five-inch stilettos and a tight mini skirt could trot.

"What's up with Billi?" The brunette craned her neck, trying to see over the heads of the crowd. People surged into the laneway to see what had Billi in an uproar.

"Mayhap she's caught one of her testicles in that suspender-belt," Meyer speculated. Mikey's legs wobbled and the tension left his body as a fit of laughter shook him.

"I'll catch you later, Greg." Mikey wiped a tear from his eye and pushed through the crowd back to the Phoenix Pearl.

A barrage of squeals greeted him as he entered his club, Screaming Sally romped around the stage and wreaked havoc on the pituitary glands of the girls at the front, Swift and Parker already had their shirts off and Gerry Romano strutted along the edge of the stage shaking his skinny arse.

Any minute now—those girls will have him on the floor.

38

Midmorning on Sunday, Mikey worked in his office, finishing the accounts when he heard a familiar voice.

"Where's me boyfriend?"

Mikey grinned; Margie and Bessie had arrived bearing an apple pie.

"In here ready for you, sweetheart."

"Put the kettle on, Mikey. Let's have a coffee."

"Coffee coming up, girls. There's plates and stuff in there." Mikey pointed to a cupboard in the tiny kitchen-come-staffroom that adjoined his office.

"Did you 'ear 'bout Kev Dallas?"

Silly question given they scraped him off my driveway.

"No, what happened?"

"'E fell off the roof of Poppy's and broke 'is neck—serve him right, he 'ad a gun with him—Rick reckons he fell off."

"Must have overbalanced." Mikey spooned a chunk of Margie's apple pie into his mouth. "Yum, Margie. Your pies are the best."

As they sat gossiping over apple pie and coffee, Mikey asked the question foremost on his tongue since he'd first met these women.

"Something I'm curious about, Margie. How come you girls haven't gone to the police with all the stuff you know about Rick?"

For the first time, Bessie lifted her eyes to look directly into his, then her head swivelled to Margie before she resumed her surveillance of the floor.

"We stay right away from them cops."

"Why? Most of them are okay."

"Can you keep a secret, Mikey?"

"You know I can. You keep my secrets, I keep yours."

"We come from a sheep station out at Eulo."

"Where the fuck is Eulo?"

"West of Cunnamulla. Our dad didden own the place, 'e was just a manager—lazy mungrel—our mum did most of the work."

"What brought you to Brisbane?"

"A thirty-seven Chevy ute."

"Stupid question, yeah."

"It was our old man's but 'e was dead, so we took it."

"What happened to your father?"

Margie's voice lowered, Mikey had to lean closer to hear.

"I killed 'im with the back of a tomahawk."

Mikey laughed but something in Margie's faded blue eyes told him she wasn't joking. Bessie sat frozen, gazing at the floor.

"'E was a dirty mungrel, always gropin' us girls and when our poor mum died, 'e started climbin' into Bessie's bed at night. Bessie was older than me and very pretty."

"Jesus, Margie!"

"Yeah and Bessie got pregnant. 'E told everyone that came to our place that Bessie 'ad a bath in the same water as 'im and one of them sperms swum up 'er."

Mikey closed his eyes and put down the last morsel of pie. He'd grown fond of Margie and Bessie; he'd never for a minute thought they'd had such a terrible past.

"The baby came early and it was dead. Course it would be—it 'ad a lot wrong with it." Margie shuddered and stopped for a moment; she pulled her lips between her gums. "Never breed a mare back to 'er sire, Mikey; that's what our mum used to say. Poor Bessie had no sooner 'ealed up and 'ere 'e was back agen. I said to meself, 'e ain't gonna touch neither of us agen, so I went out to the meat 'ouse and grabbed the tomahawk. I come back an' wack! We waited for 'im to wake up but 'e didden. By mornin' 'e was as stiff as a dead roo. We got the tractor and put 'im on the carry-all and carted 'im orf up the 'orse paddick. We dropped 'im down the old well where we threw all the dead animal carcasses an' I filled it in. I drug up a big load of timber to cover the tracks an' set fire to it."

"Didn't the neighbours ask what the smoke was?"

"The nearest neighbours were fifteen miles away."

Mikey shook his head; he couldn't imagine this tiny woman performing such a task. Margie drained her cup and set it on the desk.

"At sundown, we loaded the motorbike onto the ute an' drove to Cunnamulla. We unloaded the bike just outa town, I left Bessie waitin' there with it. I drove the ute in to town, parked it near the railway station and snuck back to the bike. We rode 'ome—it was just comin' on daylight when we got back. 'Bout a week later, the cop from Cunnamulla turned up and wanted to know why Dad's ute was in town. We said 'e took off to town one day and we never seen 'im since. The cop brung the ute back, everyone reckoned Dad musta jumped the rattler—'e 'adn't bought a ticket. Then the owner of the place turned up, said 'e didden want no girls runnin' it an' told us to go. By then we 'ad found Dad's stash—almost thirty quid—so we packed our stuff in the ute, filled it with petrol and set orf for Brisbane. I didn't even 'ave a driver's licence—I was fourteen—but we poked along. Took us nearly a week to get 'ere." Margie laughed. "We reckoned we'd git a job in the pub when we got 'ere."

"Hah!" Bessie reanimated at her sister's laugh.

"The pub! Mikey—there were 'undreds of pubs! Me and Bessie never seen such a big town!"

"Eh! Ya wouldn' read about it!"

"So you become city-slickers?" Mikey felt a little shaky after hearing Margie's tale. These women were in their late fifties and the hard years of their lives had taken their toll. Neither had married, all those years they had clung together, surviving— tearing pages from the calendar. Margie, the younger sister the stronger of the two and she had watched over Bessie like a doting parent.

"Yeah, we know this city like the back of our 'ands, 'ey Bessie."

"Yair!"

"So getting' back to why we came to see you, Mikey, I think Rick is goin' to kill some kid, I think they called 'im Ken or somethin' like that. I 'eard 'im talkin' about it to a bloke 'e called 'Arold. I really can't tell you much but the guy called 'Arold seemed pretty upset an' didden want nothin' to do with it an' Rick said you better cooperate Bouncy cause I know stuff that could get you hung by your nuts. 'Arold kep sayin' 'but 'e's just a kid, Rick.'"

"Do you know who this Harold guy is?"

"Nah but I thought I should tell yer."

"You reckon they might kill a kid?"

"Sure sounded like it ay, Bessie."

"Yair."

"And he called the guy Bouncy? Like a nickname?"

"Yair."

"Bouncy Harold?"

"Yair."

39

Kitty had served her time in a country police station and the regional city of Rockhampton her next step up the ladder. She endured sexism and harassment on a daily basis. On a quiet Tuesday night she went to tidy a cell in the watch house. They had just bailed the occupant incarcerated there for a few hours to sober up. She screamed at the sight of Constable Steve Rodes lying on the floor covered in blood, eyes staring. She ran to press the alarm, and then checked the other cells were empty. Her male colleagues strolled in.

"What's the emergency, Olsen?"

Kitty couldn't speak, her heart raced, one hand pressed to her mouth the other pointed into the cell where Constable Rodes lay.

"Come on, girl, pull yourself together and show me what the problem is."

Kitty forced herself to walk back into the carnage. As she approached the body, Constable Rodes sat up, dripping tomato sauce.

"Gimmie a kiss, Olsen."

Kitty squealed again and her faced reddened. It seemed every officer on duty had assembled to witness her embarrassment. This kind of hazing happened to her all the time and she had long grown tired of it. She wished Lester were there to take her side;

she knew he would have. A Detective Sergeant, Roy Markem, having heard of her affair with Lester Gainsford, asked her out every other day. Kitty knew he was married and around Lester's age. Only that afternoon he had pinned her against the wall and tried to kiss her. She could feel his erection pressing against her leg. She jerked her knee into his crotch, walked away and left him groaning.

Saturday night, she and Constable Rodes were out in a patrol car when a call came to watch out for a white Datsun 180B, the getaway car used in the robbery of a service station on Yaamba Road. They sighted the suspect vehicle speeding through the backstreets of Koongal and gave chase. The car had a five-hundred metre lead on them and they lost it for a few minutes. They located it beside a house in Lakes Creek.

"We should wait for backup." Kitty worried they might be outnumbered.

"Nah! You knock on the front door, and I'll go round the back."

Kitty shook her head. "I'm calling for backup."

"Don't be such a pussy! They're just a bunch of two-bit crooks; they didn't even use a gun." Rodes pulled on the handbrake and got out. Kitty grasped the radio handpiece and requested backup.

'Sure it's not just another bottle of sauce, Olsen?' She bristled at her fellow officers' laughter on the radio and doggedly repeated her request. As she left the car a shout sounded from the house, Kitty pulled her gun, before she could take three paces she saw

Constable Rodes fall to the floor in the doorway, a man stood over him with a knife in one hand and a sledge hammer in the other. Rodes' screams, as the man hammered his legs, chilled Kitty's marrow; nauseating cracks of bones shattering reached her ears, she sprinted back to the patrol car and picked up the handpiece again.

"We need back up urgently! Officer down! Officer injured! We need an ambulance…" Nerves jangled, she tried to control the panic as she approached the front of the house. Rodes lay in the doorway, struggling; Kitty couldn't see the extent of his injuries. With a sudden whuff, flames glowed from further inside the house. The man with the knife and hammer laughed when he saw Kitty.

"Well look at this, fellas, we have Constable Cunt herself."

"Drop your weapons and lie down!" Kitty shouted, aware that people from neighbouring houses emerged to investigate the noise. Two more men followed their knife wielding leader, they too carried weapons, one with a machete, the other with a sawn off shotgun.

"Drop your weapons and lie down!"

Kitty had never fired her service revolver except during practice. Now she gripped it tight, and repeated her command. The men advanced on her. When the man with the hammer was a metre away, she fired; his companions swore, one ran at her and the other fled. She fired again and the second man fell at her feet. She didn't check to see if they lived, instead she ran up the steps to Rodes. He had multiple stab wounds to his torso and both legs broken. Smoke poured from the old wooden building and crackling flames licked the ceiling over her head, blistering heat seared her face; she coughed as acrid smoke filled her lungs. Kitty holstered her gun, grabbed Rodes under his arms, and dragged him down the steps and away from the flames. He screamed as his broken legs tumbled on the steps.

"I'm sorry!" Kitty shivered. "I'm so sorry."

"Help me, Kitty!" Rodes' voice gurgled as blood trickled from his mouth. As Kitty ran back to the patrol car, she could hear sirens approaching. She requested a fire appliance as well; as she spoke, she looked down at herself. Constable Rodes' blood drenched the front of her uniform.

As another patrol car screeched to a halt, Kitty vomited on the ground beside the squad car, her legs shook and she coughed smoke and bile. The two men she had shot lay immobile on the grass. The other had vanished.

Her commanding officer went straight on the offensive. "Why didn't you wait for backup?"

"I wanted to but Constable Rodes just went in, he wouldn't wait."

The senior officer cast a cynical eye over Kitty's blood soaked shirt. She supposed he searched for a way to blame her for the incident. "Okay, Give me your revolver and get in the ambulance."

"I'm fine." Her hand shook as she passed him her gun.

"You're going to be checked over by a doctor, Constable Olsen. I'll be talking to both you and Rodes but you need medical attention first."

The next morning, Rodes took the blame, if Kitty hadn't held her nerve, he'd have burned to death in that house. Already hailed a hero by the local media, Kitty returned to work two days later.

"You did well, pretty girl." Detective Sergeant Roy Markem's gruff compliment was one Kitty never expected; she tried not to cringe as he shook her hand.

Kitty spent an hour on the phone to Lester and cried as she told him her intention to leave the force, a decision she hadn't arrived at easily. Working with people who refused to take her seriously had worn her down and after recent events—she feared their attitude might cost her her life.

"Good on you, Kitty. One day when I pluck up the courage to try something different, I might do the same."

By the time Kitty received notice she'd be awarded The Valour Award for bravery, she had returned to Brisbane. She handed in her resignation; another month of service and she'd be looking for a new job.

40

Harold Purser, better known as Bouncy Harold because of his peculiar gait, owned a little shop on the edge of China Town. Since he had lost his job as piano teacher at a prestigious Brisbane boy's college, he'd taken to teaching privately. The income wasn't as large or as reliable so he began selling adult magazines, toys, and videos. By day, students came to his little piano studio for lessons. By night, a string of flashing lights and a sign proclaiming 'The Little Big Shop of Love' appeared in the window; an array of sex toys and illegal porn jostled with whips and leather masks for shelf space. On a magazine rack, sleazy literature held pride of place: girls with girls, boys with boys, girls with boys, and boys with girl parts, and girls with mind-boggling paraphernalia. Headlines that promised a hog wallow, an orgy, and a rout. On one cover—a freckle-faced girl with an icy pole in her throat.

The man who entered Harold's shop stood an easy six and a half feet tall; his smooth skin and blue eyes gave his face a pretty appearance.

Harold wrung his soft white hands. "Good evening, sir. What can I sell you tonight?"

The man glanced around. "Nothing. I want to talk to you." His big hand closed over the nape of Harold's neck and steered him through the door to the living area behind the shop.

Harold's bowels liquefied. "What do you want?"

"I heard it from a reliable source that Rick Campbell is planning on killing some kid and that source told me you might know all about it."

A fat drop of sweat trickled from Harold's temple. "I don't know any—I—can't—" He squawked as the man grabbed onto his ear.

"Talk or I might just twist your gungy old balls!"

"Please! I can't help you—Rick will kill me! He's a bad man!"

"How do you know I'm not worse?"

"Are you a policeman?"

"No. I want to know where I can find that kid."

"It's too late—he's already dead."

The bell on the front door tinkled. A shove propelled Harold across the room and he crashed into his little kitchen table. Hauled back to his feet, he barely had time to take a breath before the man spun him around and delivered a hard kick to his arse.

The assailant strode back into the shop and Harold heard him speak. "The shop's closed. I'd get out of here if I was you, the cops will be on their way."

The bell on the front door tinkled; seconds later, it tinkled again and the shop went silent. Harold shuddered, the last thing he needed was the law crawling all over his shop. His frayed nerves shattered as the back door creaked open, Harold spun to face a big, fair-haired man.

"Please, no—" He backed away through the door and into the shop, the man followed. Harold turned and stepped off the edge of the world.

****

Kitty had two weeks remaining as a police officer before she would hand back her badge. Around midnight on a Wednesday, she and Detective Sergeant Cramb received a call to attend an address in China Town where a shopkeeper had had his brains splattered all over his shop. They found the address; Harold's Piano Studio looked harmless enough but for the sign hanging in the window that said, 'The Little Big Shop of Love.' Inside, they found an array of sex aids, porn magazine, and videos; all liberally splattered with a Pollockesque spray of blood and brains.

"Is there a murder weapon?"

A grey-faced junior constable pointed to a plastic bag on the counter with a bloodied iron bar inside. "We found that in the bin outside the back door."

"Okay, Constable. Step outside and wait. Don't let anyone in until the forensic boys arrive."

"Sarg, the back door was unlocked and there was no sign of forced entry."

Kitty tiptoed through to the back room. Everything seemed to be in place except a broken chair. A plate, cutlery, and a wine glass stood on the sink—the wash-up of Harold's last solitary meal.

She found a smear of blood on the doorknob and another on the wall beside it.

Cramb pushed through and half-filled the tiny living room. "What have you got, Olsen?"

"A broken chair, Sarg, and a small amount of blood."

"Okay, we'll leave it to the forensics. Let's go for a walk and ask questions."

They wandered the neighbourhood making enquiries. Most showed little interest and none could tell them anything worthwhile. That was until they went into a late night café and questioned the only customer. He sat, drinking coffee and reading a magazine, which he hastily stuffed out of sight when he saw Kitty's uniform. "What—I didn't do anything—what do you want?"

"We would like to ask you a couple of questions. What's your name?"

"It's Harvey. What kind of questions."

"Have you been anywhere near Harold's Piano Studio this evening?"

"No—err—I mean, I dunno." He fidgeted under the table and the magazine dropped out on the floor and fell open at the centrefold. Kitty snatched it up; the object in the model's hand made her eyes water.

"So where did you get that, Harvey?" She dropped the magazine onto the table like a scrap of road kill.

"Um, okay—so I bought a dirty magazine."

"Was there anyone in the shop?"

"No—it was empty. I left a two dollar note on the counter and took the magazine."

Cramb laughed. "Sure you did. Did you see anything unusual?"

"No." Harvey's eyes blinked as they shifted from Kitty to Dave and onto the door.

"You're not covered in blood, Harvey, so we don't think you're our man but if you saw anyone, tell us."

"Well—now that I think about it, there was someone. I know who he is too."

"So tell us."

"That big tall bloke that runs the Phoenix Pearl—I don't know his name. I could hear noises in the back of the shop."

"What kind of noises?"

"Like a fight or something—a few thumps and a yell."

"And then what happened?"

"That big tall bloke came through from back there and told me to leave—that the police were on their way."

"Did you see anyone else? Was there anything unusual?"

"No. The place seemed deserted. So I grabbed this magazine and ran—err—I paid for it of course."

"The man you saw, did he have blood on his clothes?"

"Nuh."

"Was there any blood around the shop?"

"Nuh. Well I didn't see any."

"Okay, give us your full name and address. We might need to talk to you further.

"I didn't see anything except that big bloke. What's he supposed to have done?"

"Can we see your driver's licence?"

****

At the Phoenix Pearl, Kitty and Dave Cramb flashed their badges at the doormen and asked to speak to the manager. The doorman took them into a noisy, smoky club room and through a door beside the bar.

"He's not in his office but if you care to wait, I'll go and find him."

As Kitty glanced around the room, she froze. On the wall a large photo of the Kinane family; Mikey sat between his parents with a shit-eating grin on his five-year-old face. The Kinane family, before the firebomb tore them apart.

Kitty's heart detonated. "Um, Dave—I don't think I—"

The door open and Mikey stepped into the room. His eyes fell on Kitty and she shook her head; she inhaled as the blood drained to her feet.

Dave appeared not to have noticed the silent exchange. "Mr Kinane, where were you this evening between eight p.m. and midnight?"

Mikey frowned at Kitty, his eyes narrowed. "Apart from a quick trip to Harold's Piano Studio, I have been here all night." He dragged his gaze away from Kitty and scowled at Dave. "Why? Has Harold made a complaint?"

"Harold is in no condition to make a complaint."

"What happened to him?"

"He's dead."

The colour drained from Mikey's face. "Dead? How?"

"We thought you might know how."

"How would I know? He was alive and well when I left him—apart from a sore arse where I kicked it."

"We'd like you to accompany us to the station, Mr Kinane."

"Are you arresting me?"

"Not yet, but we'd like to ask you some questions."

"Okay. I'll just let my staff know where I'm going and I'll be right with you."

41

Mikey lounged back and watched Kitty type his statement. Somebody must have decided Bouncy Harold knew too much. Mikey had a fair idea who but he hadn't made any allegations—he didn't want the police knowing of his interest in Rick Campbell's activities. Stirring up Rick's camp might be akin to poking a hornet's nest. Mikey had already disposed of Rick's chief assassin, opening his trap might draw the wrong kind of interest. Mikey trusted Kitty but not those she worked with. If she too, began probing into the likes of Rick Campbell, the corrupt element in the police could do her a lot of harm—maybe even kill her. No. Mikey would be judge, jury, and executioner in the case of the Brisbane underworld.

Kitty stopped typing and leaned closer to the paper to read the statement. Mikey shifted in his chair, her breasts, pressed against her police shirt had drawn his gaze.

"Damn, Kitty! That uniform is doing my head in."

"Stop it, Mikey. You don't know me, okay?"

"But I do know you, Kitty. I know you very well."

Her cheeks turned pink under the fluorescent light of the interview room and Mikey grinned; that response lit a fire inside. A grown woman and tough cop—but he could still make her blush.

She rose, ripped the statement out of the typewriter, and pulled a pen from her shirt pocket.

"Read through this and if you agree it is correct, sign it. I'll be right back."

Mikey leaned forward, his hand groped for the statement while his eyes admired Kitty's slender form stride out the door.

****

Kitty hurried into the CIB and found Dave Cramb at his desk. He hung up the phone as Kitty approached.

"Kitty, come with me."

"Dave, I need to talk to you."

"Good, I need to talk to you too."

He led her into the corridor, deserted at that late hour.

He stepped close and whispered. "I know what you need to talk to me about, Kitty. Your face when he walked into his office told me everything. I've compared your background to his. He was your neighbour as you were growing up."

"Yes—I knew him—"

"And he's a Kinane, therefore I'm going to give him a break."

"Thank you, Dave. It was terrible what happened—"

"We have to hurry, Kitty. We need to get him out of the station before certain people find out we brought him in—if they don't already know. I'll take his statement and file it somewhere safe." He grinned. Kitty knew that meant he would either shred it or hide it. "First thing tomorrow I'll go and talk to his staff, we need to be thorough. I'll make sure his alibis are watertight. What you have to do is hide him for twenty-four hours."

"Why? Do you think he might be in danger?"

Dave scanned the corridor. "He might be—we can't take any chances. This has all the hallmarks of a hit and I've a pretty fair idea who—although the iron bar is new to his repertoire. I've hidden the murder weapon. It's in the evidence room but not where it should be."

"Did you get fingerprints?"

"No, there were none. Whoever did it wore gloves, but if certain people decide to drop a brick, they could easily make Mikey look like the guilty party. They will try to get his fingerprints on something that might pass for the murder weapon."

"Well, I'm off duty now for two days; I guess I can take him—"

"Don't tell me—I don't want to know. What I want you to do is go and get your car and park in the pickup zone across the street. Leave your left-hand indicator blinking so I'll know which car— I'll bring Mikey to you. Watch out for a tail, you might be followed."

"Okay. Thanks, Dave. I owe you one."

"Go."

****

Mikey hoped Dave Cramb was honest. The gruff cop led him through the front doors onto Makerston Street.

"That's her car, the dark blue Cortina with the blinker going. Get in a watch for a tail."

"Thanks for the heads up, mate—I owe you one."

"Nah—just watch out for Kitty for us. A lot of us cops think she's pretty special."

"She is. Don't worry I'll take care of her."

As Mikey jogged across the street, Kitty rolled the window down. "Drive." She climbed into the passenger seat.

He jumped in and racked the driver's seat back. "Did you have anywhere in mind?"

"No—that's why I'm getting you to drive. I hope you have somewhere you can go. Preferably not to where you live."

"Okay, Kitty-Kat. Hang on."

The tyres of Kitty's Cortina squeaked and Mikey accelerated along Makerston Street and squealed left onto Roma Street.

Kitty monitored behind them. "I think someone is following us. A car just pulled out."

Mikey brought a gasp from her as he crossed the double white line to overtake a Mini Minor and swerved back.

"Did they follow us?"

"Yes—they ran a red light."

"Well, let's see how fast this Ford can go, shall we?"

"Just get away from our tail."

"Yes Maam!" Mikey flattened his foot and swerved around a taxi. The Cortina's wheels squealed as he crossed two lanes of traffic and left onto Saul Street. The lights turned from amber to red as he sped onto the William Jolly Bridge. "Are they still following?"

"Um—don't know. Yes—they ran another red light."

"I'll see if I can lose them." The Cortina's speedo touched one twenty as they drove into South Brisbane, Mikey braked and flung the car onto Peel Street. "Good thing it's not peak hour, hey?" He glanced at Kitty, she hung on to the armrest to stay upright and whimpered as a taxi beeped and swerved to miss him.

He screeched onto Gladstone Road towards Highgate Hill and pushed the accelerator to the floor. "Are they still coming?"

Kitty checked behind. "Can't see anyone—there's some headlights a long way back—might be them."

Mikey switched off the lights and screamed into a side street down a steep hill.

"What happened to the lights?" Kitty's voice pitched up in panic.

"Switched them off so those dicks following won't be able to see us." Mikey geared down, pulled on the handbrake and turned into the drive of his childhood home.

42

Dave Cramb watched Kinane steer Kitty's car onto Roma Street and stretched. He would have loved to call it a night but he had to get back to the Phoenix Pearl and talk to the staff. He turned and hurried back inside. Ray Sims wasn't at his desk and the duty sergeant didn't know where he'd gone.

"Never mind, I'll take someone else with me."

Dave called into the men's room on his way out and as he hurried out the door, he knocked a bin flying.

"Fuck it!" He set the bin upright and gathered handfuls of paper towel and stuffed them back in. Out of a folded length of towel fell a pair of latex gloves. Dave froze. They might mean nothing or they might mean a lot. He jumped up, tore a clean strip of paper towel to wrap the gloves and stowed it in his pocket. "Another job for forensics."

****

The next afternoon, Dave leaned on the bench in the forensic lab.

The forensic officer passed a scrawled note across. "Don't know whose prints they are, Dave, but I can tell you one thing about them."

"Go on."

208

I searched back through records and found the same prints on the Shellite drum that was found in Rusty Russell's unit after the Valley Fires."

"Yeah? Rusty—but he's dead."

"These prints weren't his. If you remember events back then, Rusty's prints were all over that drum and—but—there was another print on the bottom of the drum."

"Interesting."

"Also, in the wrist roll of the gloves, I found some blood and it matches Harold Purser's."

"So those gloves were used in his murder?"

"I can't say, yes definitely—but it warrants attention."

Mikey drove the car into the carport.

Kitty looked around. "What is this place?"

"Just a minute!" he jumped out, ran to close the gates and dashed back to the car. "Quick—inside."

Mikey helped Kitty from the car and guided her through the dark.

"Is this your place?" Kitty looked around as Mikey led her through the back door and flicked on the light.

"It belongs to my family, but I don't live here—I live at Ascot. The twins live here when they're in Brisbane." He didn't mention, it was also a designated safe house for his family and closest friends.

"Is it in your family name?"

"Fear not—it's in my mother's maiden name. Her parents left it to her."

"Good—we often use city hall to find out where people live."

He pouted. "You changed out of that uniform."

"I always do when I end a shift. I never wear it home."

"I kinda liked it." He reached for her but she grasped his arms and halted his approach.

"Mikey, we can't."

"I had a feeling you would say that." He leaned against the wall. "Kitty, I'm divorced—we can be together. I made a stupid mistake and I've fixed it as best as I can. I have a daughter and I can't—wouldn't—change that, but I'm a free man again."

"Mikey—"

"Do you still love me, Kitty?"

Her blue eyes softened. "You know I do."

Mikey filled the space between them with a sigh and a smile. "You don't know how glad I am to hear that, because knowing you still love me—well—I can overcome anything else that stands between us." He crossed the distance separating them and encircled her in his arms; his mouth fumbled for her lips—missed—then covered them. A never-ending kiss would have made him happy. Kitty's arms wound around his neck pulling his face to hers. His chest heaved as they came up for air.

She pulled back to search his face. "Mikey, why? Why did you go and see Bouncy Harold?"

"Kitty, I can't tell you—I can't let you get involved. I suspect Bouncy Harold was part of some really low shit."

"I'm a cop, Mikey—at least for another week—I'm trained to deal with all kinds of low shit—"

"Do you realise that some of your colleagues are on the take. Low bastards like Harold pay them to turn a blind eye to their activities?"

"I've heard stories, Mikey, but I've not seen any evidence."

"So you don't believe it?"

"I didn't say I don't believe it. I just haven't seen it with my own eyes."

"I pay the bagman close to a grand a week to keep them away from my club."

Kitty stared. "Why—what kind of club are you running?"

"My business is completely legit. If I don't pay them, they'll send their thugs in to make trouble."

"You shouldn't pay them anything, Mikey. It makes us straight cops look bad."

"But you straight cops can't shut down their racket, can you?"

Kitty chewed her lip.

"I don't blame you guys, Kitty—I just do what I have to do."

"I'm sorry, Mikey. I won't be a cop this time next week. I'm just not cut out for it."

"You would be if the force was run properly."

"I don't know—I've given up." Kitty shrugged, her lip trembled. "I've also given up complaining about it."

His heart melted at her despair. His arms tightened around her warmth. "Take me back, Kitty. I promise I won't let you down again."

"I need time, Mikey."

"I've waited for years; I can wait a few more weeks—or months." He nibbled her ear and buried his face in her hair. "I love you, Kitty—I've never stopped loving you." He looked down as she sniffed then sobbed into his shirtfront. "I'm sorry, Kitty. I've made you cry too many times. I promise from now on I will try my hardest to make you happy."

Kitty woke to a knock on the door and for a moment wondered where she was. The door opened on Mikey's smile.

"Good morning, my pretty Kitty. Did you sleep okay?"

"What time is it?"

"Late. Ten a.m."

Kitty got to her feet; she still wore the jeans and T-shirt from the night before. "I should get home."

"Stanley and Maurie are going to escort you. Just in case those guys who chased us last night are hanging about in the neighbourhood."

"Do you think they might be?"

"I doubt it, but I'm not taking any chances."

"What are you going to do?"

His eyes traced her body. "I could come with you if you like."

"Mikey—"

"Yeah—I know. You need time." Two steps and his arms closed around her. "It was tough sleeping in the next room last night. I came close to sneaking in here and crawling into bed with you."

"I had trouble sleeping too."

"Why are we doing this again? What are we waiting for?"

"I'm sorry, Mikey. I just need time. I've got a lot going on, I'm changing jobs and—I don't know—I have a lot to think about."

As she had done in days past, Kitty wondered at Mikey's physical strength as he hugged her and her feet left the ground.

****

As happy as a dog with two tails and seven lampposts, Mikey watched Stanley and Maurie follow Kitty up the street. He took a taxi back to the Phoenix Pearl, hopped in his car and drove to Carissa's place. Their affair had faded. Since Mikey's divorce, Carissa had lost that forbidden fruit flavour.

You know you've worn the arse out of a relationship when it stops feeling good, Mikey. Time to call it quits.

Carissa greeted Mikey in a flood of tears.

"Hey, what's up, Riss?"

"It's Barkley. He's been hit by a car."

"Again? Um—is he okay?"

"No! He might lose his leg."

Mikey's Irish humour chose that inopportune moment to pop up and snort. "What? Another one? Ah, front or back?"

"Back."

Laughter bubbled up, unrestrained. "That'll leave him with one of each."

"It isn't funny, Mikey—the vet said he'll have to be put down if they can't save the leg. He's such a beautiful dog—he so faithful and smart."

"Well, Riss, no matter how faithful and smart he is, a dog's no good with just one leg at either end." Mikey wiped a tear from the corner of his eye.

"Why did you come here, Mikey? You don't usually come here so early on a Saturday morning."

"Actually, I came to tell you I won't be coming here anymore."

"What?"

"It's over, Riss. I'm sorry but I'm moving on."

"Get out! You bastard! My dog's been run over and you're breaking up with me."

Kind of like a country song.

"Sorry, Riss. I hope Barkley will be okay." Mikey did sincerely hope that gutsy old dog survived.

44

After two days off, Kitty returned for her last three days as a police officer. Hidden in a storeroom, Dave hid their conversation from devices with the air conditioner running full-blast; she caught up on Dave's progress.

Dave grinned. "I've hidden Bouncy Harold's file and filed a copy in the official records."

"Why did you do that?"

"I've learned to always do it for these kinds of cases. Files in the official records have a habit of vanishing."

"What did the forensics find?"

"Kinane's fingerprints were on the front door and on the door leading into Harold's living area, but not on the murder weapon, nor on the back door where the suspect obviously left."

"They didn't find the gloves used by the suspect?"

"Kitty—I found them."

Kitty frowned. "Where?"

Dave jerked his head in the direction of the corridor. "In a bin in the men's room."

"Here? In the station?"

Cramb nodded.

"How—Dave, that means—"

"What we always suspected—there are rogue cops among us."

"Were there any prints?"

"Yes and it was in our records but we don't know who owns it."

"How come it was on record?"

"Whoever it belongs to was also involved in the Valley Fires—it was on a Shellite drum found at Rusty Russell's flat."

"How do you know those gloves were used in Harold Purser's murder?"

"His blood was found in the wrist roll."

"So where does all this leave Mikey?"

Dave grimaced and shook his head. "Leaves him in the clear. I have statements from his staff stating where he was that evening. He went out, was gone for around fifteen minutes, and returned with his clothes in the same state as when he left. Then, until we arrived, he spent the rest of the night on the club floor, collecting empty glasses and talking to the patrons. The person who murdered Harold would have been splattered with blood— somebody would have noticed if he had blood on him."

"You said you had some idea who might be our suspect; can I ask who you think it was?"

Dave shrugged. "I was thinking of German Burt Campbell, cracking heads is his favourite trick, but those weren't his prints. Anyway, I checked and according to Rick Campbell and his staff, Burt was working a shift as doorman at the Capital at the time of the murder. I'm going to see if the commissioner will allow me to fingerprint all the staff on duty that night" Dave palmed his naked scalp. "Probably pointless, the Police Union wouldn't allow it anyway."

"Probably not and until we know who owns those prints, we're back where we started. Exactly nowhere."

"Yup."

"Poor old Harold."

"Poor old Harold, my arse. About eleven years ago, he got the sack from his job as a music teacher in some swanky religious high school. He was sacked for supplying LSD to a sixteen-year-old. The boy involved said Harold had molested him for three years, but there wasn't enough evidence to convict him. The boy got expelled for tripping in church."

"He was high in church?" Kitty chuckled. "I shouldn't laugh, but that is funny."

"Something to aspire to, Kitty."

****

Kitty began working for Chris McCaffery. The little inner city office had just enough room for two desks. One for his receptionist-come-bookkeeper, a forty-something-year-old woman called Ginny. Chris and Kitty shared the other. Ginny kept her desk pristine and whenever Chris and Kitty went out, she valiantly tidied theirs. When they returned with sandwiches, coffee, cameras, and notebooks, the lines of Ginny's back stiffened but she continued to work without comment.

45

Ivy Hasted

Ivy Hasted worshipped Ellie Riley, of Ellie and the Wolfmen. In half-light, she even resembled Ellie—somewhat. Her hair wasn't as perfect, she didn't have Ellie's boobs, and Ivy had hazel eyes. She longed to dress like Ellie; the fashion houses watched Ellie's outfits and fell over each other to copy them. The gay community called her Princess Ellie and followed her across the country. Ellie's road manager scathed them with the title The Glittering Horde and they embraced it. They spent a fortune on concert tickets and records. Ivy had spent all her money to be first through the door of the Phoenix Pearl to see Ellie and the Wolfmen and shrugged off her penniless status; in the early hours she would collect—big time. If everything worked out, Ivy would have enough money to get a boob job and make herself as beautiful as Ellie.

Ivy worked as a housemaid for a rich businessman, Robert Martin, who had connections all the way to parliament house. Ivy had a wide-eyed fascination for the rich and the famous—she ached to be part of the jet set. She had heard Robert organising a pool party, and Ivy longed to know what such parties entailed. On the night of the party, she had hidden herself in the shrubs of his backyard and filmed it using Robert's own video camera. She had hoped to see beautiful women, dressed in the latest fashions but there was only Robert, his wife, Ruby Landers who owned a wine bar in Fortitude Valley, a prominent politician and a couple of other men. The other guests, a boy and two girls, intrigued Ivy; all around twelve years old and scantily dressed. The boy wore tight leather shorts with braces and no shirt. The girls wore skin-tight Lurex mini dresses, fishnet stockings held up with a black suspender belt—the taller girl clutched the hem of her dress, trying to stop it riding up.

At some point during the evening, the politician had pissed over Ivy where she hunkered in the bushes, her legs stiff from sitting motionless. She filmed for hours, only stopping to change the camera tape.

She'd arrived home at five in the morning, dead tired with the stench of urine in her hair and on her clothes. She had brought with her the camera and the mini cassettes. She copied the footage onto two VHS tapes, secreted the mini cassette under a loose floorboard in her flat and covered it with the threadbare rug.

Inspiration arrived on dazzling wings; she made an anonymous, handkerchief muffled phone call from a public phone to her boss, Robert Martin.

"Fifty grand," Ivy smiled as his breath quickened in her ear. "Have it for me at four a.m. on Sunday behind Poppy's Nightclub or I'll deliver the tape to a journalist."

"You don't know who you're messing with, girl," he growled.

"Oh I think I do." She'd smiled and hung up. She knew how this worked. She had watched every episode of Sons and

Daughters; she had studied Pat the Rat in detail. Her best friend, Karen begged her to call it off.

"You're going to get into trouble, Ivy."

"I know what I'm doing, Karen."

****

Ellie and the Wolfmen were amazing and Ivy screamed as she watched the Alpha Wolf lift Ellie's limp form and carry her from the stage; so dramatic! The man looked like Elvis and gave the audience a smouldering stare. He was big and handsome and Ellie, so small and beautiful in his arms—every girl wanted to be Ellie. Then they returned hand in hand and the whole band lined up to bow, just like a theatre company. Ellie gave an encore. Ivy watched, eyes wide—trying to see everything at once.

She spent the rest of the night dancing with her friends. At closing time she made her way to the alley behind Poppy's to wait with nerves on edge.

Footsteps echoed in the early morning quiet. Ivy's heart climbed into her throat, she hoped Karen wasn't right—he would hand over fifty grand and take the video tape and that would be it, right? Her heart dived to her feet as a blond haired, moonfaced giant leered out of the dark, one eye watched her face, the other stared at the wall. A car stopped to block the entrance to the alley.

"Do you have the tape?"

"Do you have the money?" It pleased Ivy how steady her voice sounded, but a shiver danced up her spine and she manoeuvred closer to the lane.

"Sure! I've got fifty grand in my pocket. Hand over the tape and it's yours, baby!"

"I want to see the money first—"

A sweaty, smelly hand closed over Ivy's mouth and the blond giant wrenched the bag from her shoulder. He chuckled as he withdrew the video tape.

"Tie her up."

Ivy didn't get to growl threats, scream, or even struggle—this wasn't how Pat the Rat would have handled it. Tied, gagged, and blindfolded, her captors dumped her in the boot of a car like a parcel and slammed the lid. She rolled about in the car boot, choking on the dusty air until the car stopped and her captor's arm encircled her waist. She heard a door hinge squeak and voices— men laughing and joking.

"Party time, boys!" She fell to the floor with a thump. "First let's give her a little prick." The men laughed. She was inside a wooden building, somewhere a fig bird called in the night. A strap tightened on her arm and a needle-prick stung the crook of her elbow.

"Ever try speed, honeybuns?" The man spoke from close by, he stank of cigarettes and alcohol. "This stuff is extra good; I cook it up myself. It'll really make you fly."

The gag muffled Ivy's scream as a cold instrument cut away her clothes. Fingers probed between her legs, then a mouth followed. The icy prickle of fear gave way to heat, drug induced sweat seeped from her pores.

"You're a bit flat-chested, sweetie." Teeth bit her nipple, a warm trickle of blood flowed down her ribs. Ivy's screams couldn't get past the gag. A big man climbed over her, hands forced her legs apart.

"Hurry up and fuck her, man! I'm so horny my knob's going to explode."

The man was huge, he squashed the air from her lungs as he sweat over her; he thrust into her for an age, Ivy drifted, her predicament reeled into focus then oblivion returned. For hours she floated in and out of conscience, each time she woke the nightmare continued—each time a different man violated her.

"Come on, wake up, bitch—I don't like fucking a dead body!" A hard slap set her ear ringing.

"Tip some of this down her throat, Bobby—that'll make her horny."

Laughter at this remark echoed in Ivy's ears; the gag on her mouth remained tight. The effect of the drug faded, Ivy could hear sparrows and distant traffic. Time wore on, the men unmerciful. Pain burned in her pelvis and Ivy passed out. A sharp object ripped her out of oblivion. A knife pierced her breast and Ivy struggled, these men weren't content to rape her, they intended to kill.

"That's it, Honey—jeeze she's tight!" The man's breath stank of tooth decay and onions, his body smelled of sweat and dirty socks. Something crashed against her temple and their voices faded across a red tide of pain, cold steel pierced her body; again, and again. The man on top of her screamed his orgasm, the watchers bellowed encouragement. Ivy choked on tears she couldn't shed and she saw her parent's faces in a rising black haze.

****

The half-grown mud crab reared and opened his pincers at the crow that came too close to his feast. The crow hopped further along the carcass, perched on its shoulder and tore a chunk of exposed flesh.

The body appeared like a grotesque caricature of a mermaid reclining on the log that surfaced as the tide receded. A couple of early morning anglers in a dinghy pulled up alongside for a look. The naked girl looked no more than a teenager, her long hair trailed in the water. The men waved their arms at the crows and they flew away but nothing deterred the crab.

46

Chris McCaffery looked up as the string of bells tinkled and the door pushed open. His shop seemed to shrink around him as Ray Sims and Dave Cramb entered. The big detectives took up a lot of floor space.

"Chris, it's good to see you mate. You're looking well."

"Nothing like getting away from the force to put the colour back into your cheeks, eh?"

Chris McCaffery grinned at his former colleagues. "It took you bastards long enough to come and visit."

"We didn't come to visit you, you ugly bastard. Where's Kitty?"

On cue, Kitty bustled in the back door from a morning spent following an errant wife. She set her camera on her desk and looked up. Her smiled lit the room.

Ray Sims grabbed Kitty in a brawny hug. "Kitty! As beautiful as ever and decorated."

Dave shook her hand. "Congratulations, Kitty. The Valour Award is a very high honour."

Kitty's smile faded. Chris knew the traumatic memory of the call out destined to end her police career still haunted her. Shooting two men at short range was enough to discompose the toughest cop but for a twenty-three year old girl, it might yet prove too much.

"So what can I do for you blokes?"

"You heard about the girl found in the river?"

"Yes, have they found out who she is yet?"

"Yes, her name is—was Ivy Hasted. Twenty years old, had been in the employ of Robert Martin, the property developer. We Snow Whites have not been allowed near it, but I know they've given permission for Ivy's parents to remove her things from her flat, which to us, indicates they've given up searching for her killers—if they ever did. They apparently turned over her flat and found nothing to indicate why she might have been so brutally killed—she'd been drugged and gang raped, forensics reckon about five or six men. They cut her up and bled her out—" Ray glanced at Kitty, "she died of some horrific injuries."

"And then they dumped her body in the river." Dave ran a hand across his bald head.

"Like that other poor bugger a couple of months ago." Chris couldn't remember all the details of the case except he had fatal knife wounds—they had bled him out like a beast too.

"Les Jones."

Ray Sims folded his arms and nodded. "That's him—yeah, we're told the two cases are unrelated and the powers that be have steered us away from both. There are similarities in the two cases that need scrutiny. We're going to try and have a quiet word with the medical examiner."

"So they're connected?"

"Don't know. No—I doubt it. But the bleeding out thing is the same. Both victims had multiple stab wounds into major arteries."

"So, what brings you to my gin-joint?"

"There is nothing to stop you calling in and having a look around Ivy's flat. Her parents are going to clear out her stuff this afternoon. You could just happen to be a real estate agent coming to inspect or something."

"Are they saying they can't find a motive?"

Sims yawned and stretched his arms over his head. "No motive, no suspect. A gang of rapists and at least one of them is a psycho that enjoys a bit of casual butchery. There may be nothing more to it than that."

"Okay. I think Kitty and I might go and do a little bit of digging."

****

Ivy's parents had that wrung-out look that Chris had seen too many, times on the face of a murder victim's loved ones; all the worse if the police had not solved the crime. He wondered if these people were satisfied with the performance of the police. He decided he'd tell them who he was; they didn't need more torment. Chris waited until they finished packing before he approached and introduced himself.

"I hope you don't mind me looking into Ivy's case."

"Not at all. The police don't seem to be interested in finding those bastards."

"I'm sorry. I can't promise we'll find anything either. Do you know if she was in any kind of trouble?"

"No. She seemed happy—her usual dreamy self."

"Can you make a list of her friends?"

The man looked around at his wife. "The only one we know was Karen, were there any others?"

The woman shook her head, her eye's empty and her features blank.

"Do you know where Karen lived? Or worked?"

"I don't know where she lived but she works at a chemist shop in Queen Street. Ivy used to go there to get free samples."

"You don't know her last name?"

Both shook their heads, weariness stamped on their faces.

Chris passed a card to Ivy's father. "If you think of anything else, give me a call."

When the Hasteds drove away, Chris and Kitty went inside. The flat was a lowset, wooden and fibro duplex, furnished in a tired 1960s style. It smelled of cat piss and cheap perfume. An hour later, Chris was ready to give up.

Kitty stamped her foot in frustration. "Fuck it, Chris! There's nothing here."

"Do that again."

"What."

"Stamp your foot."

"If you're going to make a remark about my looking sweet when I'm angry, I'll break your arm."

"I don't doubt it." Chris nudged her out of the way and began stamping on the floor beside her.

"What are you doing?"

"Loose floorboard. Shift your arse." Chris rolled back the 1950's floor rug to unpolished cypress pine boards. He pried one loose with his biro. "Bingo!" Tied to a floor joist with a piece of string was a sandwich bag and inside it a neatly folded white paper bag.

"And that paper bag will take us straight to Ivy's friend, Karen." Kitty examined the chemist shop's logo on the bag and smiled.

"What do you suppose we'll find on this?" Chris held up a camcorder cassette. "It must be good if she hid it under the floor."

****

Kitty sat side on to the television screen with one shaky hand to her face. Her relationship with Mikey became intimate when she was just fifteen, and in hindsight, it appalled her, especially that the first time he had forced himself on her. They had loved each other and whether or not she was old enough, she consented. The kids in this video were very young, none appeared to have reached puberty. The video was dark and grainy, so facial expression couldn't be determined, but the kids' body language was unmistakable.

"Hey! What's this?"

The excitement in Chris's voice drew Kitty's eyes back to the screen. The footage had changed. The brightness of the footage flared; the picture jerked back to focus on a white kindy paper sign with large words written with marking pen: *Ruby Landers, Robert Martin and a politician. Two other men (?)'*

"If only she had gone to the police." Chris rolled the tape forward to see if Ivy had written any more notes. "Ruby. I always suspected she pimped for hookers, but kids! Shit! I didn't think she would sink that low."

"So what do we do next? Take it to the police?"

"We could."

"But?"

"This footage is too grainy and too dark. I'll get a guy I know to see if he can enhance it but I don't hold much hope."

"If it was any other profession, I'd offer to go undercover, but prostitution? I couldn't do it, Chris."

"I wouldn't ask you to. I can't unless I wear a wig and a false nose or something, someone would recognise me for sure. I've arrested a few too many felons in that neighbourhood."

"You'd make a terrible hooker."

"You know what I meant." Chris threw a crumpled ball of paper at her.

"I could take a job as a drink waitress or something."

"I don't think you should, Kitty, there are some dangerous people who hang about in The Valley."

"I'll go into Ruby's and suss it out tomorrow night."

"No, wait. Let me dye my hair and beard brown first. Then we'll go nightclubbing and suss out the whole scene."

"But you don't have a beard."

"I can grow a magnificent beard I'll have you know, it's just the colour is not real impressive."

"What colour?"

"A dodgy shade of ginger—don't laugh!"

"Well okay, hurry up and grow it."

"I'll get some glasses in the meantime."

****

Kitty waited at the door of the pharmacy for Ivy's friend, Karen. "Karen? Can I have a quick word?"

She stopped and looked Kitty up and down, "Yes, okay. What do you want?"

"My name is Kitty Olsen, I'm investigating the death of Ivy Hasted; I believe she was a friend of yours."

Karen blenched. "Yes—but—I have to catch a bus."

"It's okay. I just want to ask a few questions."

"Will I have to go to the police station?"

"No." Kitty smiled, she was dressed in black pants and blazer but she hadn't thought she looked like a jack. "When did you last see Ivy?"

"She was on the dance floor at the Phoenix Pearl—I was tired and went home after Ellie and the Wolfmen finished. She said she was going to hang around."

"Was she in any kind of trouble?"

Karen clapped her hand over her mouth and whimpered. She inhaled. "Ivy was so silly! She lived in her own little dream world—she wouldn't listen—"

"What was she doing?"

"She was trying to blackmail her boss—I told her she'd get into trouble—she wouldn't listen!" Karen sobbed drawing curious glances from passing people; some squinted at Kitty, wondering what she had said to reduce the girl to tears.

"I'm sorry, Karen—please don't cry. Come on, I'll drive you home."

47

Kitty finally found a use for the oversized crocodile skin bag her mother had given her two Christmases past. It was big enough to conceal her gun, camera, Sony Pressman and a pair of Converse sneakers. She had never been adept at running in a pair of high heels though she worried if she had to run away from anyone, they'd hardly wait for her to change her shoes. When she put on her stilettos, she topped Chris who stood a shade under six feet.

"Kitty you look lovely! Nothing at all like a sleuth."

"I can't lie; you look hilarious with that hair colour and glasses. You could pass as a real estate agent."

"Gee, thanks."

"Or a pervert."

"Which reminds me, I need to buy a bag of lollies."

****

Rick Campbell sat at the corner table beside his cousin, Naz Van Nek, opposite them his half-brother, German Burt. Rick had already snorted a line and consumed half a bottle of scotch; neither had helped ease his pissy mood. They watched the punters trickle in, mostly regulars on their way upstairs to the casino. Rick's business had suffered a downturn since The Phoenix Pearl had opened and the bagman, John Yarrow, told him there was little the police could do to shake down Mikey Kinane—he was completely legal. He didn't have gambling, working girls—not even strippers. Sending thugs in to make trouble was pointless, his bouncers were gorilla crossbreeds. Rick went down for a look on opening night and introduced himself to Mikey Kinane. He stood six foot six and resembled a Greek god—only better looking. His charm gave every female around itchy pants. Rick, for an unguarded moment, found himself lost in those blue eyes, tempted to stroke the smooth skin on Kinane's neck. Rick liked him and rather hoped Bev would crack onto him; if his wife must have other men's children, she would find no better genetics than the youngest Kinane. Many of The Phoenix Pearl's patrons had previously frequented The Capital. Rick wasn't happy that his female customers had shifted allegiance in that first week—and where the women go, the men follow. His top billing bands, Screaming Sally, and Ellie and the Wolfmen had also moved to the Phoenix Pearl and had taken their fans with them.

"That fucking Yarrow will be here tomorrow with his hand out. That cunt is still stinging me a grand a week. For what!" Burt and Naz grabbed their drinks as Rick's fist hammered the table. "Sure the cops leave me alone but that doesn't stop me haemorrhaging cash from every orifice." Small flecks of foam shot from Rick's mouth. "I'm losing a fucking fortune just keeping my doors open. Pinkie's up the road is closing—Des can't compete with those fucking Kinanes. If I didn't have the casino upstairs, I'd be closing too!"

"When I was at Ruby's the other night, she said Kinane's brothers had been in there drinking." Burt dared set his glass back on the table and pitched his voice to falsetto. "Ooh! They're such lovely men, those twins, so funny and handsome too!"

"Ruby's a cunt." Rick's voice fell to a mutter.

"The Kinane brothers are the biggest suppliers of dope in Queensland." Naz liked to needle his cousin and his info-bomb had the desired effect.

His cousin's words sent Rick's heart southward. "What? I thought I was! How do you know that?"

Naz chugged half a schooner of beer and belched. "It's hard to find anyone who'll verify it but the rumours are going around."

"What kind of rumours?"

"All those dealers that we thought had gone straight? Straight my arse. They switched straight to the Kinanes. They supply top quality stuff and keep their prices the same as everyone else."

"That fucking bagman is gonna get a phone call in the morning!"

"Well, well, well!" said German Burt, both his eyes stared in the same direction. "Make room for the hard-on of the century! Would you look at what just walked in the door?"

Naz followed Burt's gaze. "Praise the lord and suck my balls!"

Rick looked up from his gloomy contemplation, staring at his empty glass wasn't going to fill it—that fucking drink waiter was asleep at the wheel again. The woman that had his companions' testosterone pumping was a tall, slim blonde. She wore a tight, scarlet dress with shoestring shoulder straps. Rick shrugged; he wasn't into women—as much as he tried to pretend. A bearded man with glasses escorted the blonde.

****

Kitty perched on a barstool and kept her face pointed towards the dance-floor, but her eyes swept the room.

"Do you see those three blokes sitting in the corner?" Chris leaned close.

"That big lump with the blond hair hasn't taken his eyes off us since we came in." As Kitty turned from the watching the dancers, her eyes brushed over the blond giant.

"He's watching you, Kitty. Be super careful. That's German Burt. He's the biggest arsehole God ever poured guts into."

"Hey don't forget, I'm Sally Diamond and you're James Bendell, property developer."

"Yes, would you like one of my business cards?" He grinned and patted his breast pocket.

Kitty groaned. She had conned a horny printer's apprentice to print ten business cards in his employer's absence. That she had yet to fulfil her promise of a date made her teeth itch.

"Your efforts have been duly noted; you'd be in line for a promotion, only I have nowhere to promote you to."

"My own little desk in the corner, perhaps?"

236

Two drinks later, Chris and Kitty left the capital and wandered through the Friday night crowd en route to Poppy's.

German Burt had a live-in girlfriend and decided that night would be the night he'd throw her out. Burt had fallen in love with a new woman, the beautiful blonde who had walked into the Capital—she would be his. Burt's obsessions arrived at light speed and Burt's obsessions were river deep and mountain high—as dangerous as they often were fruitless. He only became obsessed with women beyond his reach.

With his brain swimming in alcohol and dopamine, he followed the girl and her escort along the street and lost sight of them in a crowd of drag queens in front of Poppy's. Back and forth he wandered in search of the blonde in the red dress. She emerged from The Phoenix Pearl with her companion and caught a taxi. They left Burt in Fortitude Valley, broken-hearted and careworn.

When he arrived home drunk and sulky, he hauled his girlfriend from the bed and beat her.

48

The two men Aiden showed into his office made Mikey's eyes water with their pungent body odour. He motioned for Aiden and Liam to remain; the pair, obviously bikies had a dangerous look about them—their smell alone might kill a brown dog. Mikey introduced himself and his brothers.

"We're Biker Henry and Harley Phil, Sergeant at Arms and Captain of the Valley Armada Motorcycle Club." Biker Henry's face resembled a busted sofa; a tangle of coarse ginger hair almost obscured the skull tattoo on his neck.

Mikey hesitated at a strangled snort from Aiden; his brother disguised it with a cough. Liam pulled out a pack of cigarettes, lit one and tossed the pack and lighter to Aiden. Mikey didn't usually allow people to smoke in his office, but anything that would drown out the stink of the men sitting opposite was worth his sufferance.

"What can I do for you gentlemen?"

Gorillas.

"We heard you were looking to hire some security."

"I am." Mikey employed individuals as security staff, they'd stay for a few months and move on. Such men were often itinerants, they liked to travel around and see the country.

"We can provide you with twenty men to work around the clock."

"What kind of credentials are you offering?" Liam spoke before Mikey.

"We have some of Brisbane's most dangerous men in our ranks. It was us who drove The Shadow Jackals back to the Gold Coast."

"Why?" Mikey had no idea who the Shadow Jackals were or why driving them back to the Gold Coast proved a significant victory.

"They were muscling in on our territory."

"I didn't know bikies were territorial."

"We have to be. There are businesses here that pay us to protect them; we ain't gonna allow no other gangs to cramp our style."

"What is your style?"

"Kick the shit out of anyone who gets in our way. You boys all ride Harleys I'm told, we'd be honoured to bring you into our upper ranks."

"Why?"

"You blokes are earning a reputation."

"What kind of a reputation?"

"You know—don't mess with the Kinanes."

"Mate, we only do what we have to do to run our business. We're not out to earn a reputation."

"We like men who don't need to skite. I think we'll get along well—you like Harleys and so do we—"

"Mate, we only ride Harleys because we like that brand of bike." Liam folded his arms. His words bore loathing sufficient to start an average war. "Our egos are in a healthy enough state, we don't need to be part of a juvenile gang to make us feel like men."

"What are you suggesting?" Harley Phil cracked his knuckles and Mikey winced—the sound of snapping joints had that effect on him lately.

"My brother isn't suggesting anything." He cast a quelling glance at Liam. The twins resented gangs of any description. "I'm sorry, but we're not that kind of operation. We like to remain above the law; I won't be hiring thugs, today or any day."

"You might find yourself regretting your decision, Kinane."

Mikey's eyes narrowed. "I regret a lot of decisions I've made, mate—I have enough experience to know this won't be one of them. Close the door when you go."

"You blokes are only young fullas—you've got a hard lesson coming your way."

Mikey smiled. "I'm always willing to learn something new." He and the twins got to their feet in one smooth action. "See them out, please—I'll see to the dressing rooms. Screaming Sally are due any moment for a sound check, got to make sure they have everything they need."

Aiden coughed and flung the window open.

"Come gents, we'll return your weapons." Liam clicked the ceiling fan switch as he passed.

****

"Mikey!" Frankie Swift stiff-armed the dressing room door.

"Hey man!" Jeff, the drummer's long blond hair was the envy of girls Australia-wide. He extended his middle finger to push his glasses higher on his nose and grinned. "Good to be back at the Pee-pee again." He sat down at the smorgasbord of 'goodies' Mikey had laid out and began to build a doobie of Olympic proportions— a five-paper extravaganza—a *cigareefer.*

Frankie saw Mikey's puzzled expression and grinned. "Pee-pee; it's what we call The Phoenix Pearl."

"Jesus, mate—we just saw a couple of big hairy bikers leaving here as we drove in, not a good look. Fabbs would faint if he saw them." Gerry Romano stood almost as tall as Mikey but a classic string-bean, Mikey outweighed him by fifteen kilograms.

"They heard I was looking for security staff and came, offering their sterling service."

"Fuck that," said Frankie.

"I am hiring security men but not that variety."

"Why don't you give Vince Wilkins a call? We use him whenever we need security here in Brisbane. He has three blokes that work for him. He's legit."

****

Rick folded his arms. "You're saying you'll work for me for free?"

"As long as it's anything that's going to send the Kinanes tits up."

"What have you got against the Kinanes?" Rick squinted. He'd met Biker Henry and Harley Phil from the Valley Armada Motorcycle Club a couple of months before when they approached him in regards to a territorial matter. They wanted to sell drugs in the area but didn't want to step on Rick's toes.

"They insulted us."

Rick stared; those were petulant words coming from a big hairy biker. He clasped his hands and pressed his index fingers to his lips. This pair had a gormless look about them but they had a reputation for wanton brutality; he might find a good use for them at some point.

"Okay," Rick got to his feet and opened the window. "At the moment, I have nothing going down, but as soon as I do I'll give you a call. Write your phone number on that." He tossed a writing pad across the desk and flicked a pen after it.

49

Monday.

Ruby's Winebar stood a little further along and across the street from The Phoenix Pearl and Poppy's. Respectable law-abiding punters frequented this end of the nightclub strip and most people who came into Ruby's assumed it squeaky clean. Chris and Kitty had just left Poppy's; the noise had become too much when The Glittering Horde minced in with Ellie Riley and various members of The Wolfmen to celebrate Ellie's birthday. Kitty wanted to get Ellie's autograph but Chris dragged her away.

"She's so tiny!"

"I think you're a little star-struck, Kitty."

"No I'm not. I used to be a fan—well I still am—but I'm not star-struck."

"A couple of years ago, me and Dave arrested her ex-husband after he tried to abduct her. Greg Meyer had already beat the crap out of him so we just had to mop him up."

"She has an ex-husband?"

"Not many people know that, but it's true."

"She's only a year older than me."

Chris laughed. "They marry young out in the bible-belt. She grew up on a farm too, you know. And you want to know something else? Frankie Swift of Screaming Sally is her boyfriend."

"Yeah? Frankie Swift!"

"Lucky bastard."

"Lucky her. How do you know that?"

"Greg Meyer told me a few months ago. He was pretty pissed off about it. Poor old bastard is in love with her, but when I suggested he just take Ellie away from Swift, he mumbled something about being too old for her."

"How old is he?"

"Not sure, he's about twenty years older than her."

"Twenty years—"

"Yeah, big gap."

Kitty smiled and thought of Lester. They had arrived at the doors of Ruby's and put the conversation on hold.

"Tomorrow you're going to tell me all you know about Ellie."

"Thought you said you weren't star-struck."

"I'm not! Just curious."

Ruby's was more sedate. A pianist played a baby grand in the corner of the dimly lit bar and beautiful young men and women served the elegant clientele. They found a table close to the piano and Chris ordered their drinks.

"Well," Kitty siphoned the last of the cocktail from her glass. "I'm going to visit the little girls' room." She glanced at the sign that pointed the way, turned and left by a door at the opposite end of the room. Walking with confidence she pushed open the door and slipped into a hallway without looking behind her. Her eyes took in a door she was sure led into the back of the bar—a stockroom or office. At the end of the hallway, a set of stairs led to an upper floor. Her heart trip-hammered as she climbed them. On the second landing, she found a set of French doors. She checked back down the stairs, no one had followed; the doors opened into a small, tastefully appointed foyer and another set of doors. Her hand shook a little as she pushed through into a hallway, she wandered through an arch and for a moment thought she'd walked into another nightclub. The music throbbed; Donna Summer moaned and sighed, *'I love to love you, baby.'* The pink lights hurt Kitty's eyes and incense caught in her throat.

Kitty, I think you just walked into a cathouse.

She saw no one until her eyes adjusted to the gloom. People sat behind lace curtains—men reclining on pink velvet couches and naked women crawled over them like fungus. The mirrored ceiling reflected the decadence. She almost fainted as her eyes fell on a girl with a man at each end; one served her from behind, the other seemed bent on choking her with his penis. Kitty's face burned—she'd never before watched other people have sex.

"Can I help you, Darling?"

Kitty flinched and resisted fanning herself. A man in black pants and red jacket appeared.

The brothel's butler?

"Um—I was looking for the ladies room."

"Back downstairs, dearie, at the opposite end of the bar."

Kitty fled. She realised she'd broken into a sweat when she resumed her seat opposite Chris.

"So, did we guess right?"

Kitty nodded and fanned herself with a napkin. "I think Monday night is orgy night upstairs."

"Caught an eyeful, eh?"

The comedy of the situation hit Kitty, she lean back in her chair and succumbed to a fit of the giggles. Chris eyed her and shook his head.

"Call yourself a private eye—pull it together, woman."

"Let's get out of here."

"A quiet drink over at The Phoenix Pearl, perhaps?"

"Let's find a coffee shop."

"Don't you want to see Mikey Kinane again?"

Kitty sighed. "I do. A little too much, but I want time to think."

"Coffee shop it is then."

50

Tuesday.

Chris went to Ruby's by himself on Tuesday night. He perched on a barstool and chatted to the staff. Ruby took the seat beside him and introduced herself, he pretended he'd never met her before and lied he was just in town for a few days.

"Patsy tells me you're looking for a special." Her eyes flicked from Chris to the barmaid and dismissed her with a jerk of her blond head.

"Depends what you call a special."

"A girl that might not be quite—ah—legal."

"My tastes lead me in that direction, yes." Chris' skin crawled.

Is it really this easy?

"I have a girl available right now, a pretty little Lolita."

"Lead the way."

Chris trembled and prayed the cops wouldn't raid that night. If they did, his life would be over; the crime of paedophilia was, in his mind, the lowest any human could sink.

Ruby led him up the stairs through the French doors and past the room filled with pink light and throbbing music. Around a corner and along a hallway to the last room.

"Oh, I should tell you, that door," she indicated the door at the end of the hall, "is locked from the outside only. If, in the rare instance we're raided, that is an escape route for our clients."

"Nice to know." Chris smiled what he hoped was a pervert's smile.

"Mind you, if someone opens it, an alarm goes off in my office."

"Hopefully, I won't have to open it."

Ruby opened the door and Chris saw a girl sit bolt upright on the bed.

"Jody, I have a nice man who'd like to spend some time with you. Now you'll be a good girl and do as he asks, okay darling?"

"Okay, Ruby."

"Remember all the rules." The girl nodded. "Enjoy." Ruby dropped her voice and rolled her eyes. Chris imagined her shedding her skin and slithering down the hallway. His knuckles itched with a desire to punch her lights out.

The pink lamp standing in the corner, reflected in the girl's eyes. She was thin—Chris thought about twelve years old. The child's face was small and pretty but her eyes disturbed him. They held a curious mix of fear, loathing, and a weariness that looked out of place in one so young. She moved towards Chris and he backed away.

"Sit down, honey."

She stopped and stared, fear of a cruel game in the offing stiffened her face and shoulders.

"It's okay. I won't hurt you. How long have you worked for Ruby?"

The little girl made a sudden dash for the door.

"Whoa!" Chris grabbed her arm. "Jody, I only want to talk to you. Don't run away."

"Ruby said I shouldn't answer questions about myself."

"I won't tell her. Do you like being here?"

The girl looked at the floor.

"You can talk to me, Jody. I won't tell Ruby, or anyone else."

The girl looked up and the eyeliner around her eyes and the transparent negligee nauseated Chris.

"Please, Jody. I promise I won't hurt you."

"What do you want me to do first?" She began to remove the negligee.

"No! Don't do that! For heaven's sake, have you got a dressing gown?"

The girl nodded, her eyes confused.

"Put it on, Jody."

"Don't you want me to play with your dinker?"

"No, put on your dressing gown. I didn't come here for that reason. Jody, sit down, sweetheart."

The girl pulled on her dressing gown and sat on the edge of the bed, her eyes limpid pools in the darkened room.

Chris pulled up a chair and sat on the edge. "My name is James. Now tell me, where did you come from?"

"I've always lived here."

"Is your mother here?"

"My mother died. Ruby takes care of me."

"Do you like it when men come to your room?"

She shook her head; her bottom lip trembled.

"Would you like to go somewhere where you didn't have to have men come into you room?"

She gazed at him open mouthed. She hesitated, her eyes flicked to the door and back to his. "I don't know."

"It's okay, I promise I won't hurt you. Would you like to live somewhere else?"

Her eyes sparkled. "I don't know."

"Do you like it here?"

She shook her head. Again her eyes darted to the door.

"Tomorrow night, I'll come with a lady. You have your shoes on and a bag packed. Please, don't tell Ruby. We'll get you away from here, we'll find somewhere you can go and be safe."

"Can I go to school like they do on TV?"

"Don't you go to school?"

The girl shook her head.

"Yes, you'll definitely go to school. Now do you have a bag you can put your things in?"

The girl reached under the bed and pulled out an old-fashioned school port.

"Does Ruby come and clean your room?"

Jody shook her head. "I have to clean my own room."

"Pack only what you really want to take, okay? You won't be able to carry much and you'll have to do what we tell you. We'll have a car waiting to take us away."

Jody nodded. Did hope now mingle with the distrust wrought on her face?

"Not a word to anyone, okay?"

"Not a word." For a moment, Chris thought she might smile.

****

Jody had lived with Ruby since her mother died, she didn't remember living anywhere else except upstairs at Ruby's Winebar. She didn't remember her mother. The only time she went outside was to go to parties with Ruby. The parties always made her sick; Ruby would give her a tablet and all the sweets she could eat; the parties blurred by. The next day she would be sick and very sore; Jody hated Ruby's parties. Since she turned twelve, Ruby brought men to her room at an increasing rate. It used to be an occasional one, now it had increased to two or three a week. Jody liked the daytime. She watched Sesame Street, Playschool, and all the fun shows on TV. Then it would be Days of our Lives. Then she could watch all the kids' shows. Jody could count to one hundred from watching Sesame Street, and she could sing the alphabet song, but she couldn't read; Jody never went to school. Ruby said she wouldn't need what they taught at school. James' visit the night before had her both afraid and excited. He told her she didn't have to have men coming to her room, that she could go to school and have friends like the kids on TV. She had put her winter pyjamas in her port, her jeans and three T shirts. She packed her toothbrush, hairbrush, and the book she had had all her life, The

Cat in the Hat. She packed her most treasured possession, her doll, on top. The other clothes Ruby told her to wear when men came to her room, she would leave behind.

Jody worried that James might have told her a lie. The people in Jody's life usually told her lies; she expected it.

****

Wednesday.

Andy Morrow hefted his bag of tools and entered the ground floor back door of Rubies Wine Bar.

"What do you want?" The woman's words sailed from her mouth on a cloud of smoke; a cigarette holder protruded from her fist.

"I'm Gavin. Your landlord wants me to do a safety check on the electrical wiring of this building. It won't take long, just a matter of checking for earth leaks." Andy passed her a business card and flashed a letter in front of her face.

"Will you need to go into any of the rooms?"

"Nah."

"Very well, I'll be in my office if you need me."

Andy grinned and went about holding his multimeter to power points and switches; as he worked, he whistled 'Sadie the Cleaning Lady.' He moved upstairs and made a beeline for the back door where he proceeded to disable the buzzer. A qualified electrician, Andy left his job as a radio technician with the

Queensland Police Force five years before. His former colleague, Chris McCaffery PI, often used his services to get inside houses of the people he investigated.

51

"I'm telling you, Rick, that guy that came in the other night with the horny blonde is a private detective. He used to be a cop and his name is McCaffery—he arrested me when I was about fifteen."

Rick Campbell squinted at Alan Ward who stood in front of his desk looking pleased with himself. In his mid-twenties with a mullet, rat-tail and home-grown tattoos—eager to prove is worth. He'd begun his career as a violent fourteen year old, wandering the streets at night, bashing and robbing any unfortunate enough to cross his path. Since he had come to work for Rick, he'd embraced skulduggery with the fervour of a seasoned gangster. Rick's main hit man, Kev Dallas, had recently fallen from the roof of Poppy's and broke his neck. Rick couldn't shake the suspicion that one of the Kinanes had snapped Kev's neck and tossed him off. Pop Francesco vowed that Mikey came into his club that night but spent a solid hour talking to Pop at the bar and couldn't possibly have had time to climb onto the roof. Pop, in Rick's opinion, was excessively cosy with the Kinanes—all neighbourly and buddy-buddy, he treated Rick with cool indifference. The police put Kev's death down to misadventure, the fact they found him with a scoped gun the only reason they investigated at all. Rick didn't believe the misadventure bit; though a narcissist of the first degree,

Dallas hadn't been a fool. Rick surrounded himself with dangerous men and he recognised that same quality in Mikey Kinane. When Rick wanted someone dead, he paid his men to do it; he suspected Mikey Kinane was a do-it-yourself man.

"Are you sure?" Rick remembered McCaffery, one of the Snow Whites. Incorruptible. He had left the police force sometime in the past couple of years, Rick didn't know exactly when. He didn't know he'd become a private investigator, and he hadn't recognised him.

"Pretty sure, yeah. He has been into Ruby's twice this week. I reckon he's up to something. Let me get him, Rick, I'll bleed him out like I did with…"

Rick's head spun and his face tingled as the blood drained to his feet. Though thus far Ruby had proven to be discreet, she made him nervous. She knew too much about him and his associates. She made money from the wine bar but her main income came from prostitution; though illegal, the police turned a blind eye as long as she paid the bagman. Rick worried, in the event of her arrest, she'd serve up Rick and his cohorts quicker than a spotty teenage cashier at Maccas served up a Quarter Pounder. Rick too paid the bagman but bribing crooked cops only guaranteed your indemnity until they needed a notorious conviction, and if that wasn't worrisome enough, the 'Snow Whites' didn't, for a minute, respect anyone's untouchable status.

"…and cut him up and redistribute him around the city in easy to bury pieces—"

Rick cut off Alan's enthusiastic proposal. "Okay, here's what I want you to do…"

****

"Where's me boyfriend?"

"I'm only your boyfriend if you've brought a pie."

"Bessie made you some Lamingtons."

"Oh, Bessie! You'll turn my head yet!"

Mikey filled the kettle as Margie and Bessie entered his office.

"I've got some news for you, Mikey."

Something in Margie's voice made Mikey look around; her face carried worry in every line and she had plenty of those.

"More skulduggery from Rick?"

"He's planning on getting rid of a few people."

"Shit, who this time?"

"A guy called Chris McCaffery and Ruby Landers."

Mikey's scalp prickled—any plan to attack McCaffery might catch Kitty in the crossfire. He didn't know Ruby Landers very well but the twins had befriended her.

"Tell me all you know."

52

A rainy night and streetlights dripped along Wickham Street. Lester Gainsford wandered through the nightclub strip for the first time in nine years. Fortitude Valley; the sweaty groin of Brisbane. A new sports store stood on the old Pearl site. Next door was The Apollo; Lester had heard through the police grapevine that Lyle Furner had indeed bought the place in his wife's name. The pale-blue neon tube lighting over the door washed out the acne-scarred features of the doorman and gave him a spectral appearance. Lester's skin prickled as the man squinted at him; Lyle Furner's hired help had a hand-picked-by-Lyle appearance—as mean as a bag of starving Tasmanian devils. Across the street, Pinkie's looked deserted. A fish and chip shop pumped grease into the exhaust fumes that hung over Fortitude Valley. Lester strolled on, watching the young people out on the town. Youthful faces shining, full of life—happily unaware of the depravity that thrived in their city. Brisbane's underbelly of pimps, dealers, hookers, thugs, and SP bookies thrived—courtesy of corrupt elements in the police and government. How many knew a gangster cop controlled the city from within the ranks of the police force? His reign of terror intimidated all: the judiciary, politicians, and his colleagues—from top to bottom. This city had no problem with the powerful mafia-style gangs that flourished in other cities. Fear of Lyle Furner kept them away.

How many of these kids know about the fire-bombing of The Pearl? Do they even care?

It happened eight years before and Lester thought about it every day, it still tore at his guts. His greatest failure.

He passed by The Capital with its overdone façade and gaudy neon sign.

Rick still hasn't mastered the art of presentation.

The doorman nodded hello and flicked the cigarette wedged between his fingers.

The traffic snarled past, a chorus of engines and exhaust gas. Across the street and on to the next block Lester ambled, Poppy's looked busy; he recalled a raid he'd participated in ten years before. They hadn't found any illegal activity—Poppy Francesco made regular payments to the bagman. Lester didn't care; he considered raiding a gay bar a waste of police resources. A few gays and drag queens on a night out with friends never hurt anyone. Their only crimes were against traditional Western apparel.

Next to Poppy's stood the aptly named, Phoenix Pearl; the once derelict Burgess Cinema never looked so good. Lester slowed for a look; the doormen were well dressed and affable. He'd go in at some stage but not that night; he crossed the street, made for Ruby's Wine Bar further along, and halted—moving into the shadow of a building as a man and a woman approached. The man wore black trousers and jacket, the woman a long black cat suit, the kind favoured by dancers. Over it she wore a black hooded sweater that covered her hair. Tall and slim; Lester knew that body well—Kitty. Dressed that way, he concluded she was working; therefore, her companion was Chris McCaffery. He watched them separate; McCaffery went into Ruby's and Kitty down a side alley towards the back of the building.

****

Chris looked back to see Kitty's dark form disappear down the alley to the laneway behind Ruby's Wine Bar. That he had to pretend again to be a rock spider gave him a sour taste in his mouth. He breasted the bar, ordered a scotch on the rocks and resisted tossing it down in one gulp; he couldn't afford to get drunk.

"Back again, Mr Bendell?" Ruby Landers' voice, crisp and deep, Throated through from years of smoking that toughened her larynx.

"Yes," he smiled as Ruby took the stool beside him and his skin crawled to think how many men did this because they enjoyed imposing their adult male's lust on a child. "My last night in town, thought I'd come back for seconds."

"Certainly, I'll take the fee and you can proceed upstairs."

Chris fished a couple of fifties out of his pocket and passed them to her.

"It's a pleasure doing business with you, Mr Bendell."

She walked with him upstairs and escorted him along the hallway, he closed his ears to yelps not quite muffled by a closed door—the sound of a kinky exchange in action. Chris hoped Ruby wasn't going to hang about too long, he was anxious to get out of this cesspool. He prayed once again that the police wouldn't raid, he only need ten minutes to snatch the girl and be well away before Ruby knew what happened.

Ruby opened the door and waved him in. "Enjoy."

Through the door ajar, he watched her disappear around the corner and snapped it closed. Jody's eyes glittered with terror; her thin body seemed thinner in a T shirt and shorts. The sight of this little girl hurt—a child deprived of a childhood.

"Are you ready to go?"

Jody nodded; fear widened her eyes.

Chris cracked the door open and peeped through; he eased his head further out. There was no one in sight.

"Give me your port." He took the cardboard case from her; it was pitifully light. "Come, quickly."

He breathed a sigh of relief as she obeyed. He opened the back door, ushered the girl outside and down the stairs to where Kitty waited. Kitty slipped her arm around the girl's shoulders and drew her away. Men appeared from behind; Jody squealed in terror as a man made a grab for her. Kitty hit him with the barrel of her gun and he fell to the ground, swearing. Chris pulled his gun and punched one of the men in the face.

"Run, Kitty! I'll hold them off."

****

Kitty hated to leave Chris but the thin shoulders of the girl shook violently. Her car was just around the corner. If she ran, she might make it. Running feet behind her lent her speed, but as she reached the end of the lane, a black Holden Torana screeched to a halt blocking her path. The window rolled down. "Kitty, get in!"

"Mikey!"

Jody squealed as Mikey fired a shot past them along the lane. A yell of pain told Kitty he had hit his target. She threw Jody into the back seat and dived after her.

"Go!" She glanced back but couldn't see anything in the dark alley. Her heart hammered in her throat with terror for Chris.

****

Mikey gunned the Torana out of the lane, across two lanes of traffic and sped towards the city. Through the cloud of tyre smoke, he saw a bronze Kingswood fall in behind him. Mikey smiled; behind the Kingswood, he caught sight of two Harleys, a Falcon, and a Valiant Charger.

"Down on the floor, Kitty! I'm being chased!"

Mikey sped, weaving through the traffic along Wickham Street, through China Town and screamed left through an amber light and made for the Story Bridge. He checked the rear-view mirror; the car that followed had run a red light and fishtailed out of the corner. It pleased him to see the guy drove a Kingswood. Stanley's five-litre SLR Torana had superior power in a smaller car; the Kingswood had Buckley's to none of catching him. He took the

Story Bridge at one-twenty and eased back on the accelerator. He needed to draw those tailing him into the back streets.

"Hang on, Kitty!"

He turned off onto Vulture Street and a sharp left onto Gladstone Road heading for the Highgate Hill house. The Kingswood made a little ground on him. Mikey led a wild chase and hoped the boys would corner his tail. As he turned down the steep hill onto the side street, he heard a frightened squeak from Kitty. The little girl with her laughed; evidently, she liked to feel her stomach rise into her chest as the car defied gravity. A horn beep later and Maurie opened the gate without Mikey losing speed. In the rear view mirror, he saw the gate close. He stopped and climbed out, passed Maurie the keys with the order, "Park it inside and put the number plates back on. They're in the boot."

****

"Hey, we're safe."

Kitty looked around; Mikey had the back door open. Somewhere nearby, a dog barked.

"Mikey! Thank you! Where did you come from? How—" She unfolded herself from the cramped space behind the driver's seat and fell against him as he helped her from the car.

"My spies warned me what was going down." His arms slipped around her and set her on her feet. "Quick, let's get inside."

Kitty turned to Jody; the girl's eyes wide on her ashen face. "It's okay, Jody. You're safe now. I'm Kitty, by the way, and this is Mikey."

"Where's James? We left him behind!"

Kitty didn't know what to say. Fear for Chris froze her blood. "James?"

She looked up at Mikey. "She means Chris. We were using false names. I'm really frightened for him."

"The twins will be along shortly, hopefully they'll know if he got away. Come on, I'll get you inside. I'm probably going to go out again; I might be gone all night."

With one arm around Kitty, he moved to put his hand on Jody's shoulder; she shrunk away from him. Confusion creased Mikey's forehead, he looked from the girl to Kitty, his eyes quizzical.

Kitty stepped between him and Jody. "I'll tell you about it later," she slipped her arm around the girl's thin shoulders. "Come on, Jody. Mikey won't hurt you. You're safe now; no one is going to hurt you again."

"I haven't got my port. My clothes—"

"We'll get it back if we can, but don't you worry, we'll get you some new clothes tomorrow."

"Where will I go?"

"For now, you'll stay with me. I'll make sure you go somewhere where you'll be taken care of, don't you worry, Jody." It upset Kitty that the little girl stiffened as she hugged her; the child had learned to fear physical contact.

Mikey led them upstairs and into the living room.

"I'll show you where you can sleep."

"I don't think I'm going to sleep. Mikey I should come—"

"You'll have to stay with the girl." He pushed open a door and flicked on the light of a large comfortable bedroom; the pale curtains shut out the city lights. "You can use this room." She looked up at the softness in his voice. "And Jody can sleep in the room next door." He pointed to a room along the hall.

Kitty drew her gun to the sound of heavy boots running up the stairs.

"Whoa there, Kitty-Kat!" Aiden raised his hands as he sighted the gun. "I swear I'm a good guy." Liam followed him into the room.

"Did Chris get away?" Kitty returned the gun to her bag.

"Nuh. We think Jack and Paul followed the guys who captured him but we've yet to hear anything."

"Shit!" Tears stung Kitty's eyes, and Mikey's arm tightened around her shoulders.

What about the blokes that followed me?"

"We got 'em," the twins spoke as one.

"Where are they?"

"Stanley and Terry have them trussed up like Christmas turkeys."

"Who are they?"

"Alan and Dale Ward—they used to be two-bit thugs. Now they're working for Rick and they're still two-bit thugs only now they have more back up."

"Well, they might tell us something we don't know. Let's go." He drew Kitty close and kissed her. "I don't know how long I'll be, but I should be back before morning. There'll be someone on guard all night. Get some sleep."

"Mikey, what are you going to do—?"

He grinned. "Interrogate them—get a statement—whatever it is that you cops do. We'll do whatever it takes to get Chris back."

Kitty listened to their boots on the stairs and heard the door slam. A few minutes later she heard motorcycles roar away. The dog barked again and a man growled a reprimand.

Kitty took Jody to her room, they talked until around midnight and they both yawned.

"I think we should go to bed, don't you."

Jody nodded. She seemed a little more relaxed. "I'm glad you rescued me, Kitty."

"Goodnight, Jody. If you need me, I'll be right next door."

<h1 style="text-align:center">53</h1>

The scene behind Ruby's winebar blurred in Chris' mind. He saw Kitty push Jody into the back of a black sedan and dive in after her, he saw the driver, Mikey Kinane, speed off after his pot-shot winged one of those in pursuit. He had raised his hands and surrendered; he would go quietly, knowing Kitty and Jody had escaped.

"Get in." The man opened the back door of a Cortina. The gun to his head incentive enough for Chris to obey.

"Come on, hurry up!" The driver called to the man who had chased Kitty.

He trotted towards them from the end of the lane. "I've been shot," he stopped by the driver's door, hand clamped over his bleeding upper arm, "Go without me. Alan and Dale are after that prick that shot me. I'll sneak off to Dr Quack's place. I think it's just a flesh wound."

"Well, hurry up. If the cops see it they'll be asking questions."

Chris knew who Dr Quack was, his real name was Fred Quirk; he wasn't a doctor but a de-registered nurse. Chris' heart hammered and his underarms grew wet; these men didn't intend him to live; they never attempted to blindfold him. He carefully took in details of their route. They stopped at the high chain-wire gate of a house in the back streets of the Rocklea industrial area. The house had boarded up windows and looked derelict. He braced himself for what impended. The driver tooted the horn; two men ran out and jumped in the car with them.

"McCaffery, it's good of you to join us."

Chris' skin goose fleshed. Bobby Higgs had a vicious reputation; his presence guaranteed he would die in agony. The driver turned back and drove towards Ipswich. When they drove through the chain wire gates of the old Coal City Meatworks, Chris anticipated a tidal wave of torment. He thought of Wendy, would she get to bury his body?

By torchlight they led Chris into the boning room and someone lit a pressure lantern, the light gradually brightened.

"Take your clothes off." Bobby Higgs' cruel mouth leered. Chris fumbled with buttons and zippers until he stood naked. His courage wavered, fully clothed a strong man might keep his dignity; he could face down the toughest adversary. Strip him naked, it left him diminished and exposed.

"Tie his wrists and ankles."

Secured with rough nylon rope, they raised Chris' arms above his head and suspended him from a carcass rail so his toes just reached the floor.

"Now, McCaffery, where did your whore take the girl?"

"What whore? What girl?" As Chris expected, Bobby took his non-cooperation as an insult. Like an old woman, Bobby Higgs looked for slights everywhere and took offense as easily as most people breathe. People described him as well balanced—a chip on both shoulders. Bobby's choice of weapon that night was a length of ten millimetre steel rope. A yell of pain tore from Chris' throat as the flexible steel lashed his back and bit into his ribs. One of his captors whooped with glee.

****

Lester picked up the old school port and looked inside. A battered one-eyed doll, a dog-eared copy of Dr Zeus' Cat in the Hat, and some clothes. He closed it again and leaned against the back wall of Ruby's Wine Bar.

What the hell was that all about?

He knew where Chris McCaffery's office was; the first thing he'd done when he came back to Brisbane was check on Kitty. He'd go there tomorrow, that kid they'd snatched was obviously a child prostitute; why else would she be in that cat house? Lester had long suspected several of the brothels in this city sidelined in children. He'd had suspicions about Ruby when he'd worked in the Licensing Branch; hers was one of the places that received special protection.

Lester didn't carry a gun that night, he'd only intended to have a drink and catch up with the changes that had happened in his absence. Concern for McCaffery gnawed his insides—bundled into a car at gunpoint didn't bode well. He didn't see the driver of the black Torana, but Lester was confident of Kitty's safety; she had jumped in the back without hesitation. The driver was a crack shot with a handgun, from that distance, even to wing the man chasing Kitty was nice shooting.

54

His brother's scream sent a shiver down Alan Ward's spine. The tape that secured Alan to the high backed chair, prevented movement and forced him to look through a hole kicked in the wall into the next room. His brother, Dale, lay blindfolded on the floor in the dust, rat droppings, and broken chunks of fibro-cement; arms bound to his sides and his legs secured with duct tape. Fat beads of sweat fell into Alan's eyes and his parched mouth tasted of bile, Alan could see only the rubber-booted feet of the big man, the leader of the gang who had taken him and his brother captive. Latex gloved hands wielded the sharp knife that split Dale's earlobe.

"No! Please!" Dale screamed, "What do you want?" A crimson stream leaked onto the filthy floor.

"Do you like working for Rick Campbell?"

"I needed a job and he pays well, that's all!"

"Is he a good boss?"

"He's okay!"

"Well, big brother in there will convey your loyalty back to Rick. You? You've got Buckley's."

"What do you want from me?"

"Where did they take Chris McCaffery?"

"I can't tell you—"

"Can't or won't?"

"Rick will kill me!"

"He won't kill you—I'm going to do that." The man's voice sounded calm and conversational. "Tell me where McCaffery is and I might change my mind."

"I heard they were taking him to some abandoned slaughter house or meatworks—I don't know!" Dale struggled against his bonds. "Me and Alan are just shit-kickers!"

"It's the old meatworks out at Ipswich!" Alan yelled through the hole in the wall, "Please! Dale knows nothing!" The man's foot pulverized the rat droppings as it pivoted in Alan's direction.

Alan heard a knock, the man strode out of view and a door squeaked open, a brief conversation then a grind of hinges and the door closed.

"Ah, so there we have it. A little late, my men have already found where he is, now that leaves me with a decision to make— what am I going to do with you two?" The voice amused; the floorboards creaked under his feet and the hand came into view. Dale screamed again as the man pushed the knife into his groin. "I'll be right back, Dale, you just stay there and bleed out for me. No—don't thrash about, you'll only die faster."

"Dale!" Alan watched as his brother's lifeblood pumped out in fading rhythm. His stomach heaved; vomit filled his mouth and fell into his lap. This was his fault, he had convinced Dale to take the job with Rick Campbell. Rick had assured him they'd be safe, promised that his enemies were weak and at his mercy, the police firmly in his pocket. Rick honoured Alan and Dale with disposing of Les Jones. The search for those responsible had led the police up a dead end street on the wrong side of the river. Les Jones' lacerated body floated in the Brisbane River, a bloated raft of waterlogged flesh; a banquet for crows—light-headed crows. Les had been an epic junkie. After the media frenzy died down, Alan and his brother continued to enjoy their freedom, believing their boss was immune to the law. Then little Ivy turned up naked and sliced up. To Alan's delight, the papers screamed serial killer. His spree had taken two lives and the police knew nothing; Alan had eagerly anticipated a repeat performance. Now, it seemed Rick had a deadly enemy backed by a small army of equally dangerous men—men who also operated outside the law.

A door closed and feet descended four steps, low voices murmured. Feet, hurried away and Alan heard a motorcycle retreat. The rubber boots clunked back up the stairs and the man re-entered the room where Dale lay in an expanding pool of blood. A chair scraped across the floor and creaked under the man's weight.

The toe of the rubber boot nudged Dale's grey body. "Come on, don't start clotting on me." The gloved hand brought a weak cry from Alan's brother as the knife jabbed into his neck and a sluggish flow of arterial blood oozed from the wound.

"Blood pressure's getting low, Dale. This is what you and your scummy brother did to Les Jones, isn't it? Bled him out like an animal? How about little Ivy? That was one of yours too, wasn't it?"

This man had a spy in Rick's camp; he seemed well informed of the manner of Les Jones' death. Ivy Hasted's too.

"Please, I'm so thirsty." Dale shivered and Alan's insides lurched as the metallic click of a pistol trigger cocked.

"I'll give you a drink if you tell me which of your cronies raped poor little Ivy Hasted?"

Alan called through the hole. "There were two of them—German Burt and Bobby Higgs! Please, don't let my brother—"

"There were four of them I'm told—you left out yourself and Dale here. Feel good did it, all dipping your wick in that helpless little girl? You bled her out too, didn't you? Low-life scum."

Alan jumped at the bang; his brother's body convulsed and went still. Alan's bladder drained onto the dirty floor.

"And Alan, take a message to Rick. There's a new power rising in The Valley so he'd better watch his step."

55

The post-kill jitters descended upon Mikey; the balaclava made him sweat. He crept through the darkness with his brothers. Liam promised the rifle slung over his shoulder was one hundred percent accurate. If all went according to plan, he would dismantle it before sunrise and throw it into the Bremer River. His handgun would follow. Creeping through the blackness in the derelict meatworks lit a fire in his guts. Aiden had already scouted the buildings and pinpointed Chris McCaffery's position. In the inky darkness, Liam stopped and grabbed Mikey's arm.

"In there," he whispered. Mikey could hear raised voices and prayed one of them was Chris McCaffery's. He could see a crack of light at the end of a long corridor.

"That leads to a gallery upstairs," Aiden whispered, "Mikey, get up there and see what's happening. We'll be ready to take out whoever you don't."

Mikey removed the Winchester .243 from his shoulder, checked the silencer and clicked off the safety catch. Mikey's jaded nerves calmed as he crept up the stairs and the twins continued towards the voices. He tried to time his bursts of speed with the voices below. If McCaffery's captors discovered their presence, they would kill him as sure as Brisbane Bitter would lose to

Fourex. Through the filth and cobwebs he crept, ahead a shaft of light beamed from an open door. He eased his face around the door jam and his stomach clenched. Hands tied above his head; red, bleeding welts criss-crossed McCaffery's naked body. The man before him panted from exertion as he swung a length of steel rope.

****

"Answer my question, Pig!"

"Suck my dick!" Chris gasped for breath and his vision blackened.

Bobby lashed him again and again. Chris came to with warm liquid streaming down his leg. For a moment, he thought he'd pissed himself but it was one of his tormentors. Stinging, foul smelling urine cascaded over Chris' body. The men's laughter cut as deep as Bobby's wire.

"Where is your whore?"

"I don't have a whore."

The wire bit him again.

"Where is the girl?"

"What girl?"

Again the wire lashed, warm blood glided down Chris' body from stinging wire cuts. Scorching pain seared his nerves. A hard fist smashed his nose and blackness fell. Chris came to with Bobby's livid face inches from his.

"Tell me where the girl is!"

Chris spat a glob of clotted blood into Bobby's face.

"You fucking, filthy, lowlife—pig—cunt!" Bobby screamed, shaking his head to flick the blood and spit from his eyes, drool flew from his outraged mouth. "You just fucking signed your death warrant you fucking—bastard—fucking cunt!" His voice pitched up to a scream.

Chris spat again.

"Let me cut his dick off, Bobby!" The man who had urinated on Chris advanced with a knife.

Chris braced himself.

Not long now, McCaffery. It'll all be over.

He opened his eyes to see a hand with a knife, the other hand reaching for his groin. A crack rent the air and the knife clattered to the concrete floor, the man who wielded it fell against Chris' legs and he swung until he braced his feet on the dead body. Bobby's scream turned to a gurgle as a knife slit his throat. A tomahawk sunk into the skull of the third man and his body kicked and twitched as it thudded to the floor. Another crack from somewhere above and the fourth man fell across his companions.

Men appeared around him, they wore all black and their faces covered with balaclavas.

"Are you okay there, mate?"

"I'm alive."

When they cut the rope that suspended him, Chris' legs buckled.

"Whoa there, mate. Can you stand up?"

"I think so."

"Let's help you get your pants on and we'll drop you to a hospital."

"No. Just take me to the nearest phone box."

"Shit mate, you're in a bad way—"

"I'll be fine. Have you fellas got some change for the phone?"

"Sure."

****

Wendy McCaffery woke to a ringing phone and pounding heart. Such an early call rarely bodes well. She fumbled the receiver to her ear and exhaled.

"Yeah."

"Wendy—"

"Chris? What's wrong? Where are you?"

"I need you to come and get me."

56

A storm approached from the ranges to the west. The humid air shifted ahead of a wind gust and distant lightning flickered. For the second time that night, Mikey poured petrol. This time on a lonely track near Swanbank. The four men he and his brothers had killed sat propped in the Cortina with their wallets open on their laps. Each drenched in petrol, he finished the scene with a dressing of fuel and a wick line to light it. He hurried back with the Gerry can and poked it in the back window.

He winked at the stiff. "Look after that for me, mate."

He retreated, applied Liam's cigarette lighter to the line and blue flames raced to the car; it exploded in a fireball. Satisfied it was well alight he ran back to where Liam and Aiden waited on their Harleys.

****

Dressed in only his Jocks, Mikey dropped a pile of clothing and boots in front of Maurie.

"Burn them."

Maurie looked bewildered.

278

"Maurie do as I say. Burn all of them and do it properly. I don't want one thread to remain; while you're at it, I want you to clean Liam and Aiden's Harleys, from top to bottom, including the tyres and under the mudguards. Do it on the grass and hose any dirt well in. It's important. I'll be checking later."

Mikey trusted Maurie, a friend of their cousin, Stanley McClurg; he had proven his worth. He watched Maurie gather the clothes and boots, and carry them to the old incinerator in the backyard. Satisfied Maurie had them well alight Mikey took a shower. As he climbed out he remembered the only change of clothes he had were in the room where Kitty slept. He wrapped the towel around his waist, crept in and eased the drawer open.

"Mikey!"

Her voice startled him. "Shit, Kitty! You frightened me."

"I couldn't sleep. Did you find Chris?" She switched on the bed lamp.

"Yeah."

She sat up, holding the sheet across her chest, Mikey's gaze dropped to where the hem met her bare skin.

"Is he okay?"

He shook his head. "They beat him pretty badly; we got there just in time."

"No! What—what did they do?"

"He'll recover. He has a broken nose and they flogged him with a piece of steel rope."

"Jesus no—" Kitty squirmed in the bed; her hands clenched. "Why?"

Mikey bit his lip. "You should get some sleep; we'll find him in the morning."

"Where did he go?"

"We don't know. He doesn't know who rescued him—we left him at a phone box, he was going to call someone to come and get him."

"Probably his wife."

"Probably." Mikey felt his growing erection push the towel; with everything that had happened in the past eight hours, it disturbed him he could still feel horny.

But Kitty is that kind of girl.

I better go and get some sleep too."

"Mikey, wait." Kitty's eyes wandered down to where his mood had grown apparent, and she opened the covers. "Don't go."

He stepped over, shut the door and let the towel fall.

57

Thursday.

Farmer, Red-Nut O'Leary found Alan Ward beside his dead brother on a lonely road near Willowbank. Trussed, gagged and blindfolded, hammer blows had shattered his right kneecap and broken both hands. Nearby, the burned out shell of Alan's Kingswood left scant evidence of the guilty party. Seven kilometres away, a condemned house near Mutdapilly burned to the ground while the neighbouring farmers slept. On a lonely road near Swanbank, driving rain beat down on the blackened remains of a Ford Cortina. It would be several hours before a lost tourist found it.

****

Some serious violence had happened the night before. Sergeant Marty Gregor drove along the narrow road near Willowbank and pulled up behind a Falcon ute. He tightened his wet weather gear and stepped from the patrol car into the deluge that had begun shortly after daybreak.

"What have you got for me, Red-nut?"

"Found this young fella lying here all trussed up—bloody terrible! His friend has been stabbed—badly cut up—and shot in the head. The poor bastard is in shock I think, he hasn't said much. Mavis Creed came along just after me, she went into town. She said she'd contact you—and call an ambulance."

"Yeah, she's still at the station." Marty squatted beside the injured man. "What's your name, mate?"

"Alan." He shivered; the skin around his mouth, grey.

"What happened to you?"

"Don't know. I woke up here this morning."

"Where are you from?"

"Mt Gravatt."

"How did you get out here?"

"I don't know where I am."

"You're at Willowbank, west of Ipswich. You must remember something."

"Don't remember anything."

Over the roar of pelting rain, Marty heard an ambulance siren in the distance. "You'll have to give us something to go on. Is there a reason anyone would do this to you?"

"Nuh."

Marty had served in the police force a long time; he could smell a rat long before it died.

"Can you give me your full name?"

"Alan Rhodes."

"What's your mate's name?"

"John Smith."

****

Mikey and the twins rode their Harleys home to the farm; they needed to tell Jimmy about the night before and would only do so in the seclusion of their family's farm. Mikey had promised himself he'd never tell Kitty what he had done. He wanted her to remain completely innocent; if the law arrived at his door, she could plead ignorance. Killing another human was a chasm he'd stepped across and could never return to join the unsullied.

With a mug of Irish coffee each, the brothers sat on a circle of logs in the shade of the mango tree. A willy wagtail flitted after fruit flies around the fallen fruit.

"I should have been there too." Jimmy raked his scalp. "We're all in this together."

Aiden grinned. "Next time we'll give you more notice."

"And there will be a next time." Mikey scowled. "We haven't caught the bastard that started the fires yet. He's going to get special treatment."

"Are you okay, Mikey?" Jimmy studied his face.

"Yeah—I dunno. When I'm out there kicking arse I'm right on top of it—like I enjoy it. Then I see you guys and the guilts get me by the throat; my catholic upbringing comes back to bite me. Maybe I wasn't born to be a killer."

"None of us were, Mikey." Aiden tossed a flying fox sucked mango at the willy wagtail; the tiny bird chattered angrily. "We swore long ago we'd get vengeance. It won't make Mum and Dad and Craig rest any easier but we'll go to our graves better men for it. We'll leave a better world behind us."

Jimmy shifted on the log. "Don't dress revenge in finer clothes than it deserves, Aiden. It's a dirty game. Blood for blood. We chose it—we're in there up to our elbows."

"The enemy set the tone for this war—no holds barred." Liam set his cup on the log and pulled out his cigarettes. "Those guys we wasted last night have been prancing around for years, doing whatever they want with no one to challenge them."

The mug burned Mikey's hands as he squeezed it. In unguarded moments, visions of the redbrick fortress of Boggo Road haunted him. "I kind of wonder when it's all over will my conscience walk me into the nearest police station and have me fess up."

"If you do that, you'll be dropping us into it too." Liam took a swig of Irish coffee. "Why did we work so hard to cover our tracks last night if you're going to confess anyway?"

"We're doing this because the justice system failed us, remember?"

Mikey nodded and smiled. "Don't worry, our secret is in safe hands here."

"Let's make a pact. When all this is over, if we're not dead or incarcerated," Jimmy stretched out his legs and gazed at a hawk gliding above the sugarcane, "we'll dedicate the rest of our lives working for the good of humanity."

"I can do that."

"Me too."

"And me."

"Mikey?"

"I'm in." He raised his mug. "Humanity."

He batted away an image of the bullet hole in Dale Ward's head.

****

Chris opened his eyes to a tap on the open door of his room. He was awake but the swelling from his broken nose made it hard to keep his eyes open.

"Don't try and hug me, Kitty."

"Chris, I feel so bad. I shouldn't have left you—"

"You did as you were told, Kitty—you took Jody and got out of there. Where is she, by the way?"

"She's in the kitchen talking to Wendy."

Chris tried to sit up, Kitty hastened to adjust his pillows. Every inch of him throbbed and ached. He had refused to go to hospital—whoever it was that wanted Jody so badly wouldn't see the hospital as a deterrent. The men who'd taken him captive were all dead, killed by men in black balaclavas—Chris had a fair idea of his rescuers' identity; there weren't too many men that tall knocking around. The Kinane brothers' secret was safe with him.

The doctor who treated him declared the wounds superficial and while painful, they would mend quickly. He'd stitched the deeper cuts, prescribed a course of antibiotics, gave him a tetanus shot and put him on a drip.

"What should I do with Jody?"

"Leave her here; Wendy will take care of her."

"She was incredibly level-headed; there were no hysterics when I dragged her away."

"She's probably used to being handed around like a stray kitten."

"Poor little girl. It took a while to draw her out but we talked for ages last night—I think she has been ignored all of her life."

"Well, we're going to have to hide her for a while."

"What do you want me to do while you're out of action?"

"Continue with the work you're doing and watch your back."

"Shouldn't I be here, guarding you guys?"

"Keep your pager on; if I need you I'll buzz."

"I'll come and check on you tonight."

"If you must."

58

Friday.

Burt popped another pill and dislodged himself from behind the wheel of his Merc. He left his lucky pick handle, he wouldn't need it for this job; Ruby would give no trouble. Rick had suggested a lethal injection of Nembutal but Burt harboured a phobia of needles. His last tetanus shot saw him passed out at the feet of a bemused little nurse. Few people inhabited Ruby's Wine Bar when Burt arrived at midnight, speeding like an express train. He took in the room; the lone barkeep polished glasses behind the bar, lost in his task. The pianist tiredly strummed chords while the resident barfly dribbled a ballad over his shoulder. Burt would kill two birds with one stone that night. Incredibly horny after spending the last two weeks obsessing over the blonde, he thought getting an old boiler to dance on his hips might be just the ticket. Then he'd carry out Rick's instructions.

Ruby appeared at his side with her ever-present tall glass of amber liquid and silver cigarette holder. "Burtie! What can I do for you, Luvvie?"

"I've been a naughty boy, Ruby."

"Well we can't have that, Burtie. Upstairs with you!" Ruby marched a contrite Burt up the stairs, past the pink room and around to the red room—red carpet, wallpaper, and furnishings. The mirrors on the ceiling reflected every inch of the spectacle.

"Now you sit down and think about what a bad boy you've been!" She swatted his bovine rump and pushed him towards a straight-backed chair. Beads of drug induced sweat popped from his big moon face as he listened to Ruby suiting up; she emerged from behind the screen wearing her black leather corset and carrying a crop. Brittle blond curls poked from under the bright red wig. The knee-high boots flopped around her skinny calves and an ill-concealed safety pin took up the slack in the elastic of her suspender belt. "On your feet, Motherfucker!"

He lumbered to his feet and towered over Ruby. The crop brought a yelp from Burt.

"Pull down your pants, boy! Move!"

The wooden floor creaked under him as he obeyed.

"Bend! Now!"

Burt exposed his arse and whimpered. Each lash pumped lust into his loins until he was rock-hard.

"Bad! Bad! Vile fucker!" Her voice rose; her lash fell.

Burt squealed. "I am!"

"You evil, devil spawn!"

"I am! I am!"

"Whore's bastard!"

"Hit me harder!"

"Harder?"

"Harder!"

Ruby circled, slapping her gloved hand.

"Please! Hit me!" Burt shifted his arse to follow her steps.

Ruby lunged. The bedsprings shrieked as she shoved him down into the red satin and straddled him, lashing with words and whip.

"Take it, scum! Take it hard!" She rode him and lashed his nipples.

Burt rather regretted what he was about to do, he loved a good thrashing and nobody in this city did punishment-fucks like Ruby.

"I'm not a bad boy, Ruby," Burt whispered. He circled her neck with his hands, a slight smile as he tightened his grip. "I'm a cunt."

She smiled back, but her gaze hollowed to the truth, her body stiffened, the whip fell to the scarlet sheet, she clawed at his fingers—tugged at his wrists. Burt's orgasm exploded as he strangled the dominance out of the dominatrix. His living semen gushed into her body as the life-light died in her eyes.

He left by the back door, red-arsed and tripping balls.

****

Saturday.

Rick sat at his desk, staring at the melting ice in his empty glass; a pale amber tinge a reminder of the stiff scotch he'd poured two minutes before. His hand trembled as he rubbed the back of his neck. Somewhere a radio cut through the silence with the faint strains of a familiar song. The wall clock ticked a disparate rhythm. The boost he'd received from the line of coke had worn off, now he needed a motorway of the stuff.

After Kev Dallas' death he had comforted himself with the knowledge that he still had the Ward brothers. Rick turned his eyes from the glass to the phone; two days had passed since Alan called him with a report. Dale was dead, Alan scared witless and physically crippled—kneecapped and both hands broken. He hadn't heard from Bobby Higgs and his team. Rick didn't know if Chris McCaffery was dead or alive. Alan had said a tall slim woman dressed like a ninja had snatched little Jody, and he saw them dive into the back of a black Torana. Alan and Dale chased it.

That's when things went guts up.

Rick surmised the tall woman would be the one McCaffery had with him when he came in to The Capital. That didn't help much—he didn't know her name. Perhaps Burt might have found out who she was—his obsessions were as legendary as they were ludicrous.

And speaking of Burt, I wonder has he taken care of Ruby for me? Rick's glance bounced from clock to phone to door. He hadn't seen Burt yet—Burt would show up when Burt showed up, that might be in one hour, or it might be one week. Rick hoped he'd turn up sometime that day and give him some badly needed good news.

Footsteps stirred him from his reverie and John the Bagman stood in the door.

Rick's face twitched, his nose prickled from the cocaine. "I suppose you want your retainer?"

"Yes, but that's not the only reason I'm here. Do any of your men drive a TD Cortina?"

Rick's chest began to burn. "Yeah—a blue one."

"Harry Redgate?"

"Yes."

"Yes I thought he worked for you. I'll take your word for it about it being blue. They found it yesterday out past Swanbank, completely burned out and the remains of four people inside. Whoever did it was an expert. Forensics got the engine number—that's all they had to go on, there were no number plates and there was nothing to identify anyone. Don't worry; the case is in safe hands."

Rick sighed.

Yarrow's eyes shifted in the direction of the drawer where Rick kept his payoff until collection time. Rick knew the drill; keep forking out money and the bent cops would keep the Snow Whites from his door. He opened the top drawer, pulled out a paper bag and passed it to Yarrow.

"So, did Bouncy Harold get on someone's wrong side?" Yarrow opened the bag and rubbed Rick's frayed nerves by counting the money.

"I had nothing to fucking do with Harold's death! It was probably one of the kids he fiddled with somewhere along the line—don't fucking try to pin it on me!" The clock seemed to have stopped.

Where the fuck is Burt when I need him?

"Okay—okay. Don't get off yer bike—I was just askin'."

"I've had the jacks on my door step twice now, asking questions. Tell Furner to fuck them off!"

"I can try. Furner doesn't have much influence over the Snow Whites."

"If you don't mind, Yarrow, I have work to do."

"Okay—okay. Hospitality is getting thin around here." Yarrow snatched a glance at the bottle on Rick's desk, turned on his heel and stumped out.

Rick scowled after him and poured another slug of Scotch. "Hospitality my arse."

****

Yarrow tucked the bag under his arm as he exited The Capital; he too had work to do—today was payday for the grafters. He was a little disappointed though; he had hoped Rick might give him some clue who was responsible for all the violence. Such information could bring a small profit. The events of two nights before had made some in the police force nervous. Lyle Furner, however, was unconcerned.

Ah well, on to Ruby's next.

59

The doormen stood like sentinels in front of the Phoenix Pearl. It was 7:30 and Fortitude Valley remained quiet, the action didn't start until much later. Lester didn't plan on hanging about, he only hoped to find Kitty; he'd called Chris McCaffery's office and the receptionist said Chris and Kitty were both out; she didn't seem disposed to give him a clue where.

The doormen waved him through, and he joined the sparse patronage sitting at tables or leaning on the bar. The DJ had the volume at a comfortable level. He bought a beer and looked around; there was no sign of Kitty.

****

Kitty and Mikey spent all afternoon in bed. They'd reunited and neither wanted to spend a moment apart. At the Phoenix Pearl, they locked themselves in his office and began again.

"Quick, get this off." Kitty laughed as he tugged at the blue chiffon, whipped off her dress and dragged her free of underwear. His hand was warm on her leg as he lifted it, opening her to him. Kitty sighed as he laid her across the desk. Her legs wrapped around his hips pulling him in, his arms held her tight.

They redressed and composed themselves. Kitty reapplied her lipstick and ran a comb through her hair.

"How do I look?"

"Like you've just been fucked one time too many."

"Oh no—do I really?"

"Of course not. But if you did I'd be happy—I want the world to know the prettiest woman alive is mine."

"I love you, Mikey Kinane."

"And I love you, Kitty Olsen."

Kitty clung to Mikey's hand and they emerged into the clubroom; to her left she caught a glimpse of the blond giant she had seen at The Capital, then from her right a man descended on her.

"Kitty!" Lester Gainsford's arms clamped around her and he kissed her hard on the mouth.

"Lester!" She allowed him to hold her a few more seconds before she eased out of his arms. The confusion on Mikey's face turned to displeasure as he looked from Kitty to Lester.

"Mikey, this is Lester Gainsford—we worked together at Longreach."

"You did more than work by the looks of it."

****

Lester extended his hand but Mikey Kinane didn't move.

"Mikey, I'm pleased to meet you." He'd been so happy to see Kitty, it hadn't occurred to him to look at who stood beside her.

Kitty had never told him just how big and imposing Kinane was. "Hey—sorry, Mikey. She's yours; I know that—I'm just happy to see her." He kept his hand out and watched the murder slowly leave his eyes. The hand that shook Lester's was strong and hard; he hoped Kinane would never raise it against him.

"I'm pleased to meet you, Lester." He didn't look especially pleased.

"I'd like to talk to you and your family some time."

"You would?"

Lester looked at Kitty; she had obviously not mentioned him to Mikey.

"I owe you all an explanation."

"About?"

"About the investigation into the death of your parents and brother."

Mikey's face froze, a muscle in his jaw twitched.

"I'm sorry, Mikey—forces beyond my control obstructed the investigation. I want you and your family to know exactly what happened, because the court case didn't uncover the truth. I still don't know who was responsible, but I haven't given up."

"I see."

****

"Come and dance with me."

The voice beside Kitty startled her, a sweaty hand grabbed her arm and she jerked out of his grasp. German Burt's face darkened as Kitty shrunk away.

"No—thank you, I don't dance."

The garlic on his breath would kill a vampire at forty paces. "You will with me—"

Mikey planted himself in front of Kitty. "You heard her mate, now off you go."

Lester pulled Kitty away, "Keep out of the way, Kitty—this bastard is German Burt—he's as mad as a March hare."

As Burt closed in on Mikey, Kitty noticed he had one eye that looked at the wall. His teeth bared and he butted at Mikey's face with his enormous head. Mikey jumped aside and slammed his fist into Burt's midriff; the blond giant grunted and his eyes narrowed.

"You're gonna regret that!"

"Fuck off, mate." A chill shook Mikey's voice and the nightclub security appeared. Burt swung a roundhouse punch; Mikey ducked and slammed his fist against Burt's ribs.

"Mikey!" Kitty yelled a warning as a switchblade clicked in Burt's hand and he advanced again. Vince and his security team closed in, Vince's truncheon struck Burt's arm with a dull clunk. He snarled as the knife fell from his stunned hand. Purple faced, he glared as Mikey stepped back in front of Kitty. Lester helped the four security men halt Burt's attack.

"Put him on the floor." Lester pulled a set of handcuffs from his pocket. He cuffed Burt's hands behind his back. "Alright, call the cops. You're under arrest for affray, by the way," he nudged Burt with his foot, "so just lie still until the law gets here."

"Are you a cop?" Vince Wilkins looked closely at Lester.

"Used to be." Lester turned back to Kitty and smiled. "Well that went better than I feared it might."

"Who the fuck is that big ape?" Mikey's arm trembled as it settled around Kitty's shoulders.

"German Burt—professional thug and all-round nutcase. He's Rick Campbell's little brother and one of his attack dogs."

"He didn't sound German."

"He's not. He just likes to pretend he is. He comes from a small town out on the Southern Downs where the gene pool is a bathtub."

Kitty laughed and slipped her arm around Mikey's waist. "Lester, it's good to see you. Have you really quit the force?"

"Long service leave actually, but I'm thinking I might not go back. It's high time I branched out and became a human being."

60

Sunday.

Lester knocked on the door of the well-cared-for Queenslander. He thought he might buy a house like this one, now that he contemplated a career change. He spent the last eight years living in police force accommodation and hadn't mowed a lawn or tended a garden for quite some time.

"Hello, can I help you?" A slim, blonde woman with a path of freckles across her nose greeted him. She looked him over with sky-blue eyes that had patches of gold sprinkled across the iris; Lester had never seen such spectacular eyes.

"My name is Lester Gainsford; I'm looking for Chris McCaffery."

"Just a moment." She turned back inside. It worried him a little that she left the door wide open.

Being a cop has made you paranoid, Lester.

Soft voices reached him where he waited and a moment later, she returned.

"Come in, Lester. I'm Wendy—Chris' wife."

"I'm pleased to meet you, Wendy."

"Detective Inspector Gainsford, I believe that is your rank these days." Chris McCaffery rose painfully and shook Lester's hand. With his black eyes and broken nose, he looked like he'd done a few rounds with Tony Mundine.

"A promotion that didn't come without a fight, McCaffery."

"Kitty said you might drop by."

He held out the old school port. "I believe this belongs to a friend of yours."

"Oh!" Wendy McCaffery's eyes widened. "Jody!" She called then added in a whisper, "she's been fretting about that port."

A thin girl appeared in the door of the living room, the lines of her body stiffened when her eyes fell upon Lester.

"Come on, Jody—it's okay. Lester won't hurt you."

"Hello Jody," Lester smiled. "I just dropped around to bring you your port."

The girl's eyes rounded as he passed it to her. Lester took a seat and watched as the girl set the port on the floor and opened it. She took out the Dr Zeus book, set it on the coffee table then gathered up the one-eyed doll and hugged it. "Thank you," she whispered, rose and left the room, taking the doll with her.

"Poor kid," Chris shook his head. "She's had a shitty life."

"It will get better," said Wendy. "Chris and I are going to foster her and hopefully adopt her."

"Good, I'm pleased to hear that." Lester picked up the dog-eared copy of Cat in the Hat. An inscription inside the cover said, *To Jody, Merry Christmas, from Nanna Creevey.'* He flicked through the book and listened as Wendy told of her hopes for Jody. As he closed the back cover, he caught a glimpse of some shaky handwriting and fumbled it open again.

*Tonit eval peple are gon to burn the purl and valley star.
Pinkie told me all ebout it. He nos who, I can't rember.'* The shaky
hand had dated the statement and signed the name: *Carla Creevey.*

"Jesus!" he jumped to his feet.

Wendy stopped midsentence. "Sorry?"

"Sorry, I didn't mean to interrupt—look at this, McCaffery."
He passed the book to Chris and watched as he read the statement.

McCaffery blinked at the words before him; his body frozen
but Lester could sense the cogs turning, gears clunking into place.

"Young Rusty Russell did not set those fires, Chris—nor did
Daryl Reid. Daryl was about to tell me everything but Furner and
Doyle got there before I did."

"But they testified in your favour."

A cynical laugh bubbled up out of nowhere. "Oh yeah—
Lester couldn't possibly have done it—wink, wink; nudge, nudge. I
could have done without their 'help.' I can't be completely sure,
but I'm certain that Furner's prints are all over the whole sordid
story." Lester sighed, resumed his seat and recounted that evening
to Chris McCaffery. Kitty was the only other person in the
intervening years to whom he had voiced his suspicions. He
finished to silence and rubbed his temples.

"Ah fu—" Lester cut off the curse as he remembered where
he was and sighed. "Now I know where Carla Creevey's little girl
ended up. Her so-called friends said an aunty had taken Jody but
Pinkie must have handed her straight to Ruby Landers. Bloody
scum! They treated her like a stray puppy, just hand her over to

anyone who had a use for her." Lester's eyes shifted to Wendy as she sniffed. "I'm sorry, Wendy." Tears prickled his eyes.

As soon as I find him, Pinkie Pinchester is in for a straightener.

****

Chris studied Gainsford, apart from greyer hair, he hadn't changed. "And I thought my experience with the Police Force was bad. I remember all the rumours from back then; I was still a constable at the time. You sure had the boot sunk in, didn't you?"

"I did. In a way, it was the best thing that ever happened to me—that transfer out of Brisbane. Once I got out into the outback, I was able to get on with the job and actually make a difference."

"Kitty spoke very highly of your work out there."

Lester's eyes crinkled, affection for Kitty evident in their golden brown. Kitty had never said so, but Chris suspected she and Gainsford had been more than friends.

Lester got to his feet. "Well, I guess I'll go and find Pinkie."

"I'll come with you."

"No! No, your reputation is still intact, who cares if I come out of this with egg on my face? I can handle Pinkie. He won't be expecting a visit from me after all these years."

"When you find out who is the guilty party, or parties, what will you do then. You can't take it to the police."

"No, Chris, the time has come to take a leaf out of Furner's book and deal with it myself. Mikey Kinane is an impressive young man; I think I might enlist his help. What do you think?"

Chris swallowed the words that teetered on the tip of his tongue. How could he tell a man so obviously in love with Kitty, that he suspected the one who ruled her heart was a cold-blooded killer? He waged moral ambiguity, from what Gainsford had just told him, Lyle Furner was also a cold-blooded killer whose actions justified the Kinane brothers' violence. "He'd be the man for the job. He and his brothers are a force in themselves."

"He's awfully quick for a big bloke. German Burt couldn't land a blow on him."

"German Burt?"

"He was in the Phoenix Pearl last night; he came up and asked Kitty to dance, when she said no he started to get a bit wild-eyed—if you get my drift."

"So what happened?"

"Vince Wilkins, Eddie Holt, and their security team got him down on the floor and I cuffed him. The cops took him away." Gainsford puffed out a breath. "I'm worried about Kitty, having that arsehole getting obsessed over her is the last thing she needs."

"You're right there. Dammit! I picked a bad time to get beaten up. Kinane's more than a handful but he can't be with Kitty all the time."

"I'll try and keep an eye on her." Lester's fingers furrowed his hair. "Well, you get yourself mended, McCaffery. I'm off to pull

Pinkie out of his rat-hole." He took one more look at Carla Creevey's last statement and shook Chris' hand.

61

Pinkie scratched his crotch and unlocked the back door of his defunct nightclub, he'd come to pick up his personal effects. Pinkie's Discotheque; his respectable façade to disguise his links to the skin trade. In its first year, Pinkie's showed a healthy profit; now, he bemoaned a fickle public. He'd cut the live bands after two years and employed a wannabe DJ who cost far less. From chic to bleak.

But it's all over now, Pinkie—back to running pros for a living.

A hard blow across the back of his knees came out of nowhere and Pinkie fell on his back. He recognised the man who loomed over him with the axe handle; he had changed little in eight years since he last saw him from his hidey-hole in the ceiling of the brothel.

"Gidday Pinkie, you're under arrest for being a lying cunt."

"What—what did I lie about?"

"It would be quicker to list what you told the truth about."

"Hell, Sarg, I'm a law abiding—"

Pinkie screamed as his shin stopped the axe handle with a sickening crack.

"Another lie, Pinkie." Gainsford smiled and broke Pinkie's forearm with his waddy. Pinkie suspected most detectives got some kind of a thrill from breaking things. Immediate results unlike much of their work. "Now, you made yourself scarce when I needed to ask you questions about the fires. Interstate were you? More likely hiding behind some hooker's skirt. If you don't want me to break every bone in your ill-bred body, you'd better start talking. Who set those bombs?"

"You got the guy who did it—" Pinkie howled as Gainsford belted his broken forearm; he swallowed the bile that rose into his mouth.

"Hurt didn't it? I'm not a cop anymore, Pinkie, I can kick the shit out of you with impunity. Cough up the names, now!"

Pinkie panted, sweat poured down his face. "I can't—Furner will kill me!"

The axe handle smashed his humerus and Pinkie fainted. He woke to Gainsford poking him hard in the ribs.

"Come on, Pinkie, pay attention! I want those names." Gainsford tapped various parts of Pinkie's anatomy as though trying to decide what to break next. Pinkie cringed; drops of cold sweat trickled from his skin.

"I'll tell you, but you have to protect me from—"

Another blow from the waddy and Pinkie squealed as his collarbone snapped. He puked up a bit of his breakfast.

****

Fury surged through Lester's veins; he controlled the urge to keep hitting the whimpering dog of a man at his feet.

"Like the way you protected poor little Jody after you murdered her mother!"

Pinkie's eyes widened. "Murdered? No, she died of an overdose of pure heroin."

"Funny you should know what killed her."

"I—no—it was all over the news! They said it was pure heroin"

"Which you shot up her arm. I checked. There was another set of prints on that syringe and on the spoon; I know they were never fully investigated. Do you want me to have them re-examined? I lied, Pinkie, I'm only on long service leave." Lester also lied about the existence of the prints; he merely exercised a hunch which had the desired effect. Pinkie's face blanched whiter "I can bring you in if that's what it takes, but you know who runs the police force, don't you?" Lester pressed his advantage. "You want to be banged up in a cell knowing you might get a visitor in the middle of the night?"

"Please, no. Not Furner."

"Then start talking, you fucking weasel."

****

Jack Walker listened, his heart beating in his throat. He had only dropped into Pinkie's to pick up the records he'd loaned the young DJ. He'd been sitting quietly in the DJ's booth, sifting through the albums when he heard the back door open, then Pinkie's panicked voice. He had sneaked around to see the cause of the commotion. A tall, grey haired man beat the crap out of Pinkie with a piece of wood. Jack shrank back to listen, his skin crawled and rage mounted; this was the information he had sought for eight years.

62

Monday.

A sea breeze cooled the front veranda of Mikey's farmhouse. Mikey, his brothers and sisters gathered around the table. Lester Gainsford had asked to speak with the whole family.

"Now, tell us what this is all about." Mikey's voice almost failed him. They were about to hear who had murdered their parents and brother.

Lester's mouth tightened and he inhaled. "First, I must stress—I don't want you boys to go off half-cocked—"

"We'll decide that—"

"Mikey! Stop it." Nola laid a hand on his arm. "Tell us, Inspector."

"I've got the names of the men who planted the bombs that killed your parents and brother."

"Let's have them then."

"Mikey, you're not going to like this—now listen to me, bugger it!"

"Okay—I'm listening." Mikey breathed the fresh air and tried to calm himself.

"They're working for you."

"What?"

Gainsford tapped a fist against the palm of his hand and sighed. "Vince Wilkins and Eddie Holt."

"You're joking." Mikey felt the blood drain from his face.

"They planted the bombs but they didn't make them nor detonate them—someone else did that and I haven't been able to find out exactly who. What I can tell you is who organised the whole show."

Mikey's hands clenched. "Jesus-fucking-Christ, how could I be that easily fooled? I thought they were okay."

"I'm as stunned as you are, Mikey. I honestly thought Wilkins had gone straight; he probably has been straight for the past eight years but Pinkie wasn't lying—by that stage he wasn't capable of making up a lie. He said Wilkins and Holt were blackmailed. A kind of honey trap he said—the oldest trick in the book. Furner got incriminating photos of them and forced them to do the heavy lifting—"

"I don't care what made them do it; I'll kill those bastards."

"First we need to kill Furner and Doyle."

Their heads turned to Gainsford, was he suggesting murder?

Jimmy folded his arms on the table. "Furner and Doyle? Who are these guys?"

As Gainsford told them about Chief Superintendent Furner and his lapdog, Detective Inspector Doyle, the monster inside Mikey reared, ready to strike.

"Okay, so tell us what's the best way to trap these guys?"

"Trap them? Mikey we'll go to the Commissioner—"

Gainsford laughed. "I'm sorry, Nola. What you have to understand is everyone, all the way up to the top live in fear of Furner. He has a dossier of everyone—if he hasn't got it, he'll get it—he'll fabricate one. The minute it looks like an inquiry might happen he'll destroy the reputation of the person responsible. Daryl Reid and Rusty Russell just happened to stumble on what was going down and look what happened to them. They weren't the first witnesses to fall foul of Furner. No, there isn't going to be an easy way—a legal way to do this."

"Nola and you, Fiona, you better go." Jimmy's face looked pale.

"Do as he says." Mikey didn't often give orders to his older sisters but the less they knew the better. Nola's face protested but Fiona took her sister's arm.

"Come on, Nola." Tears glistened on Fiona's pale face.

Mikey stared at his hands as he waited for his sisters to leave, neither of them had the stomach for deadly violence; Mikey hadn't either until their parents and brother were murdered so brutally.

"Alright, Gainsford, tell us how to do it."

63

Tuesday.

Mikey resisted tearing out his hair; his ex-wife had that effect, even now when he only had to suffer her company once a week when she came to collect their daughter.

"You lied to me!"

"Yeah, I did—so what are you going to do, divorce me? Again?"

"I've already done that. I was right about her, wasn't I?"

"Yes and no."

"You were unfaithful to me with her too, weren't you?"

"On one occasion, yes."

Kitty had fled upstairs to the bedroom when Barbara walked in and found her in Mikey's arms, buried to their ears in a kiss that had them both trembling. Barbara reacted as though Mikey was still her husband.

"You told me there was nothing going on!"

"There wasn't at the time, Barbara. Kitty was my girlfriend before you got knocked up."

"I—she was a child!"

"She was fifteen—yes, a bit young—her father thought so too. That's how I managed to let you get your claws into me—"

"My grandmother warned me I was marrying beneath myself when I married a Kinane—"

"But we Kinanes kept you in pretty good style, didn't we? We still do."

"I can do without your money!"

Mikey scratched his forehead; almost every time he spoke to his ex-wife it ended in a shouting match.

Fuck this shit.

"Barbara, don't be ridiculous—I don't mind—Danielle is my daughter too—" Mikey cut off. A shadow in the open front door distracted him.

"Where's me boyfriend?"

Mikey cringed; Margie had poor timing.

Danielle charged to the door. "Margie! Bessie! Come and see what Daddy made for me!"

Barbara gaped in horror as Danielle dragged Margie and Bessie to see her doll's house.

"Who are they?"

"They're friends of mine."

"Friends?"

"Yes, friends. And before you start judging, they're good, decent people. They worked for my father for years."

Barbara hissed like an angry wallaby. "Well, tell Danielle to hurry up, I want to get home."

"Barbara, I need you to stay here, where I can watch you."

"Here? Why?"

"There's a few things going on—you and Danielle might be in danger."

"Now who's being ridiculous?"

"I'm not kidding. I want you to leave Danielle here, go home, get your things, and come back. Please, Barbara, I'm not joking."

****

Wednesday.

"Jack," Paul sat beside him on the couch and took his hand. "What is it? What's wrong—you've hardly spoken for days."

Jack swallowed his emotions. Pinkie's confession tested his self-control. Tonight, when he arrived for work at the Phoenix Pearl, he'd have to walk past Craig's murderers, Vince Wilkins and Eddie Holt. He'd hadn't yet talked to Mikey, to tell him his trusted doormen had killed his loved ones. If Jack followed his instinct and murdered Wilkins and Holt, he fully expected he'd be imprisoned; he worried what that would mean for Paul.

"You said you saw the men plant the bomb under the stage of The Pearl, can you remember what they looked like. I know I've asked you this before, but I have to know."

"I don't know—I was only ten at the time." Paul was quiet, deep in thought. About to speak, Jack halted when Paul drew a sharp breath. "I do remember something! One of them had a bad limp, like one leg was shorter—fuck! Oh shit! Jack! Eddie the doorman! I think it's him!"

"Yes, it's him." Jack's voice faltered. "I'm going to kill him—and Vince Wilkins."

"Kill—Jack? How—how did you know?"

Jack told him about going to Pinkie's and hearing Lester Gainsford beat a confession out of the pimp.

"Pinkie! He's the bastard that put me to work for Ruby."

"Really?"

"I always wondered if he made my mother disappear. She was one of his toms. She was furious after I told her about Ruby's parties—as she left to go to work she said she had a bone to pick with Pinkie. She never came home that night and I never saw her again." Paul sunk low on the couch; his lip trembled. "I'm lucky I found you. Ben thought he was lucky too—for a few years but then he got too old for that bastard. I wish I knew what happened to him. Shane reckons Billy murdered him; he got rid of him because Ben knew too much. Shane says Billy's not his real name."

"Then who is he?"

"Don't know. I'll ask. I'll help you—we'll kill all of them."

"We need to work out how to do this without being caught."

Paul opened his hands, sniffed and smiled through his tears. "Just rock up and blow the bastards away with a shotgun."

"Sounds easy enough."

<h1 style="text-align:center">64</h1>

"Where's me boyfriend?"

Mikey rubbed his face, he wasn't really in the mood for Margie and Bessie.

"Hello Margie—Bessie."

"'ave you got time for apple pie and coffee, Mikey?"

"Sure, Margie."

Bessie moved to fill the kettle and take plates from the cupboard. Margie sat opposite Mikey and peered at his face.

"Ya look tired, Mikey."

Mikey sighed. Twenty-eight, but he might have been a thousand years old. Vince Wilkins and Eddie Holt lived on borrowed time; Mikey would do as Gainsford instructed. The file would land on Furner's desk in about one hour, the twins, and Gainsford would stake out, waiting for Furner and Doyle to appear. Gainsford was confident Furner would find their 'bait' irresistible. His brothers had agreed to let Mikey take care of the Chief Superintendent and his lapdog. He wanted it done that day but he knew it would not. He did not intend to give Furner the mercy of a quick and painless death.

"Yeah, I'm tired, Margie. Having a new girlfriend is playing hell on my sleep patterns."

"Hah!" Bessie set a mug of coffee and a slice of apple pie before him.

"Ya prob'ly don't wanna 'ear this then, Mikey."

"Lay it on me, Margie."

"Rick 'as lost all 'is men, six of 'em in one night I 'eard 'im tellin' Naz and Burt."

"Clumsy of him."

"The only ones left are German Burt and Naz Van Nek—Naz is useless."

Mikey took a sip of coffee; Margie's shrewd eyes fixed on his.

"'E reckons you dunnit."

"Me? I'm just a harmless farmer." Mikey grinned, "You've excelled yourself with the pie, Margie."

Margie brushed aside his Irish.

"Anyway—'e's enlisted that bikie gang, the Ready Tomatas or whatever they call 'emselves."

"Smelly Armada."

"Yeah, them."

"Let me guess, he's going to send them after me?"

"Ya got it right, first time."

And I'm about to rub out my head of security.

It never rains…

****

Liam and Aiden hurried into Mikey's office.

"You called?"

"I did. I need you guys to get down to the Gold Coast and find the Shadow Jackals and hire them. I've heard they're spoiling for a straightener—this can be their opportunity. Rick has just recruited the Smelly Armada to put us out of business."

"But we're about to meet Gainsford."

"I'll do that—is Jimmy here yet?"

"Yep, I'm here." The eldest Kinane brother appeared in the door.

"Jimmy, can you go to my house? Take Stanley and Maurie with you. I need you to sit guard on Barbara and Danielle. Tell Barbara to stay put. She's got the shits with me. Big time—but she'll have to put up with it. Kitty, Wendy and Jody are all over there too. I have to assume Rick knows where I live." Mikey pulled open his desk drawer. "Here's the key to my gun safe. Give Kitty a rifle if there's any trouble."

65

The unused boat shed on the Logan River belonged to Mikey's Uncle, Ryan McClurg, Stanley's father. The twins used it sometimes to warehouse the marijuana before on-selling it to dealers. Mikey and Gainsford sat for hours, watching and waiting.

"Here he comes!" Gainsford jumped down from his vantage point. "He just turned up the lane."

"Has he got his mate with him?"

Gainsford laughed, "Furner doesn't commit any skulduggery without Doyle there to lick his boots clean."

"Okay, I'll take Furner. You get Doyle."

"Furner is going to be so pissed off when he finds out there is no amphetamine El Dorado in this boat shed. Just calf formula and chook pellets."

"Well, I'll give him a couple of days to let the heartbreak wash over him."

"Shoosh! They're here." Gainsford renewed his grip on his waddy and took his position. Outside, car doors thumped; the enemy's approach.

The shed door rattled. "It's locked." The voice sounded discouraged.

"Well of course it's locked—if you were storing half a million bucks worth of cocaine and speed, you'd keep it locked away too, wouldn't you? Force it."

The door shook and remained closed. Gainsford shook his head; a wry smile lit his face. Another hit on the door to no avail. Mikey leaned against the wall and looked at the roof and he too shook his head.

Put your shoulder to it, dickhead.

Furner's voice grew impatient. "Come on, Charlie, didn't you eat your Weet-Bix this morning?"

****

Lyle Furner watched as Charlie Doyle shoulder charged the door for the fourth time; it sprang open, bounced back and collided with the side of Charlie's head.

"Well, well, well. Now doesn't this look promising?" Furner strolled into the shed, as his eyes adjusted to the dark they feasted on shelves laden with packages of powder and jars of pills. On the floor lay boxes, still taped closed. When the official and confidential report of this bonanza landed on his desk, Lyle Furner sniffed a sizable profit on the wind. This enterprise was new, the owner didn't pay protection money; normally he would move to discover who owned it and dispatch John the Bagman to sign them up. However, when he saw the potential value of merchandise listed on the report he decided he might look it over; take delivery of some first class goods. For the past ten years, Furner had averaged eight-hundred dollars a month in kickbacks, the contents of this shed would pay for a nice yacht. "Someone has a very nice business going on here."

"They did," laughed Doyle. "Now we have a steady supply for the next six months by the looks of this lot."

"We'll get the boys over to—" Furner stopped; a hard arm encircled his neck, choking off his words, steel chilled the skin behind his ear. Behind him a struggle and a thud; Charlie Doyle fell to the concrete floor with a grunt of agony.

"Lie down, arsehole, or I'll blow your head off."

The man forced him to his knees and down, his face pressed to the floor. A pair of handcuffs secured his hands behind him.

"Well hello, Superintendent Furner. Still out here policing from the ranks I see?"

"Policing you call it? This prick would put Ned Kelly to shame."

Furner struggled to see who spoke; a man crouched beside him.

"Gainsford!"

"I'd tell you, you're under arrest and read you your rights but let's face it. If I took you in, you'd be out in five minutes flat."

"What makes you think you can take me in, Gainsford?"

"He isn't taking you in, mate."

A pair of R M Williams boots appeared in front of Furner's face and fear crawled over him on prickly feet.

"Let me go and I'll forget all about this."

"What if I don't?"

"I'm a rich man, I can pay you—"

"Forget it—I don't want your red shillings."

"Who are you?" Sweat pooled between Furner's shoulder blades.

"I'm the youngest son of Tom and Mary Kinane. It's taken me eight years but with the help of an honest cop, I've finally caught up to you."

"What are you going to do?" The man's voice chilled Lyle Furner's marrow.

"Dispense the justice you denied my family."

"I didn't deny it, the court—"

"The court, like everyone else, did your bidding." Gainsford's voice was almost as dangerous as Kinane's. "You thought you had silenced me, and for a long time you did. I hope you've enjoyed the fruits of your evil career because today it all ends. Tie their legs."

"Today?" The man in the R M Williams spoke.

Furner rolled on his side to look on the son of Tom Kinane. His stomach clenched; tall and handsome, the young man's blue eyes held pure hatred. His mouth smiled but his eyes didn't.

"Lester, I'm not going to kill these guys today, I'm going to make them suffer first. Then I'm going to burn them alive, like they did to my parents."

"No, please—"

****

"Relieve him of his gun and anything that will identify him." Lester got to his feet and watched Mikey rifle through Furner and Doyle's pockets.

"You carry two guns, Furner? Do you think you're Wyatt Earp?"

Gainsford gave a short laugh. "One gun for police business—the other for Lyle's business, that's how it works, hey Furner."

They tossed everything into an old steel toolbox with a couple of bricks. "That can be dumped out to sea." Gainsford flicked the lid shut with his foot and clipped it closed.

"Lester, please—"

Fuck off, Furner—you've done the exact same thing to how many people? How many witnesses have you had killed? People pleading for their lives? Begging will get you nowhere."

Mikey walked to a shelf at the back of the boat shed and returned with a hammer and a cold chisel. A spike of horror speared Lester's gut.

"What are they for?"

"Hold his mouth open."

Lester had to this point in his life, thought himself unshockable but he shuddered as Mikey Kinane pinned Furner's head to the floor with his knee and wedge the cold chisel against his molar. The hammer clinked on the chisel; Furner screamed and sprayed blood across the floor. Kinane flicked the tooth out with the chisel tip.

"Mikey, what—"

"Removing everything that might identify him—that's what you said."

"Yeah—I did but—"

"Dental records can identify people. Hold his gob open!"

Furner coughed, choking on blood and bone chips. Again, the hammer clinked and Furner passed out.

"There's another one. Fuck, this guy has kept his dentist busy over the years."

Lester's skin crawled as Mikey removed all the filled teeth from both men's mouth.

This has to be the cruellest man I've ever met.

By the time Kinane had finished the dental work, both his victims had lapsed unconscious. Lester's stomach churned as Mikey severed Furner's ear, tossed it on the floor in front of its owner and went to wash his hands and utensils.

Mikey returned, dead-eyed. "I'm sorry you had to see that, Gainsford, but now you know the kind of torture me and my kin have lived with these past eight years."

Lester nodded; no words could express the chaos inside his head.

66

Thursday.

In the middle of the night, Barbara pushed open the door of her ex-husband's room.

"Mikey, I've had enough of this rubbish—"

"Barbara, what do think you're doing?" Mikey sat up, switched on the bed lamp, and looked down at the blonde in the bed beside him. The sheet covered him from the hips down. "Give us a bit of privacy."

"I'm going home, I've been here more than twenty-four hours and no one has tried to kidnap me."

"Well if you're going to go, go—but leave Danielle here. I won't have her in danger."

"These people make me nervous. Those rough old women and these guards, your brothers—"

"No, that's not the problem, Barbara. These people just won't bow and scrape to you; that's your problem. Now go back to bed— I need to get some sleep."

Barbara shut the door; she did not intend to go back to bed. As she turned back towards the guest bedroom, she stiffened as Mikey's cousin, Stanley, trotted soundlessly along the hallway, a rifle pointed at the ceiling. He tapped on Mikey's door and cracked it open.

"Mikey! Come and take a look at this—"

"Oh fuckin' Jesus!" Mikey growled. Barbara gasped as the naked form of her ex-husband pulled the door wide. "What now?" he snapped.

"Get some duds on, man, and come and have a look at this pair of clowns!"

Mikey's eyes narrowed as they fell on Barbara. "Get back to bed!"

****

Kitty stirred and rolled onto her back. "What's all the yelling?"

Mikey smiled as Kitty sat up, dishevelled and beautiful. "Go back to sleep, Baby—Stanley wants to show me something." He pulled on his boxers and followed his cousin.

"Don't switch on the light." Stanley held the door of his bedroom open for Mikey and passed him the gun. "Take a look at the two guys in the driveway."

Mikey exhaled, took the gun and high-stepped across his cousin's untidy room. In the dim streetlight, at the end of his forty-metre driveway two men moved, one dug a hole in the gravel wheel-track, the other held a flat box. Mikey squinted through the telescopic lens.

"Is this gun loaded?"

"Yep."

"Is it accurate?"

"Sure is."

"Is the silencer tight?"

"Yep, just checked it."

"Good. You wanna see some fireworks?"

"Yep."

"Then pin your ears back."

Mikey clicked off the safety catch and aimed for the box the man eased into the hole his companion had dug. He squeezed the trigger and a blast drove him backwards. A shock wave hit the house like an oversized fist, Mikey flinched as the window shattered, glass tinkled to the floor.

"What in fucking hell was that?" Stanley picked himself up and gingerly approached the window.

"A crude land mine. Good thing you weren't sleeping on the job, mate."

"Mikey!" Barbara's baby doll voice pitched up to bat-range. "What was that? What are you doing?"

"Barbara, get back to bed right now! If you had driven out of here like you were threatening to do, you wouldn't be here."

Kitty appeared wearing Mikey's shirt, her feet and long slim legs bare.

"Was that an explosion?"

"Yep. Two wankers were trying to set a land mine in the driveway—"

"Guess it must have blown up on them." Mikey cut off Stanley's explanation of what caused the explosion."

Mikey and Stanley went for a closer look; the mine had blasted a shallow crater in his driveway. The police and fire brigade arrived as Mikey found an arm in the torch light. His front yard looked like a warzone with bits of bikers scattered across the lawn. A couple of Harleys lay prone on the street. Mikey picked up a piece of a torn leather jacket.

"Smelly Armada and one of them is an expert bomb maker by the looks of that hole. Pity they hadn't learned how to handle such a dangerous device. Sometimes they can go off without warning."

"Ah well, you won't have to fertilize your lawn this year." Stanley could always find the upside.

Mikey and Stanley told the police the explosion woke them; the police could find no reason to doubt their word. Even Barbara did as Mikey asked and lied to the police. She shellacked them for allowing violent criminals to walk the streets and finished off by informing them her father, Bill Matheson, the Minister for Main Roads, would hear about the incident.

Mikey shook his head.

Sometimes I almost like you, Barbara.

67

Friday.

The smell of faeces, urine, and stale blood filled Lyle Furner's nostrils. He didn't know how long he and Charlie had lain in the lonely boat shed. He had given up calling for help, no one could hear. Charlie had gone still hours ago, Lyle thought he might be dead. Early that morning he had watched with dull horror as a rat made off with his severed ear. A shaft of sunlight shone through a window high on the wall, Furner watched its progress across the dusty floor, as it moved up the opposite wall it turned dull orange and died. Darkness fell again. Pain and exhaustion crushed the Chief Superintendent and oblivion fell.

A loud click woke him and the door creaked open; the tall figure of Tom Kinane's youngest son strode into the shed and flicked on the light—a single dim bulb high above. Four men accompanied him, the shortest and he guessed, the eldest looked exactly as Lyle remembered Tom Kinane. Furner's eyes bulged, for a moment, his fevered brain feared the ghost of the Valley Star publican had come back to torment him.

"Good evening Superintendent Furner. I trust you slept well?" Mikey Kinane approached, dead-eyed and menacing. "These are my brothers, Jimmy, Aiden and Liam. The guy with the dogs is our cousin, Stanley. We had another brother, Craig, but you've forgotten him, haven't you, scum?"

Furner tried to speak but his tongue had swelled from dehydration and the injuries inflicted by the cold chisel. Infection had set in and to swallow was torture. Oblivion claimed him once more. He woke; someone dragged him across the concrete floor, abrading the skin on his face. Ropes bound hard, heavy objects to his body. Rough hands lifted and swung him side to side.

"One, two…"

Furner landed painfully on a slanted wooden surface, his legs elevated. It rocked about, the sound of water sloshed around him. He was in a dinghy. His eyes widened in terror as he raised his head, coughed and spat as a warm flow of blood seeped into his mouth. Beside him, Charlie struggled against his bonds and made frightened-animal sounds. The sky above was the deep blue of twilight with the orange glow of Brisbane to the northwest. The dinghy rocked as the boat's motor rumbled and gurgled in the slipway. Someone tied a fishy smelling tarpaulin over them.

****

Mikey and his brothers watched Stanley steer his father's boat out into the main channel of the Logan River. He'd made this trip hundreds of times and knew how to avoid the sandbars. They wound their way between Russell and Cobby Cobby Island; around the bottom end of North Stradbroke and out to sea.

"Old Furner's going to be pretty sea-sick by the time we get him far enough out to burn him."

"I just hope one of these waves doesn't swamp the dinghy, I'd hate for him to drown."

"I hope they won't see the flames from Straddie."

"By the time anyone gets there, the boat will have burned to the water anyway."

"Good night for a boat trip." Liam leaned against the railing and sniffed the cold ocean breeze.

The Coral Sea became choppy as they moved away from the coast and across the dark water. The glow of Brisbane faded and the Milky Way blazed white above.

Stanley killed the motor. "Okay fellas, we're seven nautical miles off the coast—now what?"

"Burn them."

****

Furner had never been one for boats or planes; they made him queasy. The ride in the wooden, tarpaulin-covered dinghy had him choking on bile, overcome by pain, dizziness, and nausea. He had tried to roll over, but the heavy objects tied to his back prevented it. Someone ripped away the tarp and Furner could see the silhouette of the youngest Kinane brother standing on the stern platform, one of his brothers used a hook pole to pull the dinghy around close to the back of the boat.

"No!" The word tore from Furner's inflamed throat, his heart hammered and he thrashed against his bonds. Petrol fumes filled the dinghy; the cold, volatile fuel splashed over him, the fumes seared his lungs. "Please! No—wait. We can talk!" Furner rasped and coughed as more blood seeped into his throat. Panic conquered agony and he screamed, pleading with his tormentors. "Please— what—what did you say your name was?"

"Just call me Lucifer, and no, it's way too late to talk about it. You showed no mercy when you burned my kin alive, don't expect mercy from me."

****

"Is that extinguisher ready?" Mikey climbed back onto the poop deck and unhooked the rope that secured the dinghy to the stern.

"Standing by." Liam braced himself against the taffrail.

Stanley fired the engine.

"Ready?" Jimmy held a stubby bottle with a kerosene soaked rag stuffed in the neck.

"Do the honours, big brother."

Aiden lit the rag and Jimmy tossed it. With a whuff, a small shockwave shot across the Coral Sea and a fireball engulfed the dinghy. Stanley gunned the motors and drowned out Furner and Doyle's last screams.

"Well Uncle Ryan will be happy we didn't set fire to his boat." Liam hung the fire extinguisher back on its hook and clipped it in place.

68

Mikey and his kin arrived back at the safe house after eleven p.m. As they mounted the stairs, Chris greeted them.

"Jesus you guys! I was just about to take off—"

"What's the matter?" Mikey's heart dropped to his boots at the fear on McCaffery's face.

"Mikey, I'm sorry. Barbara took off with Danielle; we got a phone call about half an hour ago. German Burt has got them."

"Shit! What does he want? Where has he taken them?"

"Rick is demanding we hand over Jody. I'm guessing—hoping they've taken them to the house at Rocklea. Kitty, Lester, and Maurie have gone after them. I'll draw you a map."

The two-way radio crackled. *'Come in, Chris?'* Gainsford's voice scratchy and breathless.

"Yeah, Lester—go ahead."

'You were right—he's in there—there's only a couple of men. But Chris—Kitty's gone in—I couldn't stop her—have you seen Mikey yet?'

Mikey snatched the handpiece from Chris.

"I'm here, Lester."

'I'm sorry, Mikey. I think Kitty is going to offer herself in return for Barbara and Danielle—'

"Ah—shit—alright, stand by until we get there."

"I'll contact the Shadow Jackals—we're going to need some backup. They were in town this afternoon." Chris reached for the phone.

White faced, Mikey's legs trembled, dread chilled his blood; he could not marshal his thoughts.

Jimmy laid his arm across his shoulders. "It'll be okay, Mikey. Chris, you stay here and look after Jody and Wendy. Stanley, leave both your dogs here with Chris. Come on, Mikey. Stanley, you and I will take your Torana. Mikey, you and the twins follow on the bikes in case we need to chase anyone."

"Let's go," the twins spoke and moved as one.

Mikey rode his Harley to the industrial complex at Rocklea with every fibre of his being taut, ready to tear someone apart. Kitty and Danielle. Danielle and Kitty. The two people Mikey's happiness—his life—depended on. The cold hand of murder again gripped his heart; German Burt would die, as would Rick Campbell.

Nobody touches my daughter. Nobody touches my Kitty.

****

"Daddy!" Danielle threw herself into Mikey's arms. "That man was scary, Daddy. He's ugly."

Mikey couldn't speak as he clutched his daughter against his chest and kissed her forehead.

"Mikey," Barbara appeared beside him, tears streamed down her pale face. "I'm sorry I didn't listen to you. I hope you can get Kitty back, unhurt."

"Barbara, take Kitty's car and go back to the Highgate Hill house. Drive carefully, lock the doors and don't stop for anyone—can you do that?"

"I can."

Mikey gave her a brief hug—her white face evidence of a lesson learned the hard way He let his anger settle for the sake of their daughter, grateful Barbara had learned an ounce of remorse.

"I'll drive her, Mikey." Lester Gainsford's face carried the strain of fear. "I'll come straight back. It's only twenty minutes' drive."

"No, Maurie can do it—we might need you here, Lester."

Mikey kissed Danielle and strapped her into the back seat. As Maurie sped away, Mikey ran with Gainsford along the street to the entrance of the industrial complex and joined his brothers and cousin where they peered around the open gate of a high corrugated iron fence.

"That pair of dickheads haven't twigged that we're here yet, they're too busy craning their necks for a look inside."

A distant flash of lightning revealed the two men. Mikey guessed they had orders to keep watch, but both peered intently through the window. His jaw clenched; Kitty was for his eyes only. The temptation to sneak up and snap their necks overtook him, only Jimmy's calming hand on his arm stopped him. Jimmy nodded to the twins who dashed across the tarmac yard in their socks. A few thuds and grunts, the distracted guards fell to the ground unconscious, bound and gagged.

69

Kitty trembled as she watched Barbara flee with Danielle. Lester would take care of them. Kitty silently pleaded with Mikey to, by some miracle, arrive and rescue her. The realist in her knew her only chance was to engage Burt in conversation and convince him to take it slow. His moon face glistened with sweat as he advanced on her. His wayward eye fixed on her a moment then pivoted to gaze at the wall.

"Couldn't resist me, eh?" Lightning flickered through the window and incandesced his face.

"I guess not." Kitty gulped, her heart climbed into her throat.

Burt chuckled deep in his chest; he reached for the front of her shirt and Kitty shied away.

"Don't you think we should get to know each other first?"

Burt stared, and Kitty feared she might have spoken some foreign language. He pulled off his shirt and the blond fuzz on his shoulders shone orange in the lamplight like an orangutan. His huge arms clamped around her and hauled her against him.

"No—wait—" Kitty's voice lifted as she pushed against him. His body had the texture of a full bag of flour, unyielding—a dense layer of fat covered the muscle and bone; Burt held no hollow spaces. He reeked of garlic and cheap deodorant. "Getting to know each other is half the fun!" She wished her voice didn't have that tremor. Burt squeezed her bottom and ground his erection against her.

"Just shut up—I hate women who talk too much!" His mouth clamped over hers, his lips had the consistency of a dead jellyfish. Kitty tasted vomit in her mouth and tried to pull away. Her shirt ripped loudly and the buttons popped off. He tore her bra away, his tiny pale green eyes fixed on her breasts.

"No don't!" Kitty tried to cover herself. The backhand came fast; Kitty flinched and took the blow to her temple. The wooden floor shook as she went down hard; cold air on her bare skin brought her back to consciousness, she was naked and face down. The only lighting came from a kerosene lantern and between the cracks in the floorboards; Kitty saw unmistakable signs of dried blood. His hard hands squeeze her flesh; she tried again to move away. Burt lifted her and slammed her down on her back, his penis dripped semen on her leg as he pinched her nipple between his finger and thumb. He forced her legs apart, probing with his fingers then his mouth. Kitty kicked at his groin and Burt's fist slammed into the side of her head. Kitty's vision swum with stars and she vomited on the floor.

"Like it rough, do you, cunt? I'll show you what a real man feels like—"

Kitty heard a thud but felt nothing, Burt roared in pain. Kitty opened her eyes to the face she had loved since childhood. Mikey kicked Burt in the face and jumped away. Burt dived after him and

Mikey aimed a pistol at a point between his eyes, it clicked as he cocked it. Burt's nose dripped blood.

"Kitty, are you okay?" Mikey kept his eyes on the giant before him.

"Yes." Kitty stumbled to her feet and gathered her clothes.

"Get your pants on, scum." Mikey's voice shook and Burt's harsh laugh made Kitty's scalp prickle.

"Why? Don't like to see what a full size cock looks like, eh?"

"I'd put them on if I were you, my trigger finger is itching to shoot your knob off."

Kitty shivered as she pulled on her jeans and Jimmy Kinane wrapped his jacket around her shoulders. She looked around for where she had dropped her gun when Burt had let Barbara and Danielle leave. Outside the sound of motorcycles filled the air and Burt laughed.

"Looks like the Armada's here, Kinane—let's see how you stack up against them."

"Feels good does it, hiding behind a gang of bikies."

"I don't hide behind anyone!" Burt's eyes bulged in his red sweaty face. He swiped the trickle of blood from his nose on his bare shoulder. "I'll fight you, one on one pretty boy. No guns, no weapons, just you, me, and the floor. Whaddya say?"

"You don't have to, Mikey." Lester appeared at Kitty's side. "Just stick a bullet in him, it's all he deserves."

"Sure—what are the stakes?"

Another voice called, "We'll call off our fight with you, Kinane—if you can beat Burt, we'll walk away." The Captain of the

Valley Armada's bulky frame filled the door. "We'll always stand behind bravery."

"You'll also call off your war against the Shadow Jackals—if they're happy to let it go—"

"We can do that, but I doubt you'll beat, Burt." Biker Henry, the gang's sergeant at arms' sceptical voice cut in, he muttered to Harley Phil who snorted; his hairy face shimmered with mirth.

Their leather clad subordinates pushed past them. "Well, I'm backing Kinane—"

"My money's on Burt."

"Nah—Kinane."

"How much ya wanna bet?"

While the biker's lay their money down, Jimmy and the twins moved to cover Burt. Their guns all pointed at his blond head.

Mikey removed his jacket. "Okay, we're on. Outside where there's more room."

Kitty stood numb, clutching Jimmy's jacket close to her body. Mikey came alongside, slipped his arm around her, and led her outside. "Did he have you?"

Kitty shook her head; she knew Mikey could not say the word, 'rape.'

"No—you got here just in time."

"Are you okay?"

"I will be."

Kitty pulled back from Mikey's kiss, she could still taste Burt on her lips.

"Sorry, Mikey—I can't—"

"I'll make it better, Kitty."

Kitty pushed her face to his shoulder, breathing his scent. His lips pressed against her temple.

"Watch me kick his arse, sweetheart."

"Mikey, I'm scared—"

"Don't be. I'm not. I'm going to kill him, Kitty."

Outside the high tin walls, more motorcycles roared to a stop. The Shadow Jackals had arrived.

70

Mikey watched Lester lead Kitty towards the gate; he knew if he didn't survive this fight, Lester would in a way, win. If it came to it, Gainsford was the only man in the world he'd be happy to have replace him in Kitty's life.

Jimmy and the twins surrounded him.

"Don't attack his head, Mikey."

Mikey laughed. "Yeah—I won't. His head is the toughest part of him."

"I suspect he's not very fit, but he's a good thirty pounds heavier, so don't let him get on top of you," said Jimmy. "Your best chance is run him ragged, wear him out and then get a hold of him—snap his neck. He's got girly hands and his arms are soft, you have the advantage of being taller—"

"He doesn't look very bright," said Aiden.

"I've seen more brains on a butcher's shop floor," Liam added.

Mikey nodded. "You guys, stay out of it. If I can beat this arsehole we might all be able to live in peace."

"We won't let him kill you, Mikey."

"You might have to. If you finish him off, these bikies will attack like mongrel dogs."

"There's only eighteen of them." Liam and his twin were optimists.

"Anyway, the Jackals are here now," Liam added. The younger bikie gang filed in and took their place behind the Kinanes.

"Are you ready?"

"Yep."

"We've got your back, Mikey."

"Brothers in arms." The twins chimed.

Mikey grinned. "You blokes are the greatest. This one's for Craig."

"Come on, cunt—stop cuddling your big brothers! I'm gonna rip your heart out!"

Burt's words brought scattered applause and a whistle from the ranks of the Valley Armada. Lightning strobed the yard white. Mikey hadn't taken a close look at him when they threw him out of the Phoenix Pearl; he quickly sized him up.

So this is the great German Burt—a big, loose-pizzled blimp.

Mikey's face grew impassive; he stood relaxed and ready, watching Burt's eyes. Burt's shoulders lifted, his legs bent, he fluttered his fingers and narrowed his eyes; his lip curled into a snarl. His feet slipped a little as he charged; Mikey jumped aside and kicked his knee as Burt hurtled by. Dancing on one foot, Mikey turned; he daren't take his eyes off him.

****

342

Burt stumbled to a stopped, turned and appraised his opponent. He'd been drunk when he tried to head butt him in the Phoenix Pearl. He'd forgotten how tall and quick he was. Kinane's face portrayed boredom, except for his eyes—that had something deeper, something threatening.

"Come on pretty boy, have a go!"

"You first, Burtie." A flash of lightning silhouetted the youngest Kinane.

Adrenaline and anger flooded Burt's veins, he'd smashed this man into the ground and then he'd take the blonde—Kitty. Never in his life had Burt so badly wanted a woman and he meant to have her. A growl rumbled in his throat and he charged again, Kinane jumped aside, his fist shot out and smacked Burt's ear; over and over, Burt charged, each time Kinane stepped out of the way and his fist or foot connected. After taking three hard kicks to the arse, Burt stopped; his mouth hung open dragging in oxygen.

"Come on arsehole, fight like a man!" Burt trembled with adrenaline, his loose eye darted around; the man before him remained unflustered.

****

Lester's arm around her comforted Kitty as he drew her away from the baying crowd and into the dark, deserted street.

"You okay, Kitty?"

Kitty nodded. The sting of vomit in her throat stopped her speaking.

His smile barely reached her in the gloom. "I never thought I would see the day when I'd throw the oath I swore out the window, knowing it was the right thing to do. Not the legal thing—but the right thing. Mikey Kinane is a good man, Kitty. Whatever happens in there tonight, I hope you understand the kind of man he is."

"Lester?"

"He has risked everything, trying to tear down those evil…"

Movement behind him distracted Kitty. A big man strode towards them.

"Ray?" A gear shifted in Kitty's mind—something wasn't right. Detective Sergeant Ray Sims clutched his service revolver, his eyes on Lester. "Ray? What—"

Roaring filled her head and time slowed to a whirling nightmare. Kitty watched Sims raise his gun and squeeze the trigger as Lester turned; a dark hole appeared in the side of his head. Hot blood sprayed her face and Lester dropped to the bitumen. The world sank and twisted out of shape. Kitty hit the ground and woke to strong tape binding her wrists and ankles together. The scream stopped in her mouth; Sims had her gagged. His brawny arm encircled her waist and hefted her along the street. He tossed her into the backseat of his car and strapped her down with the centre lap belt. He jumped in the car and sped away. Kitty couldn't tell which direction he travelled; tear-blurred streetlights, the glow of traffic lights—red, yellow and green. She slid about as the car turned corners—right then left. Braking and accelerating through the city. Rain began to fall as Sims increased his pace.

Lester. Is he dead?

She hoped with all her heart that somehow he had survived.

How could he survive? That bullet went right through his head.

For the first time in this whole, horror evening, Kitty cried. Raw sobs shook her; tears flowed unchecked across her face onto the vinyl seat, wetting her cheek and hair.

****

Mikey's mouth twitched and he forced his face back to impassive. Burt launched at him again, this time he caught Mikey with his shoulder and knocked him down. Burt staggered sideward. Heavy breathing and ponderous footfalls—Burt closed in. Mikey rolled. Sprang to his feet and ducked. Burt's roundhouse punch grazed Mikey's head. The momentum of his punch spun Burt side on and exposed his flank. Mikey's fist sunk into his kidneys, Burt grunted, dropped to his knees and moaned. Mikey swung his boot at the monstrous jaw and Burt's teeth clacked.

"Nice work, Mikey!" Jimmy's voice cut through the cheers and whistles of the bikers. Mikey had no time to take a breath, German Burt staggered to his feet; his eyes wavered and fixed on Mikey's face.

"I'm going to kill you for that, you little pansy."

"Who are you calling a pansy? I've seen harder nuts in a Christmas stocking."

Burt snarled; he charged and roared; a great bull of a man. Mikey skipped aside and Burt lumbered to a stop, turned and prowled back, this time circling.

Well look at that—he is capable of learning.

Red-faced and sweating, Burt puffed and his mouth gaped. Mikey sensed an easy win; evidently, Burt had earned his reputation from surprise attacks on carefully picked opponents. His bulk was mostly fat; the underlying muscle soft. Around Mikey's age, Burt had grown lazy.

Burt closed in, his hand jabbed for the face, Mikey grabbed his wrist, pulled him in and rammed his elbow into Burt's throat. Burt fell back, coughing and Mikey's fists hammered the point of his chin. Burt fell on his back and Mikey dropped his knee into his groin. Burt curled into a foetal position and Mikey kicked his tailbone. Burt howled, rolled face down, clenched his butt cheeks and twisted the length of his legs together. Mikey smiled and jumped on Burt's calf and hyper-extended his knee. A quick sideward kick smashed it completely. German Burt roared in agony. Mikey regained his balance, gripped Burt's wrist, stuck a foot on his shoulder blade and jerked his arm skyward and twisted, a satisfying pop dislocated Burt's shoulder. Mikey gave a hard kick to the back of Burt's elbow and snapped the joint. He dropped Burt's limp arm on the ground and turkey-tromped his hand.

"Had enough?"

"I'm gonna kill you, cunt!" Burt panted and struggled to regain his feet. He bellowed in pain; flecks of foam flew from his mouth as Mikey body slammed him face first into the bitumen. He took hold of Burt's neck and head, twisted until he had Burt's head poised—ready for the final neck-snapping jerk.

The spectators' feet scuffed all around as they closed in for a better view, none spoke. Expectation bristled.

"Now, all I have to do is give one little tug and your neck will snap. Do you want to die?"

"You haven't got it in ya!"

Mikey pulled and Burt's neck cracked. The big man yelled in fright.

"That'll put you in a neck brace. The next one will kill you— *auf wiedersehen*, German Burt—do you want to die?"

"Go on, Kinane—snap his neck for him!" The bikies were a bloodthirsty mob.

Burt grunted; subdued by the pain in his neck. He breathed in loud gasps, his mouth hung open. Mikey tightened his grip. Where was Kitty? Did he really want to kill a man while she watched? Did he even want to kill again? He'd taken so many lives in the past few months—would this be one too many?

"Okay—so you want to die."

"No! No."

"You want to live?"

Burt's voice a harsh whisper, "Yes."

"I can't hear you."

"Yes!" The word croaked from his injured throat.

"You want to live? Say it so everyone can hear!"

"Yes!" Burt rasped, "I want to live."

The bikies bayed like a pack of hounds. A lone voice cut through the melee. "Ah boo! Ya gutless bastard!"

Mikey thought it rich coming from a group of men who drew their courage from the safety of the pack, fighting as a gang, never as an individual.

"Do you give up?"

"Yes!"

"Say it louder."

"I give up!" Burt screamed.

"Good. Stay away from me and mine! Next time I will kill you."

Boos and whistles; disgust and celebration. Fists punched the air. Their roars might shake loose the roof timbers.

Mikey let him go and regained his feet. As Burt lay struggling on the ground, a demon made Mikey grab his uninjured leg, twist his ankle and kick his knee. The cheers of forty bikies failed to mask the crack.

"Someone get him an ambulance." Mikey walked back to his brothers and looked around for Kitty.

71

Grief over Lester screamed for attention as Kitty dragged her mind to her dilemma, survival in the shadow of certain death. She rubbed her face on her sleeve, slowly the edge of the tape lifted, peeling back from her mouth. The tape on her wrists and ankles presented a bigger problem. She wriggled her legs, spreading her knees and elbows. One thread at a time, she loosened her sticky shackles. Rain lashed the car, crashing thunder and lightning. On and on, Sims drove through the night. His pace slowed and began winding. Gravel spattered in the wheel arches and water dashed the underside of the car as the wheels cleaved puddles. Lightning flashes silhouetted trees against the stormy sky. Kitty slid forward against the seatbelt as the car slanted and braked.

"So." Sims killed the motor to darkness. A crash of thunder followed by a flicker of lightning. Rain and eucalypt leaves lashed the windows. "Here we are. We're going to get wet but you're a tough lady, aren't you, Kitty?"

"Ray, what are you doing? You killed Lester—"

Sims climbed out and opened the back door.

"Clever girl, to remove the gag. Won't help you out here though."

"Where are we?"

"Somerset Dam. We're going to spend a night in my private island shack, Sweetheart."

Terror jacked up Kitty's heartbeat. "Ray, please—"

"Ah, pretty damsel, I've always wanted to see what you have between your legs. But fear not, I'm usually not as violent as my little brother, Burt."

"Burt?"

"German Burt—my little brother. Rick just knew he'd stuff up so he put me on the case. I never stuff up."

"What—why? Why are you doing this?"

"My older brother, Rick Campbell wants little Jody back. Your big stud, Kinane would do anything to get you back, wouldn't he?"

"He won't give up Jody—he's not like that."

"We'll see. I don't care—I get to fuck you and he's going to die anyway. Old Biker Henry is going to release Kinane from this vale of tears tomorrow night. Stick a bullet in him when he arrives at his nightclub. Rick has it all arranged—all mapped out, right down to where old Henry needs to wait and what kind of gun he'll use…"

Kitty's neck cramped as she gazed up at Sims, lightning flashes backlit his head, shoulders, and his protruding ears; he seemed impervious to the deluge that plastered his hair to his head. If she could unshackle herself, she'd attack. She'd had her gun tucked in the waistband of her jeans but it was gone.

"…just wait behind the building outside the loading dock, he said. Kinane always parks his car in there, he said." The storm crackled and boomed. "Yep. Bang, bang. The big stud dies."

Kitty shivered and cold rain blew in on her face. "Why?"

"Kinane knows too much. Knowing too much about my big brother, Rick, will get you killed every time. He's the state's top tier drug trafficker with unusual appetites, how do you think he has survived this long?"

Kitty swallowed her terror. "And where do you fit in?"

"I'm the middle brother, the one he calls on when he can't afford to have any fuck-ups."

Her skin crawled. "Ray, please let me go."

"So you can rescue your big stud? So you can give evidence against me? Don't think so, honeybun."

"Please, Ray—don't do this—"

Sims unbuckled the seat belt and dragged Kitty into the deluge, through sheets of water, pricked and dimpled by the storm. Rain striped his torch beam as he carried her down a steep embankment and dropped her on the ground. Lightning flashed over the floodwaters—a creek or river. Kitty could hear the rustling of heavy fabric and the whip of ropes. His arm encircled her waist and dropped her into an aluminium dinghy; stars exploded in her brain as her forehead hit a hard seat edge. An oppressive sound roared in her ears—was it rain or her own blood pumping? The boat rocked as Sims climbed in and pushed it away from the bank. A sprocket whirred as he attempted to start the outboard motor. Something hard moved under Kitty's fingers, a sharp metal object. She scrabbled her fingers along its length and grasped a handle—a knife.

In the dim glow from his torch, her eyes strained for some sign of what lay ahead. She squirmed to a seated position, arms and legs still bound together. A lightning flash lit the world for snap glimpse of surging floodwater.

She raised her voice over the chatter of the rain. "Ray, you can't take this boat out into that—it's too dangerous."

Ray swore and pulled the cord again; the tiny motor spluttered, fired and died. Rainwater deepened in the bottom of the boat. The knife cut her fingers as she tried for a better grip. She flexed her ankles and slowly severed the tape; wriggle, scrape, ignore the stinging cuts. The outboard motor gurgled to life. The little boat reversed into the water and turned. Kitty freed herself as Sims accelerated; the torrent flung them off course. He cursed again and revved the motor. A loud thud shook the boat and it lurched and stalled. The branches of a dead tree held the boat in its grip.

"Fucking bastard!" Sims gained his feet and tried to work it free. As he leaned over the side of the boat, Kitty rose and kicked him headfirst into the water. Sims' weight rolled the tree, forcing the little boat under. As it submerged, sinking from beneath Kitty, she clambered into the branches. Sims surfaced and Kitty kicked him in the face. The movement made the tree roll again; it took Sims under and Kitty clambered along the trunk away from the branches. The tree swung lengthwise to the current, Kitty a reluctant figurehead on the root end. Lightning flashed and she glimpsed Sims trying to free himself from a branch that had tangled in his shirt. Kitty stood up, grasped a vertical root and swung on it; once again, the tree spun and dragged Sims under. Too late, Kitty realised the danger as the tree continued to roll and took her under as well. She let go and kicked away. Something pushed her deeper; she held her breath and fought to free herself. Everything went red, a flame curled in the pit of her stomach. Her lungs burned. Brain in overdrive, she slipped out of Jimmy's jacket. Her muscles stung as she resurfaced, coughing and gasping. Lightning flashed, the tree drifted beside her, indifferent to her plight—it hadn't deliberately tried to kill her—on it floated, destiny unknown.

Still coughing floodwater from her lungs Kitty clambered back onto the tree. With each lightning flash, she looked around, trying to see where Sims had gone. A metallic bang of thunder tore at her jagged nerves; golden hooks of lightning forked and snaked overhead. The after-flashes lit the world around her and she looked down into Sims' cold dead face, wide eyes blurred by the surface of the water. The tree lurched and Kitty slipped into the water, her feet found the river bottom. The tree snagged on a sandbank.

The water chilled as she splashed through deep sand and tea trees to crawl exhausted to the muddy riverbank.

72

Lightning gashed the sky and left a jagged purple line across Jack's vision. He steered the van off the bush road onto a narrow track. Deep into the Imbil State Forest he drove and parked off the side of a timber cutters track.

"Okay." Paul smiled at him in the dim light of the van's dash. "We're going to do this."

"We are." Jack stepped out into the aromatic forest air. With one small torch for a light, he pulled the back doors of the van open and lowered the ramp. Paul rolled his Suzuki down the ramp to the ground and the plan rolled out in seclusion. A piece of black tape obscured the logo on the fuel tank; a false registration plate covered the existing one. Jack opened the sawn-off shotgun and pushed a couple of shells into the breech.

"Right, we're ready to go?"

"Crash hat." Jack leaned in to the back of the van and passed a full faced helmet to Paul. "And zip that jacket."

"Yes, Dad."

Jack smiled as he buckled Paul's chinstrap. "Don't be naughty, Ducky."

Paul swung his leg over the bike, kicked the stand back and started the motor. Jack climbed on behind.

****

"No sign of them yet?" Rick stood beside Trouncer the Bouncer and gazed along Wickham Street. He'd checked the street at regular intervals, for hours. How long would it take Burt to retrieve Jody? He went back inside and got a bottle of Scotch and a glass of ice from the bar. Shut in his office he snorted a line of coke and sat but couldn't relax; snatched up the phone and dialled. No answer.

"Where the fuck are you?" His brothers from other mothers did not hold Rick's predicament in high enough regard. He slammed the receiver back into its cradle and recommenced worrying.

What if Ruby had some insurance hidden away? Evidence of Rick's appetites?

The door flung open and his cousin, Naz Van Nek staggered into the room wearing yesterday's clothes and a cloud of alcohol; his face mottled crimson.

The door slammed behind him. "You dirty fuckin' cunt!"

"What's up your arse, Naz?"

"All these years I thought you were just a fag."

Rick's face rippled as the blood drained to his boots. "Get to the point, Naz."

"I'll get to the fuckin' point alright." Naz wove across the room and Rick saw the knife in his cousin's hand. "I'm gonna fucking kill you, you dirty bastard. I'm gonna cut your nuts off!"

Keep your poker face, Rick.

"What did I do to you, Naz?"

"It's what you did to all those little kids—the same thing your old man did to you and me and Ray and Burt and who-the-fuck-knows else? You dirty fuckin' rock spider."

"You don't know what you're talking about."

"The hell I don't! I went and visited Pinkie—he's in the hospital all busted up after some cop beat the shit out of him. He told me all about how he used to recruit little kids for you and your mates." Naz's eyes grew distant, his back straightened. "I remember now—that's what all that shouting was about—you helped organise the Pearl fire. You helped kill the Kinanes and their boy!"

"I didn't know anyone would die—you've got to believe me…"

"You're a cunt! You're a fuckin' rock spider!"

Rick's lower lip trembled. His worst nightmare had arrived, drunk and wielding a knife. "I can't help it, Naz—it's the way I am."

"You shoulda killed yourself before you fucked up all them kids, you dirty cunt. I always looked up to you, I thought you wuz a good bloke. But you're nothing but a stinkin' pervert."

Rick slid open the top drawer of his desk and his hand closed over the Derringer. Naz lumbered around the desk and slashed; Rick threw up his forearm and deflected his cousin's swing. He poked the little pistol in Naz's face and fired, the knife thudded to the carpet and Naz fell beside it.

Rick flopped into his chair and cradled his head; his heart banged against his ribs. Tears flowed as the memories flooded back. For as long as he could remember his father had molested him—in the shed, in the calf pen. Once he did it behind the pigpen. Rick had hated it, but when he reached puberty things changed. The smell of semen, body odour, and filth became his biggest turn on. Forcing himself into a gagging throat tipped him over the edge. Children were his thing, especially little boys. Soft skin and prepubescent bodies. In his younger days, he could get it on with a woman; he thought marrying Bev would cure his problem. Every man alive would love a romp with his wife, but no matter how he tried, Rick could not go there anymore. As he swallowed a mouthful of his drink his head swivelled to his cousin's body— cousin and half-brother. Burt and Ray were also his cousins as well as half-brothers. Rick's breath shook as he brushed away the tears and thought about his father. He'd died when Ray shoved his head into the fly-wheel of a Ruston Hornsby engine. The coroner concluded misadventure; the old man must have tripped. Rick shivered and grimaced. He could not feel sorrow over his father's head pulverised by a spinning cast iron wheel. Ray had mastered the art of torturing, terrorising, and murdering. His trembling limbs proved Rick had not; he would get Ray or Burt to dispose of Naz's body later. The thought brought him back to the worry that had plagued him before Naz burst in. Where the hell were Ray and Burt? Why hadn't they called with a progress report? He needed to retrieve Jody before she had a chance to tell her story, if she hadn't already. Kinane was dead meat. A mere five hundred bucks was all

Biker Henry asked for the privilege. They knew Kinane parked his car in the loading dock at the back of the Phoenix Pearl every night; Biker Henry promised he'd easily put a slug in Kinane's head.

He tossed back his drink, slipped the Derringer inside his jacket and closed the door on Naz. The noise from the disco had masked the crack of the tiny gun. Once again, Rick's feet carried him towards the street. As he emerged from The Capital's front door, he feared the world had gone crazy; a regalia of drag queens swooped and carried Trouncer the Bouncer away down the street. They disappeared around the corner, a yellow feather rolled along in their wake. Their whoops and cackles faded against the roar of a motorcycle. Rick turned, the bike mounted the footpath, slowed, and drew level, the pillion passenger thrust a sawn off shotgun at Rick's throat and fired both barrels. The motorcycle roared away and Rick hit the pavement, jets of crimson sprayed the walls; his limbs thrashed, weakened and stilled, blank eyes stared at the flashing neon sign.

****

As Paul accelerated, back onto Wickham Street and away from The Capital, Jack cracked the shotgun and reloaded.

That one was for Paul, and Ben, and all the lost boys and girls.

Along the street, Paul slowed a little as they approached The Phoenix Pearl. The absence of the Kinanes, away on family

358

business made Jack's task less daunting; he and Paul overstepped the mark but they would not stand by to Mikey and his brothers' lone stance, to risk everything for the ones they'd lost. He gripped the shotgun tight as Paul mounted the pavement. Vince Wilkins and Eddie Holt stared as they approached. The first barrel went off in Eddie's eyes and Paul came to a stop; Vince Wilkins seemed frozen as Jack pointed the shotgun at his head and fired the second barrel.

Those two were for Craig and his parents.

Paul accelerated away, Jack held on tight as the Suzuki weaved through the traffic and sped along Turbot Street, through the city and onto North Quay. As they weaved across the city, Jack reached around Paul and pulled the tape off the fuel tank. He checked behind; no cars followed. He tapped Paul's shoulder, the signal to pull into a side street where Jack removed the false numberplate. With the gun and numberplate tucked in his jacket, Jack climbed on the pillion and Paul sped back to the Imbil State Forest.

73

The sight of Lester Gainsford, dead on the darkened street burned into Mikey's brain. The absence of any trace of Kitty gave him small hope and much foreboding. An ambulance took Burt away and the police arrived to investigate the death of their colleague. Jimmy dispatched every available man to search for Kitty. Everywhere they thought she might be. The police frustrated Mikey with their lack of concern.

"Just because she accompanied Gainsford," a jack had said, *"doesn't necessarily indicate her disappearance is cause for concern."*

"Come on, Mikey—we'll go back to the Phoenix and wait."

"Wait? Jimmy I have to find her."

"You've got McCaffery leading the search, if anyone can find her, he will. And besides, we probably should call her parents."

"Oh shit if her parents knew half the things I've done—" His hands covered his face.

"But they don't."

"No, I doubt they even know we're together—Kitty hasn't told them yet. Her father's going to go apeshit."

"Come on, let's go."

With nerves jagged, Mikey accompanied his brothers back to The Valley. Anxiety nailed Mikey's heart against his ribs as they

360

approached the Phoenix Pearl. The sight of police cars and ambulances out front set his worried mind into a tailspin. Was this something to do with Kitty? Or did they know about Furner and Doyle? If so, how? Had they come for him? He still had to dispose of Vince Wilkins and Eddie Holt, but exhaustion sapped his rage— years of anger sloughed away like dead skin. He wanted Kitty home, safe. The vile threats that had motivated Vince and Eddie didn't make their involvement less abhorrent; they deserved punishment but while taking down German Burt, Mikey lost his appetite for revenge. *'An eye for an eye makes the whole world blind.'* Too much stolen sleep and bitter tears.

But where is Kitty?

The music had ended, the waltz finished. The band had packed up and gone home. Lucifer leant on the bar with a wink and a drink, saying, "You did me proud, young Kinane. You did me proud."

But where was Kitty?

His head barman hurried towards him, pale and shaking. Vince and Eddie lay dead. Mikey and Jimmy pushed through the crowd of bystanders, two body bags lay side by side on the pavement; other hands had taken the lives Mikey had chosen to spare.

"What happened?"

"Two guys on a motorbike shot them."

"What? Did anyone get a look at them?"

"Nuh—they wore full faced helmets and they were gone before anyone could move."

"Shit 'eh?"

Ah well, somebody took the decision out of your bloody hands, Mikey.

74

Saturday.

Sunlight and a savage little ant woke her. Kitty had climbed free of the raging floodwater to collapse, exhausted in the pitch-black and fell into an uneasy sleep. Propelled by a cool breeze, the last golden rags of clouds sailed towards the early morning sun. Naked from the waist up, Kitty's sleep-fuddled mind cleared and the nightmare flooded back. Lester was dead and tonight, Mikey would die too if she didn't get back to Brisbane by sundown. Sims had driven on a sealed road until only minutes before he stopped. The muddy current still ran from left to right so she hadn't crossed the river. If she walked upstream, she might find his car. Her watch said six thirty five. The sun rose like a gold coin into the blue. Her stomach rumbled with hunger as she set off, fighting her way through the undergrowth. A rolling tumbleweed of despair and anger; revulsion and terror spurred her on. She fought back the flood of tears—nothing must distract her from the task ahead. Sims had gunned Lester down in cold blood. Sims. He'd identified himself as one of the snow whites. Events of the night before dropped into place like pieces of a puzzle. *'My big brother, Rick Campbell wants little Jody back.'*

Kitty picked up the pace. She had to get to a phone.

Her legs shook from exhaustion and hunger; she'd been walking for nearly an hour. The river had taken her a long way; she began to worry that somehow she had walked past Sims' car. The dam of tears burst and flooded the chasm of despair that opened over the years of her life. The loss of Mikey's kin had wounded her on the sidelines and devastated the Kinanes. Why did evil things happen to good people? Why did other good people allow that evil to happen? Nausea swirled in her empty stomach. Her mind swam with misery and regrets. Blood pulsed through her head like tar. Birdsong persisted and grated her nerves like the discordant mallet fall of a child's glockenspiel thrumming in her ears. She swayed and sobbed in the humid morning air, crying herself to imminent collapse. The crow cawed in a nearby tree and brought back her present predicament; a flash through her tears caught her attention. Ahead, through the trees, sunlight reflected on glass—Sims' car.

****

The coming day glowed in the east as Jack and Paul arrived back at Mikey's farm where they enjoyed a romantic weekend getaway. While Paul scrubbed his Suzuki, Jack borrowed a pair of tinsnips from Mikey's shed and cut the numberplate in tiny pieces. He dismantled the shotgun, packed it in a paper bag of rock salt, and stashed it in a picnic basket.

On a road trip to Rainbow beach for a day in the sun, Jack drove and Paul tossed the numberplate fragments out the window.

On the sandy bank of a deserted estuary on the Inskip Peninsula, they buried the shotgun deep in the wet sand.

"Do you think the drag-queens will turn us in?"

"They didn't know what was going to happen. They were just told to get Trouncer out of the way."

"Why did we need to get him out of the way?"

"Paul, he's a quick thinker—he would have taken us down before I could line that gun on Rick."

"Well, it's done. For better or worse."

"For better or worse. Let Craig rest in peace."

"He would have been proud of you, I'm sure."

Jack smiled. "He was really something. So, let's go get some fish and chips, and I'll show you the propeller from the Cherry Venture." He took Paul's hand and led him across the deserted estuarine beach, the marble-like soldiers crabs stampeded ahead and vanished as one into the grey sand. They let go hands as they emerged from the scrub and onto the road where they left the van.

"I'd rather see the Cherry Venture itself."

"You'll need a four-wheel-drive for that, sweetheart. Someday we'll do it."

****

Kitty slipped in the mud, cursed and struggled to her feet. The floodwater had risen and swamped the floor of Sims' car. With feet sliding and squelching, she picked her way around and opened the driver's door.

"Fuck you, Sims!" He had taken the keys with him. The car's carpet squished with muddy water as she got in and searched for a second set. She grabbed a smelly black T-shirt from the passenger seat and pulled it on; it was big enough to fit two of her but fashion wasn't top priority. Sims' aviator sunglasses might be handy and the console full of coins she would use to buy food and call Mikey—if she could find a payphone.

The absence of keys left her with only one option. She would have to hot-wire the car and break the steering lock.

What a pity I didn't pay more attention when they showed us how crims steal a car.

Her imagination ran wild when she opened the glovebox on a pack of latex gloves and stained bowie knife wrapped in a black balaclava.

A sharp knife is good. My gun would have been better.

In the boot, she found a Gerry can and a quick sniff told her it contained petrol. From a toolbox, she grabbed a screwdriver to remove the steering column cover. The latex gloves protected her from the currents while she stripped the battery wires and twisted them together. Using a wheel spanner, she tapped the screwdriver into the ignition slot and unlocked the steering. Stripping and connecting the ignition wires, the car started and Kitty punched the air.

Voila!

A minute later Kitty had added several new swear words to her inventory as the car slipped about on the muddy ground and went nowhere. She turned the motor off and battled self-pity as she broke branches from tea trees and wedged them under the back wheels, building a twiggy bridge over the slippery mud. Hours and countless tries later, Sims' car finally shot out of the mud and up the riverbank.

75

As he investigated the previous night's debacle, Dave Cramb grieved for Lester Gainsford and wondered why Ray Sims had not fronted for duty the night before. Reliable Ray, that's what they called him, though lately, he hadn't been so reliable. Where was he? And where were Furner and Doyle? The Licensing branch said they had left in a hurry around lunchtime four days prior and hadn't been seen since. Their wives weren't overly concerned, Furner and Doyle often stayed away for one or two nights. Headquarters had issued an alert but they remained missing. Someone had beaten German Burt to a pulp, and of the fifty-odd witnesses, none would say who did it. Even Burt wasn't talking.

I never thought Burt had an honourable bone in his thick skull.

"It's a shame, really," said a grizzled old uniformed sergeant, "the bloke who beat him deserves the keys to the city. He rid us of German Burt and his pickhandle."

Then there were the three bullet-ripped bodies in Fortitude Valley. Trouncer the Bouncer pointed his finger at the city's drag queens as those who carried him around the corner but given the nature of their attire, identifying individuals among them nigh on impossible.

Poppy's staff stuck to the script and formed a brick wall of non-cooperation. Poppy Francesco's statement read. "I heard they were just mucking about. Trouncer would never let them into the Capital so they pranked him. I was told he came back wearing a frock and had lipstick kisses all over him. I never saw a motorbike and I never heard a gunshot. Buggered if I know."

Nobody could confirm the colour the motorbike—blue, maybe. Some said black, other's said red and one, green. The black clad rider and his passenger had vanished before anyone could raise the alarm. Nobody could give a registration number or make.

"Definitely a four stroke," said one helpful bystander.

Dave grunted, "Well that narrows it down a bit."

Congratulations boys, you just committed the perfect murder. Three perfect murders.

The discovery of Naz Van Nek, unconscious on the floor of Rick Campbell's office, seemed Dave's last hope. A doctor told him the tiny bullet that lodged at the base of his brain would likely remain *in situ.*

Dave shrugged. "Ah well, it won't matter much, Naz doesn't use that part of his body anyway."

76

Kitty swore and hung up the payphone. Mikey's home number wasn't answering. His work number diverted to his home number. Chris' number wasn't answering either. Kitty couldn't remember the number of the Kinane's safe house in Highgate Hill, and as it was an unlisted number, the dog-eared phone book was useless. Tired of sweating in the pissy, graffiti covered phonebox she gave up; time was running out. Sims' balaclava was hot, she kept it rolled back off her face to cover her hair and the bruise on her forehead; the aviators were too large for her face but they concealed her blackened eyes. The coins jingled into the hopper and Kitty retrieved them. Across the street at a dilapidated roadhouse, Kitty bought two Chico rolls, a bottle of milk, and a cheap cigarette lighter.

"Been out bush-bashing, have you Darlin'?" A paunchy man asked as he passed her change of fifteen cents and eyed her mud-caked clothes.

"Yep, got bogged too."

Back in Sims' car, the greasy Chico rolls filled a yawning void in her stomach. The milk reminded her of home and family. She could call her mother but she didn't want her worrying; Kitty worried enough for herself, given her plans for that evening. Five dollars and twenty-seven cents of Sims' spare change remained.

She hadn't time to worry over which bridge to cross and which bridge to burn. The road sign ahead warned how little time she had to save Mikey's life.

****

Biker Henry had spent the day watching TV and sleeping. He hadn't heard from any of the gang; for most of them it was a day of rest—family time. The Valley Armada had called off their fight with the Kinanes and the Shadow Jackals but he'd already been paid for this mission and he wanted to prove his loyalty to Rick. It grew dark as he took up his position behind the loading dock of the Phoenix Pearl, and waited. Kinane drove a gold Fairlane. The Australian symbol of success.

Henry held the semi-automatic pistol, relaxed and muttered, "Successful or not, Kinane, your end is nigh."

****

Night came early under the dark clouds. Kitty parked Sims' car in disused parking lot behind a vacant shop in the cluster of buildings behind the Phoenix Pearl and made her way into the shadowy laneway. The stiff fabric of the T-shirt itched. Sims had spilled something down the front. Kitty shuddered, the balaclava smelled of sweat, stale breath and the coppery tang of blood hung about on Sims' assassin outfit. Slipping into the shadow of a lillypilly, she rolled her shoulders and renewed her grip on the knife. With leg

371

muscles tense, she swallowed the bile and fear that burned her throat, to stop them from shaking. The headlights of Mikey's car lit the lane as he swung into the loading dock. Did she shout a warning to Mikey? Henry would almost certainly shoot her if she did. Could she live with what she was about to do? Would guilt eat her from the inside? Kitty refocussed on her mission—to save Mikey's life. She'd deal with the consequences later.

****

Mikey steered into the laneway. The front of the club was a no-go zone after the murder of Vince and Eddie. A night and day spent worrying about Kitty left him feeling one day older than humanity. The twins had suggested they call a staff meeting and Mikey could find no reason to disagree.

****

Kitty crept silently behind Biker Henry as he eased his head around the corner, gun poised. Speed was her only hope. Henry wasn't tall but thickset; he resembled a cane toad on hind legs, wearing jeans and leather jacket. Kitty's hands and feet tingled; a ghost hand gripped the back of her neck. Her heart hammered murder through her veins.

You've killed before—you can do it again. That time she defended herself and an injured colleague. This time she defended

372

the most important person in her life. She had lost Lester in this war; she would not lose Mikey.

****

Mikey pulled into the loading dock and stepped from his car, the back door of the club burst open and the twins swooped. Behind them, three bar staff slewed to a halt.

"Mikey, get inside quick—we just had a call from the Jackals. Biker Henry is gonna—"

"Look out!"

"Ah, Shit!"

****

Her foot scuffed a pebble at the same time Mikey's car door slammed and she heard excited voices; the would-be assassin raised his gun. Kitty's arm snaked undetected over Biker Henry's leather-clad shoulder, the blade glided into the whiskery skin under his jaw and he recoiled; his gun sprayed bullets as she slit his throat ear to ear. Air hissed from the wound and blood spurted onto the concrete. Kitty fled into the dark as Biker Henry's body fell, thrashing and spurting.

****

Automatic pistol shots gouged chunks from the bricks above; one ricocheted, and hummed past Mikey to carve a dint in the car's hood. The three brothers froze as a splattering and hissing came from behind Mikey's car. Biker Henry pitched forward, his throat a red fountain; the gun hit the concrete and spun away. Henry kicked and flopped like a drunken break-dancer. Mikey's heart stilled with astonishment; he stared as the bikie's limbs slowed and went still. Mikey searched the deserted lane.

"What the hell?" Liam's face paled.

"Oh god!" A junior drink waiter coughed and vomited across the driveway and into the gutter. "So much blood!"

"Jesus, Mikey—somebody just saved your life."

Aiden dashed along the lane and stopped, peering into the dark. "But there's nobody here."

"Whoever did it sure moved fast."

"Did you see anyone?"

"Nuh."

A barman narrowly avoided stepping in the dam-burst of arterial blood and succeeded with the junior waiter's abstract gut spillage—his foot slipped a little and he threw up a balancing arm. "Maybe Henry accidently cut his own throat."

"With a gun?"

"Dunno. Probably not. Do you think we should call the cops?"

"Well I'm not going to clean him up."

"Me either."

The junior drink waiter gagged again.

Clutching the Bowie, her hand covered in blood, Kitty sprinted along the lane and ducked between two buildings. Relieved to roll the balaclava off her face, she glided through the dark, high on adrenaline. Up and over a high brick wall, she landed lightly in the empty carpark and sprinted to Sims' car. She debated the merits of returning the car from where she'd taken it. City people are too busy watching where they're going to notice a stray woman wandering around in filthy clothes but such things fascinate country people. She would need to buy fuel if she were to return to Somerset Dam.

"You have five dollars, Kitty. Forget it."

She cast her mind around for somewhere to dispose of a car. Her grandparents once owned a farm near Petrie. She and her brother had played on a grassy bank of a tributary of North Pine River, at the end of a two-rut road through the coastal scrub she recalled her mother's warning of how deep that tidal creek could be.

On her third try, Kitty found the right place, parked on the steep embankment and thanked her lucky stars for the low tide. She scouted around and found a sturdy branch to chock the wheel. Back in the car, she tipped the last of Sims' coins into her jeans pocket and knocked the gearshift into neutral. Her head spun with petrol fumes as she emptied the Gerry can over the interior of the car and tossed it on the back seat. Destined for a single job, the cigarette lighter flared with the first strike; she plied it to the balaclava and waited until it was well alight then she tossed it into the car. Whether it was the explosion or just fatigue, Kitty didn't know but she picked herself up to watch the inferno destroy the interior of the car. The flames seared her face as she pulled the branch from under the wheel. Praying the fuel tank wouldn't explode, she leaned against the boot, the car inched forward then, as if it decided the water looked inviting, it plunged down the embankment, sizzling and steaming it disappeared beneath the black surface. Kitty blinked her eyes to remove the smoky ghost of the flames and knelt by the water to wash Biker Henry's blood from her face and hands.

77

Twenty-four hours later, his doctors deemed Naz Van Nek fit enough to talk to the police. When Cramb arrive at his bedside, Naz poured his heart.

"You know who did this?" He pointed to his puffy face; one eye sparkled at Cramb from the depths of swollen eyelids.

"Yep, your cousin Rick."

"Have you arrested—you wanna arrest the bastard quick, Mr Cramb. He's not like us—he's abnormal."

"He's dead."

"You—he's what?"

"He's dead. Some guy on a motorbike blew his head off with a shotgun, right out front of the Capital."

"Shit ay?"

"We know he shot you because the kind of gun he had in his pocket."

"I forgot he had that itty-bitty gun."

"Well, he gave you a timely reminder, didn't he?"

"He was a fuckin' rock spider. I only found out the other day, Pinkie Pinchester told me. I went to visit Pinkie in hospital and he told me to warn Rick that Gainsford was coming after him. When I arks him why, he told me about Rick and his mates. Fred Donnelly, Robert Martin and old Bouncy Harold. Fuckin' rock spiders. Fuckin' Ruby Landers supplies them with kids. I wanted to kill him. His old man used to like rootin' kids—he was a mean bastard. He'd fuck us and lock us in the feed shed until we was so hungry—then he'd make us swear to say nothing, otherwise he'd starve us some more. All the time the dirty bastard use to feel us up. I can still taste his cheesy cock." A tear oozed from the bloated corner of Naz's eye. "He was a scary man, Mr Cramb. I danced and sang all day when the old cunt tripped and stuck his head in the flywheel of his irrigation pump. They reckon it busted his head like a watermelon. Always, Mr Cramb, you hear of bad things happenin' to good people but this time it happened to a real arsehole."

"So getting back to Rick and his mates. What else did Pinkie tell you?"

"He didn't. I took off, I was gonna get pissed and kill Rick. I dunno how he could do it. Me and Rick and Ray and Burt—he should have known better!"

"You're talking about Ray Sims?"

"Yeah, not many people know it but he is Rick's brother."

Cramb sighed. On days like this he wished he'd chosen a job at the hardware shop. "Ray is also dead."

"What?"

"I'm sorry, Naz. His body was found in the Somerset Dam. He drowned."

"Ah shit. That's sad. Poor Ray. He was the one what found his father's body and all the blood and brains sprayed all over the pump shed. It was tough on the poor bugger but in a way it were a good thing, Ray was like Burt, really. He was fucked in the head."

"Burt's career as a thug is over."

"Why, did you arrest him?"

"We will, but at the moment he looks like an Egyptian mummy, bandaged from head to foot."

"What happen to him?"

"According to fifty bikers, he tripped."

****

Dave found Pinkie in his mother's living room watching a movie on TV, his broken leg propped on a grubby pillow. She cleared a pile of newspapers off a chair for Dave to take a seat, turned the TV down to zero, and left the room.

"Gee, Pinkie. You look like you've been playing in the traffic."

"Police brutality, that's what this is. Fuckin' shouldn't be allowed. I'm going to make a complaint against Gainsford."

"Inspector Gainsford is dead."

"What? I didn't do it—how come—who killed him?" Pinkie scratched behind his ear.

"What makes you think someone killed him?"

"Well—dunno, I just thought—" Pinkie scratched his nose and added, "Oh that's sad."

"Naz Van Nek told me a very interesting story and you had a supporting role, kind of like Cagney there." Dave tilted his head at the TV.

Pinkie scratched his nose. "Naz is an idiot."

"He seemed to know what he was talking about actually."

Pinkie lowered his eyes. Cramb could imagine the cogs turning in his devious brain.

"I've been putting two and two together, Pinkie. It was you responsible for the Valley fires, wasn't it?" Dave played his bluff hand; all the while he watched the pimp's face. "You set those bombs and framed Rusty and Daryl."

"No! No, it wasn't me—I swear."

"You better start talking, Pinkie, because I'm warming up my handcuffs. I want to know, from the top down—who did it?"

"Rick Campbell and his mates, Harold Purser, Robert Martin and Fred Donnelly were all in a big panic. So was Ruby Landers because Tom Kinane apparently had all their names and was going to take it to the newspapers. They're a bunch of perverts. Furner saw it as an opportunity to make some big bucks and told them to pay up and he'd take care of it for them. Rick set up Vince Wilkins and Eddie Holt and forced them to be the ones to carry the bombs in. They were security guys, they had keys to a lot of places, they could go in and the cops would say nothing." *First count, Pinkie. Accessory to murder.*

"So if they didn't make the bombs, who did?"

"Sims I think, he was pretty handy at that sort of stuff."

"Sims? Ray Sims?"

"That's him."

"Ray Sims is a police officer."

"He's also Rick's deadliest assassin—a real bad bastard."

"Do you have proof of that?"

"Nothing solid but it was always understood, if you pissed Rick off badly enough, he'd send Ray after you."

Dave exhaled.

Sims. All those years I worked with that scum thinking he was a good man.

Pinkie continued. "The shit nearly hit the fan when Gainsford arrested Rusty and Daryl. They never did it, but they knew all about it."

"Who told them?"

"I did, I got pissed and shot my mouth off." Pinkie raked at his ribs.

"Then what happened?"

"Rick panicked and called on Ray Sims to sort it for him. Sims tortured Rusty and scared him so bad, he confessed just to get put in jail and away from Sims." Pinkie shrugged. "He was only in there a few weeks and the screws done him in."

"Who killed Daryl Reid?"

"Dunno, I know that Furner cleaned up the mess. Gainsford blundered in while they were at it and Furner being the cunning bastard he is, he managed to turn it around and cast suspicion on Gainsford."

"Pinkie, you wouldn't happen to know who killed Bouncy Harold? And why he was killed?"

Pinkie scratched and plucked at his crotch. "Rick had a rent boy living in a little unit on the beach at Redcliff. He got too old for Rick's tastes and so he was going to do him in. Bouncy got wind of it and tried to talk him out of it, Bouncy liked the boy apparently. He threatened to go to the cops and blow the whole thing wide open." *Second count, Pinkie, accessory to murder.*

"So what happened?"

"I reckon Sims or maybe Burt killed Bouncy. Rick wouldn't have done it. He always got someone else to do his dirty work."

"That'd explain the matching fingerprints on the glove and the drum."

"Huh?"

Nothing. Just thinking aloud. Okay, Pinkie. Don't leave the country. I might have some more questions for you."

Dave got to his feet as Pinkie's mother shuffled in the door and began beating Pinkie with a rolled up newspaper.

"You should be ashamed of yourself!" She swat her son across the ear. "If your father was here he'd take the strap to you!

"Lay off, Mum!"

"You're going to get your backside out of that chair and get over to the church. Father Joseph will take your confession."

Dave grinned, tempted to stay and watch the old lady's demonstration of tough love but he had work to do.

"I'll talk to you again, Pinkie." *When I come back to arrest you.*

"Yeah okay—gawd Mum! Lay off!"

78

Kitty succumbed to exhaustion and fell asleep in the long grass. She woke as a truck on a nearby road snorted in the early morning light. Cursing the truckie and his exhaust brake, she staggered to her feet; her body sore and dirty. Her blond hair was a dull straw colour. She looked feral with no way to hide the lump on her forehead and two black eyes. Sims' aviators and balaclava were in his burnt-out car under twenty feet of water. At the edge of Old Petrie, she found a payphone on the edge of a park and dialled Mikey's number. As the call trilled softly in her ear, she watched a flock of rainbow lorikeets, already drunk as they ate fermented fruit under a mango tree.

****

Mikey arrived home with Kitty and worried he hallucinated. Barbara sat on the couch drinking beer with Aidan, Liam, Margie, and Bessie.

"Mikey, I need to talk to you."

"Just wait a few minutes." His first priority was Kitty. He led her, tired and stumbling, to his room. He longed to hold and kiss her but she resisted. Kitty had never resisted his kisses or his touch. She touched his hand and made for the bathroom, the door closed on his confusion. Mikey sighed, his brain buzzed from a lack of sleep. A day at the coalface of revenge, fighting German Burt and then a twenty-four hour search for Kitty had left him reeling. When she turned up, alive but battered the tension eased from his muscles and left him drained. He longed for stillness, undiscovered in the seething rapids of youth. The deaths of those who bore him had carried him to the edge of mortality, to gaze into the darkness that awaited all. He cast a hungry glance at the bed then went to find Barbara.

"I'm so sorry for what I put you through, Mikey. I've learned a lot in this past week."

"I'm sorry too. I was a terrible husband and I—"

"We both made a mistake but we've got our baby."

Mikey smiled. "Yeah, the silver lining."

"Mikey, Dad asked me to sound you out about standing for his seat at next year's election."

"Barbara, I'm not politician material but I know someone who is."

"You do?"

Mikey raised a heavy arm, unfurled his index finger and tapped Barbara's collarbone. "You."

"Me? But I'm a woman—"

"So? You're strong. You're sharp, you're a good organiser, and you're a good speaker—you could use some elocution lessons to strengthen your voice."

"What's wrong with my voice?"

"Um—I—"

"Well?"

Mikey scratch his chin, the chuckle sapped his strength. "Your voice is fine, but if you're going to compete with a chamber of yobbo politicians it needs strengthening."

"But what about Danielle?"

"I'll take care of her when you can't. We'll work it out."

Barbara's mouth opened and closed. Inspiration lit her eyes, her face shone with excitement.

"Do it. Show our daughter what a woman can achieve. I'll back you."

"Mikey, do you really think I can do it?"

"Bloody oath."

"Bloody oath. Yes. I can do it, can't I? I will."

"You've got my vote."

His ex-wife flung her arms around him. "Thank you, Mikey. I'm going to go and talk to Dad."

"Call if you need my help."

"I will."

"Where's Danielle."

"She's playing poker with Aiden and Margie."

"That's my little girl."

****

Warm bubbles enveloped Kitty as she lay back and luxuriated in a warm bath. She forced her tired eyes open; she closed them to gashed throats, red hands and sharp knives; the terrifying face of

German Burt loomed. His groping hands had left invisible welts on her skin. The terrible thrill of slicing into Biker Henry's leathery throat played on an endless loop; mild resistance and release as sinews and cartilage succumbed to the razor-sharp steel—the gush of hot blood over her hand. Sims. He had broken her heart and sloughed away her trust in humanity. The world had grown darker for the loss of Lester Gainsford. Her lip trembled and tears fell. He died because he stood between her and a maniac. She cried herself numb. As the tears subsided, she ran hot water into the scented bath until it burned her skin; slowly she washed away the revulsion. Her fingers had pruned as she slipped under the water, held her breath then resurfaced to a soft tap on the door.

"Kitty?"

"Come in." Kitty had yet to meet a man more attractive than Mikey Kinane. Being here with him, safe and sound was her reward for cold-blooded murder. She would do it again without hesitation. His blue eyes held sadness and love. He sat on the bath's edge; Kitty rose to her knees and unbuttoned his shirt.

He tilted her face. "Are you feeling better?"

"A little, but pushing you away is not helping me either."

"I'll make it better, Kitty. I beat Burt once; I'll do it again if I have to."

"I'm glad you didn't kill him, Mikey. I really feared you would."

"That was my intention, but after I beat him so easily I felt sorry for him. That and I couldn't—not while I thought you watched."

Kitty peeled Mikey's shirt from his shoulders and kissed his chest. He stepped out of his jeans and joined her, bubbles slopped onto the floor. Her back against his front, his legs either side of her, Kitty lowered her eyelids and allowed him to kiss the length of her neck and across her shoulder. His arms enfolded her, the warp and weft of their lives pulled tight.

"I have a guardian angel somewhere."

A tingle spiral down Kitty's spine. "Why do you say that?"

"Biker Henry had his gun trained on me and before he could get off a shot, someone slit his throat."

"Oh, really?"

"You wouldn't happen to know something about that would you?"

"Me? Of course not."

"Of course not." His lips pressed behind her ear. "So, you haven't told me how you got from Somerset Dam to Petrie."

"Hitchhiked. I'll tell you about it when I've had eight hours sleep. My nerves are shot and I'm knackered."

"It's over now. It's all over."

As Kitty towelled his back, she sensed the tension there and led him to the bed. Her fingers eased the knotted muscles of his shoulders, inwards and up to where his dark hair spiralled to a peak at the nape of his neck. She smiled as his breathing deepened and slowed; her lips pressed to his cheek as she stretched out beside him and willed herself to sleep.

Das Ende

BIOGRAPHY

A. Isobel Sutcliffe lives in Western Queensland, Australia with her husband, two dogs and two cats. She has an adult son and daughter. A child of grazier parents, she grew up in remote rural Queensland. She spent thirty-three years as a working musician. A visual artist she turned to writing in 2015.

www.ingramcontent.com/pod-product-compliance
Lightning Source LLC
Chambersburg PA
CBHW070349170726
48291CB00001B/238

9 781946 675316